THE PENGUIN POETS

BAWDY VERSE

A PLEASANT COLLECTION

Ephraim John Burford was born and educated in
the City of London. As a journalist he has led an
adventurous life and has travelled extensively in
Europe and Africa. A research historian, he has
written several books on the social and sexual *mores*
of 'old' London and his view is that his 'books
reach the parts that other histories do not reach'.
His other publications are *Queen of the Bawds* (1973),
The 'orrible Synne (1974), *Bawds and Lodgings* (1977)
and *In the Clink* (1979). He is currently preparing a
book on the rise of organized bawdry in London.
He has also lectured on London and particularly
old London Bridge for the City of London Society.
He is married and lives in London.

BAWDY VERSE

A Pleasant Collection

❧

Edited by E. J. Burford

PENGUIN BOOKS

Penguin Books Ltd, Harmondsworth, Middlesex, England
Penguin Books, 625 Madison Avenue, New York, New York 10022, U.S.A.
Penguin Books Australia Ltd, Ringwood, Victoria, Australia
Penguin Books Canada Ltd, 2801 John Street, Markham, Ontario,
Canada L3R 1B4
Penguin Books (N.Z.) Ltd, 182–190 Wairau Road, Auckland 10, New Zealand

First published 1982
Copyright © E. J. Burford, 1982

Set in Linotron Palatino by
Rowland Phototypesetting Ltd
Bury St Edmunds, Suffolk
Printed in Great Britain by
Hazell, Watson and Viney Ltd
Aylesbury, Buckinghamshire

Title page illustration by Brian Grimwood

Contents

Contents

Contents

Contents

Contents

Acknowledgements

The author wishes to thank the following for kind permission to publish poems in this collection:

The Bodleian Library, Oxford, for the Rawlinson MSS. (Poetry); the Lewis Walpole Library of Yale University, for extracts from *The Letters of Sir Charles Hanbury-Williams*; the Osborn Collection, Yale University Library, for *Advice to a Cunt-Monger*, Yale MS. b.105.f.394; the British Library, for the Harley MSS., 7318, 7319.

Sources

TEXTS

The Academy of Complements by Philomenus, London, 1650.

Choyce Drollery – Songs and Sonnets. Being a Collection of Divers new excellent pieces, Poetry never before published. London. Printed by J. G., for Robert Pollard at The Ben Jonson's Head behind the Exchange, and John Sweeting at The Angel in Popes Head Alley, 1656.

Jyll of Brentford's Testament, ed. F. W. Furnivall. The Ballad Society, Extra No. 11, 1871.

Merry Drollery or A Collection of Joviall Poems, Merry Songs & Witty Drolleries & Catches, collected by W. H., C. B., R. C., & J. G., Lovers of Wit. Printed by J. M. for P. H., March 1661 and are to be sold at The New Exchange, Westminister Hall, Fleet Street & Pauls Churchyard.

Merry Drollery Compleat – a Collection of Joviall Poems, by W. N., C. B., and R. S., Lovers of Wit. Printed for William Miller, 1691.

The Merry Muses of Caledonia, attrib. Robert Burns. 1827 edition.

Musarum Delicae, or The Muses' Recreation, containing severall poems of Poetique Wit. By Sir J(ohn) Mennes and Ja(mes) Smith, printed for Henry Herrington and are to be sold at his Shop at the Signe of the Anchor in the New Exchange. London, 1655.

A Musical Miscellany, being a Collection of Choice Songs and Lyric Poems by and for J. Watts. London 1729–31. 6 vols.

National Songs and Ballads: Merrie Songs and Ballads to 1800, compiled by John Stephen Farmer, 1897.

The New Academy of Complements. Compiled by Lord Buckhurst, Sir Chas. Sedley and Sir Wm. Davenport. London 1671.

The Percy Reliques: Loose and Humorous Songs (1868) (unexpurgated extra to Hales and Furnivall, *Percy Folio Reliques of English Poetry,* 1865).

Ane Plesant Garland of Sweet-Scented Flowers, ed. James Maidment. Edinburgh, 1835.

Poems for Severall Occasions. John Wilmot, Earl of Rochester. 1732 edition.

The Roxburghe Ballads, ed. C. Hindley. Reeves and Turner. London, 1874.

Shakespeare's Youth, ed. F. J. Furnivall, 1882.

Westminster Drollery, Songs and Poems by a Person of Quality, Printed for H. Browne at The Gun at St Pauls Church Yard, 1685. [NOTE: The Person of Quality was Sir J. Mennes.]

Windsor Drollery, being a more exact Collection of the newest Songs, Poems and Catches now in use – than any yet extant. Collected by a Person of Quality. London, 1672.

Wit and Drollery – Joviall Poems, by Sir J. Mennes, Ja. S., and Sir W. Davenport and the Most Refined Wits of the Age. Printed for Nath. Brook at The Angel in Cornhill, 1661.

Wit and Drollery – Joviall Poems. Printed for Obadiah Blagrave at The Bear in St Pauls Churchyard, 1682.

Wit and Mirth – An Antidote Against Melancholy. Printed by J. P., and Sold by Henry Playford near to The Temple Church, 1682, third edition 1684.

Wit and Mirth, or Pills to Purge Melancholy, compiled by Thomas D'Urfey. Editions of 1707, 1709, 1719, 1720.

MUSIC

The British Broadsheet Ballad and Its Music, by Claude Mitchell Simpson. New Brunswick, U.S.A., 1966.

A Collection of the Songs of Robert Burns, ed. C. Thomson, Edinburgh, 1822.

Popular Music of Olden Time, ed. W. Cramer, Beale and Chappell, 2 vols. (1855–7).

Abbreviations

Introduction

> Say, Puritan! can it be wrong
> To dress plain Truth in witty Song?
> What honest Nature says we should do
> What ev'ry Lady does or would so.

The first duty of a modern editor of early literature is to reproduce the old texts without bowdlerizing or omitting verses because they use language unacceptable to the *unco guid* or deal with sexual activities in explicit terms. Gone are the days when such were regarded as tidbits to be privately published in small editions for the delectation of the few wealthy *cognoscenti*, or printed in a foreign tongue – usually Latin – so that ordinary men and women could not read them even if they had access to them. Moreover it is not fair that only classical scholars should enjoy the privileges denied to ordinary people. These ballads and verses have therefore been chosen because they reflect the standpoint of those ordinary people who were our ancestors, and are in the language used and understood by them.

There is a lot of poetic licence in licentious poetry, the popularity of which is shown by the immense number of bawdy ballads, lubricious lyrics and salacious songs in existence. Although a great many of them are parodies of current 'straight' poetry, a great number were deliberately composed for bawdry's sake. But however couched or spelt, their theme is common to all races – the perennial chase of the male after the female.

19

Assuredly such ballads and songs have been in existence almost from the time when man first learned to speak. The earliest epics and sagas known to us from the ancient civilizations of Sumer and Egypt were clearly also parodied into sexual terms. For example the famous *Epic of Gilgamesh*, first composed some seven thousand years ago, has as its hero the randy Sumerian prince of that name whose amorous exploits were faithfully chronicled. Gilgamesh '. . . took sons from their fathers and maidens from their lovers . . .', thus evidencing both sodomy and rape – although he was canny enough to avoid carnal copulation with the Great Goddess, Ishtar, sexual congress with whom would have ensured his death in very unpleasant circumstances. As it was, the goddess was much displeased with his prevarication. For upwards of three thousand years this hero's sexual exploits must have been sung lustily in Babylonian and Assyrian taverns and brothels, in parodied forms conforming with the political changes in the godheads, such as when Babylonian Marduk was replaced by Assyrian Asshur.

A thousand years or so later, the Egyptian story of *The Two Brothers*, wherein a lustful wife tries to seduce her honest and honourable brother-in-law, in clear language, must have been a smash hit in the cities of On and Thebes, while the similar exploits of Potiphar's wife with the (probably) homosexual Joseph must have had them rolling in the aisles in about 1400 B.C.

Inevitably a great number of love songs and ballads were parodied, originally esteemed by the nobility and gentry for their elegance and beauty but in a language too rarified to be enjoyed by the *hoi polloi*, whose notions – and experience – of sexual behaviour and enjoyment were much coarser and simpler. In the ages when the majority of men and women were illiterate, these coarse ballads would be disseminated by the travelling story-teller or minstrel, and sung with supporting gestures and nuances at interesting points in the action. The same troubadour (to jump a few centuries) who sang to his mistress's eyebrows (as Shakespeare sardonically remarks in *As You Like It*)[1] also sang for the delectation of audiences of a lesser sort, although with no less sense of enjoyment. We can be sure that Blondel sang bawdy songs to his lecherous master, Richard the Lionheart, extolling the theme of his loins rather than the lions. The ballads would have had even greater impact when rendered in such a form as to require audience participation at certain points or as a chorus at the end of each stanza.

Indeed, the importance of such audience participation must very early have been realized by the priestly castes in their rituals, and remains vestigially in the hymns sung in churches and the sung responses in certain parts of synagogue rituals. To this day bawdy ballads are sung to hymn tunes, much to the distress of the clergy, perhaps tempered by the thought that at least the tunes are sacred and thus the religious background not completely lost.

In mankind's earliest days religion and politics were inextricably interwoven. Politics too were earnestly discussed, since innumerable wars, convulsions and revolutions have occurred in the history of every people. Thus ballads were adapted to criticize and satirize their rulers and ventilate their grievances, and, like people, they come in all shapes and sizes – good and bad, long and short, clean and dirty, loyal and rebellious, candid and hypocritical, pious and fraudulent, adulatory and denigratory, pure and bawdy. They had, however, all to be of topical interest, no matter what the theme, and to give pleasure as well as understanding to the listeners.

Of all the subjects, sex was the most popular. Love, sacred and profane, was in turn exalted and ridiculed. While love poems and ballads glorified one or other physical aspect of womankind in the most beautiful, imaginative and poetical phraseology – albeit often too cloying and thus boring – the bawdy ballads were more honest. They reflected the ordinary

1. Act II, Scene 7.

man's attitude towards his womenfolk – the eternal search by his virile member for entrance into the ostensibly mysterious female pubic triangle. So they were male ballads composed by men for men's enjoyment and reflected male standpoints only, eschewing fine words and phrases, contenting themselves with descriptions of female parts and copulative activities in the living vernacular – the vulgar tongue. There are very few reflecting the woman's point of view, or indeed written by women. And, because life among the commonalty was generally hard and dirty – so to speak at ground level – the principal primary functions were always mentioned in stark terms, reflecting the ancient axiom that 'between piss and shit we are all born', both being normal vernacular words and by no means 'dirty'.

Moreover, in the main, little element of love entered into the lives of the poor; their women were for copulation and created for that purpose, and bought, sold and married for that purpose. Marriage of a sort was from the earliest times recognized as a copulative instrument for the breeding of children – preferably males – to suit the contemporary economic and religious ethics. Hence the preoccupation in much bawdy literature with the excretory functions. Since these functions were done openly they occasioned no special comment; colloquial words were coined to describe them and their organs in matter-of-fact terms, and even ascribed to places such as Pissing Alley, Shiteburne Lane and Gropecuntelane, without the residents seemingly objecting until hundreds of years later, when a change in attitude had come about.

It would be of great value if we could know the vulgar version of, for example, Solomon's Song, since it would certainly have been sung in less elegant terms by drunken young Hebrew men in the wine-bars on festive occasions, as well as broadside songs (*vide* Psalm 69) when important persons could be shamed and bawdy songs sung about them at the town gates by drunkards. Soldiers' victory songs are usually more explicitly obscene when describing their vanquished enemies, and it will assuredly have been something like this that so upset King David's wife, Michal, when she castigated him for explosing his genital apparatus while dancing in the streets 'before his handmaidens like any common fellow' (2 Sam. 6:20).

Moreover, singing to music is incredibly ancient. All can see the seven-thousand-year-old harp of the princess of Ur in the British Museum. Perhaps the earliest martial ballad known to us is Miriam's triumphal song over the vanquished Egyptians, which must have been chanted for centuries after the event. Because of the tones and inflections and the way a ballad is always sung, it nearly always leads to the formation of the *double entendre* for the delectation of the vulgar. In this way, Miriam's (and later, Deborah's) ballad would have been parodied and debased centuries later in less traumatic days, when King Solomon ruled in concupiscent peace.

In the western world the earliest bawdy ballads come from Roman poets such as Ovid, Catullus, Tibullus, Juvenal and Martial, all of whom were certainly using material known long before their own times. These poets are regarded with esteem today, but in ancient Rome the status of poets was somewhat ambiguous. In about 150 B.C. it was not regarded as an occupation for Roman gentlemen, but for freedmen and servants, and upon occasion literate slaves. Most of the poets were *clients* of nobler or richer Romans, writing sycophantically for their bed and board. Hardly any poet went out on to the streets to sell his poems to the public.

Bawdy poetry could, however, be found as *graffiti* on the walls of taverns and brothels, to be read by and read to the commonalty and sung drunkenly by them in both types of hostelry, and verses such as the *Priapae* – which extolled the *phallus* in its ceaseless quest and conquest of the *cunnus* – were more to proletarian liking. They can be likened to the rude ballads sung at football matches or at rugby clubs today. In Caesar's time salacious verses were sung to the mobs in the stadium by naked female actresses, helping the plebs to forget their woes and political demands by concentrating their attention on sex.

The usual English definition of a ballad is a song that tells a story, dramatic, satiric or comic. The word derives from the Latin *ballare* – to dance; hence a ballet is a story told in dance. The first known balladeer in Britain was Caedmon, a monk of Whitby who lived about 680 A . D . It is said that the gift of song came to him late in life 'by heavenly inspiration' and was his only claim to fame; fellow monks then told him to turn parts of the Scriptures into verse and sing them so that Christian belief could be easily assimilated by the English pagans, who, like Caedmon, could neither read nor write. Hence these ballads would have been brief, simple and easy to remember and pass on to other pagans.

Indeed the lives of the heroes of Christianity would have brought a new element to the listeners, whose lives were brief, painful and often intolerable. All they knew was that the sun rose and sank each day, and the moon at night – although sometimes the sun was taken away for a while. They knew that part of the year was hot and part was cold. Their brief life of some twenty or thirty years was a constant struggle; they had neither knowledge nor time nor opportunity for philosophical speculation about the meaning or purpose of life, but if they were at times happy they would sing. If work went well they would also sing – probably the ancient painters in the caves sang if their work was going well. At a very early date they would have had the lute as an accompaniment; and as their principal pleasure was copulation, they would undoubtedly have sung its praise in some primitive manner.

Very few of Britain's most ancient bawdy ballads have come down to us. There are a few in this present collection which date back to the fourteenth century. Ballads about Robin Hood were known then. The length of some of these early ballads may tire the modern reader, but in olden times the listener was a willing participant; in the absence of any other source of diversion or amusement he would memorize the contents (he would hear them many times), altering them when memory failed but still transmitting them. One of the earliest is the famous ballad of *The Nut Brown Maid*, first printed in 1503.

It was the invention of the printing press which revolutionized the English ballad. For the first time oral traditional songs and verses could be put on permanent record and made available for wider distribution. Indeed, ballad singers are first illustrated in William Caxton's *Mirroure of the Worlde* in 1481. Sadly, no copies of a ballad printed earlier than 1513 remain. In that year the poet John Skelton's *A ballad of the Scotish Kinge* appeared, and it can be assumed that his satirical-bawdy ballad *Cock Lorells Bote* was printed as early as 1508. Both were certainly sung to a musical accompaniment. His friend and patron, Henry VII, could apparently take his satirical comments in good humour – he nicknamed the king 'Old Penny Pincher' – but things changed when Henry VIII came to the throne.

At first Henry encouraged the singing of ballads, but when they were used against the Reformation he reacted vigorously with a Proclamation in 1533 to 'suppress foul bookes ballads rhimes and other lewd treatises in th'Englishe tonge', especially if sung 'with a crowde or with a fyddell'. Fiddlers were of course musical balladeers and purveyors not only of bawdry but also of politically subversive information to the largely illiterate man and woman in the street. In 1542 Henry enacted that the realm must be purged of all such books, ballads, songs and rhymes 'as be pestiferous and noisome'. This edict may perhaps be linked with his attempts from 1535 onwards to close down the Bishop of Winchester's licensed whorehouses on the Bankside in Southwark, wherein assuredly many a right bawdy and politically pestiferously seditious ballad would be sung by day and by night in the taverns and brothels in the Clink Liberty. Eventually in 1546, a few months before he died, Henry closed them down. His endeavours were in vain, for his son, Edward VI, relaxed many of his father's laws; the whorehouses re-opened (this time however, with their frontages painted white for easier recognition), while the output of ballads multiplied vastly.

Many of these outpourings were so violently anti-Catholic that when Edward's sister, Mary I, succeeded him she instructed Bishop Edmund Bonner in 1554 to order 'the suppression of ballads and hurtful devices', by which was meant such as were sung by her Protestant subjects.

There was also another very important development which affected ballads. This was the incorporation in 1556 of the City of London Livery Company of the Stationers, who were given the privilege of licensing all printed material. However, the fee for registering a ballad was fourpence per copy. The poorer printers thus preferred to dispense with registration. Since most ballads were printed on single-sided sheets – broadsheets – for cheap mass distribution at a penny or twopence a time, payment of such a tax would effectively put them out of business. Evasion therefore was widespread, and forced the Stationers in the very next year to secure from Queen Mary a Royal Charter to protect their monopoly. This required, among other things, that all books and printed material be entered in a Register at the Stationers' Hall, giving the name of the author and of the printer as well as the title of the work.

As might be expected, a large number of illegal presses sprang up, mainly for profit-making purposes but also for the printing of seditious 'underground' pamphlets against the regime and the Catholic religion. Religion and politics being however more dangerous than bawdry, the bawdy broadsheets flourished like the green bay tree to meet the insatiable demand for ballads with sexual content, even though the perpetrators might spend a while in prison in between. But this was nothing to the fate of those who printed 'seditious libels'; they (in Queen Mary's time) would get their ears cropped while being stood in the pillory in addition to a spell in prison. The Stationers were losing a great many fourpences through anonymous printers. Nonetheless the size of the outpouring may be gauged from the report that in December 1560 no less than 796 (respectable) ballads were in the cupboard at Stationers' Hall awaiting entry into the Register.

Queen Elizabeth I was also bothered with seditious libels. She quickly enacted that 'convicted minstrels' (i.e. ballad singers) 'be grievously whipped, then burnt through the gristle of the ear with a hot iron', and for a third offence be put to death 'without benefit of clergy'. In August 1579 two men were hanged 'for singing satirical songs and ballads'. A contemporary drawing in the Bodleian Library at Oxford depicts a number of fiddlers hanging from the gallows, with their fiddles swinging from their feet, after they had been tried and held in the Clink Prison.

In Queen Elizabeth's day it was said that 'Tinkers sang Catches, Milkmaids sang ballads & Carters whistled'. There were also special songs pertaining to particular trades and professions – including beggars – while Puritans sang songs and hymns to popular tunes. Henry Chettle in *Kinde Harte's Dreame*, published in 1592, remarked that ballads were 'abusively chanted in every street'. By 1600 it was reported that penny ballads made for better sales. The bawdy street ballads were usually vulgarly romantic to reflect lower-class manners and morals; when they were politically orientated they brought alarm and dread to many a man and woman in high positions. As early as 1632 Sam Rowland in his play *A Woman never vex'd* (Act I, scene 1) says 'And I'll proclaim thy baseness to the Worlde', and John Ford, in his *The Ladies' Trial* (Act II, scene 2), demonstrates how calumny was spread in the phrase 'You are grown to tavern talk!'

Then, as now, a great deal of hypocrisy was evident. Highly respected and respectable versifiers would descend to street level. For example in 1596 the well-known poet and playwright Thomas Nashe (1567–1601), who constantly fulminated against sexual manifestations, wrote one of the best pornographic ballads, entitled *The Merrie Ballad of*

Nashe His Dildo. This vividly describes the failure of his own virile member to satisfy a nymphomaniac strumpet whom he had chosen for her prowess from a brothel which he frequented – possibly 'Hollands Leaguer' in Old Paris Gardens. His failure and his unsuccessful attempts to revive his flagging friend – graphically and lengthily described – caused the lady to discourse at even greater length extolling the virtues of her faithful dildo, which could be used at all times while men's natural dildos often flagged through exhaustion.

Robert Herrick (1591–1674), renowned for his delicate love lyrics, did not hesitate to compose scabrous couplets against lovely strumpets of his acquaintance, not for their sexual proclivities but for their bad breath or other physical unpleasantnesses. Later, Henry Purcell, renowned for his sacred music, nonetheless did not think it beneath him to compose the music for a number of dirty ditties and catches which were sung in the Georgian 'Mug Houses' in Cheapside and Long Acre, wherein gentlemen in both trade and the professions gathered after their daily labours and sang bawdy songs to the accompaniment of musical instruments. At a much later time, even the highly respectable and god-fearing Gilbert and Sullivan were reputed (by George Augustus Sala) to have composed a lewd pastiche of the Earl of Rochester's panegyric upon buggery, *Sodom*, entitling it *The Sods' Opera*. In this 'The Brothers Bollox' were wittily described as a 'pair of Hangerson', and other characters similarly named.

During the reign of King James I the flimsy broadsheet ballads poured off the presses and were sold by the thousand to avid buyers in the streets for a penny, or sometimes twopence. The ballad-monger was not necessarily the balladsinger, but both had regular customers in inns and taverns, in barbers' shops and whorehouses, and indeed anywhere where people congregated, such as Gresham's 'Old Exchange' in the City of London and the 'New Exchange', built in the newly fashionable area of the Strand in 1690. They were always thronged with men and women seeking excitement and diversion, and particularly those selecting partners for every sort of sexual gratification.

As may be expected from such mobile and clandestine printers, both printing and setting-up were execrable; the broadsheets were ill-spelt and used different type-faces indiscriminately, while lines might be incomplete and so disorganized that they sloped to one side, with uneven margins.

There were also innumerable chapbooks – *cheapbooks* – to be sold in the *cheaps* (markets). These were sheets of paper folded to make twelve pages, which, together with the broadsheets, were sold by chapmen moving through the countryside to the markets in the small towns and villages. These chapbooks are the ancestors of today's gutter press; they recorded all the more scabrous and scandalous events of the day, uninhibited by any libel laws inasmuch as they were printed and published anonymously to avoid the fourpenny registration fee.

Parodies of religious tunes and verses were very popular, and even more so when they were anti-religious or recorded the unbelievably immoral activities of the Court. Indeed, sometimes the bawdy ballad is the only clue to happenings not published elsewhere. A good example is *Panders, Come Awaye*, which lists all the courtesans and procuresses in and around the Court of King James I, with, for good measure, their individual perversions.

Then as now, sex and crime were the principal interests of the ordinary man and woman; hence these effusions pandered to their prurience. Autolycus, in Shakespeare's *The Winter's Tale*, says that the chapman had songs for man or woman as well as the prettiest love-songs for maids, adding 'so without bawdry, which is strange', thus attesting that the bawdy ones were the most popular.

The Long Parliament from 1640 onwards passed many measures to make life less burdensome for the commonalty, in the teeth of bitter hostility from an obstinate king, a dissolute nobility and a rapacious bourgeoisie, all resenting any interference with their God-given rights to absolute domination over the less fortunate. The Long Parliament was composed of men of quite separate political and social ambitions, uncongenial factions such as Presbyterians and Independents as well as various nondescript sects who were united for a time only against the monarchy and nobility, but as long as the farmers were left alone to oppress their peasantry and the merchants left alone to make their profits, they cared little about the Divine Right of Kings. Indeed Puritan interference with the maypole upset them more than the death of an unpopular king.

In 1640 this Parliament had already reduced many felonies to misdemeanours, with correspondingly less harsh penalties. In 1641 they abolished the Master Printers' monopoly, enjoyed since the days of Henry VIII, relaxing some of the restrictions on the trade although not lifting the censorship: indeed in 1643 Parliament set up a Committee 'to seek out scandalous sheets', and ballad-singers risked the pillory and the whipping-post for any anti-Puritan broadsides. Nevertheless the flood of 'unofficial' news-sheets and ballads continued unabated.

Perhaps the most curious period is that of the Commonwealth. The popular impression is that the land was stifled by puritanism, but the Roundheads were not all bigoted fanatics. Many of their marching-songs were very free when they were not actually bawdy, since the old tunes and libretti – even when banned – could not be suppressed, and remained popular during the whole Commonwealth period. The Roundhead Josh Gisling was permitted to keep bears in Old Paris Gardens, although Colonel Pride's soldiers had destroyed them on the nearby Bankside. In 1650 John Playford's famous work *The Dancing Master* was published, containing the music and lyrics of many of the olden ballads, the tunes of which were used in bawdy ballads with the words parodied to satirize the times.

Indeed it was during the Commonwealth period that the first collections of the popular and off-beat ballads were published, the most popular being *Choyce Drollery* in 1656. After their defeat at Boscobel this book became a sort of talisman to the Cavaliers, who (according to one contemporary writer) literally hugged it to their breasts. The Puritans' hatred of this book was so fanatical that almost every copy was hunted down and burnt by the public hangman – only six copies are known to exist today. Their hatred was not because it offended against good taste or was coarse and immoral – a vulgar phrase or so did not upset Puritans, who were themselves not afraid to use the common speech. Colonel John Hutchinson's wife, Lucy, was renowned for her forthright streams of abuse against the monarchists. In particular the Puritans hated *Choyce Drollery* because of its attacks upon 'that certain mechanic fellow by name Oliver Cromwell – the Usurper'.

Many of the ballads in *Choyce Drollery* can be traced back to earlier days, two to the time of the Gunpowder Plot in 1605 and several to 1637. In 1656 another collection, entitled *Wit and Drollery*, was published, containing some quite openly bawdy material, yet this did not encounter the same venomous response. About this time, too, John Selden began to collect broadside street ballads and so did the Oxford scholar Antony à Wood, who, although an ardent Royalist, admits some very human behaviour of Roundheads.

With the succession of Charles II the lid came off the pornographic press and the ballads became more and more explicitly bawdy, modelling themselves upon the merry goings-on at the Court and the immense spread of organized whoredom in London and elsewhere. Both *Choyce Drollery* and *Wit and Drollery* were reprinted in 1661. The popularity of this bawdy balladry is attested by Samuel Pepys, particularly in the diary entry for 11 April 1661, when he was enthusing over a lengthy and turgid ballad entitled *I Prithee Sweetheart*, in the third verse of which were the words 'Shitten come Shite the beginning of Love is'. This phrase so imprinted itself upon his mind that he sang it to himself for a week, diarizing it again on 17 April after a drunken carousal at the 'Mitre' tavern. Indeed, most of these ballads were meant to be sung in ale-houses and similar places of resort, and the broadsheet would be pasted on to the wall for all to follow. Very popular too were the 'catches' or 'rounds', which ensured that although many a ballad was very long, a refrain could be caught and repeated by the crowd while being prompted by the singer. Many were scurrilous and subversive as well, so that in 1662 Charles II was compelled to enact the Licensing Act to control the flood. He appointed Sir Roger L'Estrange – himself no mean lecher and profligate – to be Surveyor of the Press, and as a good example of thief turned policeman he proceeded to require that ballads had to be licensed too. The attitude of this gentleman, a close friend of the notorious procuress Mother Elizabeth Cresswell, towards women can be summed up in his own words in *Poor Robin's Vision* (1677):

A Woman's honesty is pen'd up in a very little room.
It is confin'd only from her Apron strings downward.
Yet there are no imperfections in a woman but want of Chastity . . .

Notwithstanding this alleged supervision, the flood of bawdry did not diminish, and during this time there appeared *Merrie Drollery, Westminster Drollery, Windsor Drollery, Choice Drollery, The New Academy of Complements* and *Musarum Delicae*, all of which contained a number of bawdy ballads interspersed with current popular songs and verses of mainly turgid material, of little interest today. The last of these appears to have been *Merry Drollery Compleat* (1691).

The essence of all these compilations was that they must give the mainly illiterate listeners an easy understanding of complicated matters. Hence there was great scope for half-truths or even outright lies, with the most anti-social propaganda wrapped up in seeming protests demanding political changes. Often the most ribald gibberish is found cheek by jowl with good poetry; however the most breathtakingly lovely poetry would be boring to the mob. It was only when it was parodied and put to a popular tune that it often became a smash-hit. Music has the power not only to make nonsense seem reasonable but also to make hypocrisy as well as obscenity acceptable.

Ballads also had the lucky facility of being adaptable to a large number of tunes, given only that the scan of the verse matched the rhythm of the tune. Hence the same ballad can be found over a long span of years with different tunes, a good example being the lampoon *The Four-Legg'd Elder*, first aimed against the Puritans and fifty years later against the Quakers. Another is the *double-entendre* ballad of *The Joviall*, or *Merry Tinker*, which can be traced back in many forms and tunes to Elizabethan times. Frequently the ballad gave a social picture not to be found elsewhere, for example *The Long Vocation*, which details the sexual habits of Londoners and gives the locations of the red-light districts during the Long Vacation when the Court and the *haute bourgeoisie* left the sweltering city for healthier climes, leaving the citizenry clear to enjoy many other popular outlets for their energies and recreations.

The first comprehensive collection to include unexpurgated old bawdy ballads and poems was that of Thomas D'Urfey, who in 1698 published his first edition of *Wit and Mirth, or Pills to Purge Melancholy*, which also included snatches of music to some of the songs. He was of course fiercely attacked by the Establishment, but his work was so popular that it was printed many times in his lifetime, each edition being larger and more compendious. The editions of 1707 and 1719 are the most complete.

There were many bawdy ballads and off-beat songs to be found in other collections, for example the *Bagford Ballads*, collected by the self-educated cobbler Bagford (1650–1716), and the later collection of John Kerr, 3rd Duke of Roxburghe (1740–1804), who presented his collection to the British Museum in 1788. However the *Bagford Ballads* and the *Roxburghe Ballads* were 'laundered' to make them acceptable to Victorian readers.

Likewise, when Bishop Thomas Percy published in 1765 a collection of ancient ballads under the title of *Reliques*, he claimed that his object was to popularize the old-time balladry, but he deliberately omitted such as he considered unsuitable for the eyes of the commonalty. Still, posterity was lucky to see any of it. Many thousands of the flimsies had perished – he discovered that hundreds of them were being used by his maids to light the fires! The original manuscript was 'a scrubby shabby paper book' about fifteen and a half inches long and two inches thick which was found 'lying dirty on the floor under a bureau in the parlour of his friend Humphrey Pitt at Shifnal in Shropshire'. It was thought to have been written up before 1642 – some of the compositions go back to the time of Chaucer. These flimsies were also in great demand as waste paper, much used by bookbinders to stiffen hard covers.

Similar ill-fortune dogged the subsequent history of the worthy bishop's papers. In the 1850s J. W. Hales and Frederick Furnivall collaborated in the fine three-volume edition of these *Reliques* which is now regarded as standard, but they parted company when Furnivall insisted that a number of the items should be published unexpurgated, on the grounds that it was the editors' duty to give the reader the stark originals, while Professor Hales upheld the Victorian Christian principle of omitting or laundering anything that was 'not nice'. Furnivall then published these ballads at his own expense in 1868 as a sort of annexure to volume three, entitling it *The Percy Reliques, Loose and Humorous Songs*.

Ill-luck also dogged the volume of manuscripts which James Maidment found in the Library of the Faculty of Advocates in Edinburgh. From these miscellaneous flimsies he compiled in 1835 a small collection which he entitled *Ane Plesant Garland of Sweet-Scented Flowers*. The original volume cannot now be found, and the contents would have been lost to posterity had not John Stephen Farmer included some of them in his monumental *National Songs and Ballads: Merrie Songs and Bal-*

lads, which includes a very large number of unexpurgated items, culled from many different sources.

But in Victorian England Farmer could not find a publisher to take the risk, so he published them in a private edition at his own expense in 1897. He included items from other collections which had been expurgated, bowdlerized and laundered, and he had access to many manuscripts in private hands or otherwise inaccessible to the man in the street. He also included many of the very explicitly bawdy Scottish ballads collected before 1796 by Robert Burns – some of which may actually have been written by Burns or parodied by him. These had been privately printed as a collection in 1800 in a very limited edition under the title of *The Merry Muses of Caledonia*. It will be seen that in sexual matters the Scots are much less inhibited in expression than their southern neighbours. The *Merry Muses* have been published several times since 1800, especially in the United States of America, in special expensive editions to keep them out of the hands of the *hoi polloi*. Those which appear in this collection are taken from the privately printed edition of 1827 – although it is thought that this was deliberately ante-dated and was actually printed much later in the century. The items published here are taken from the section marked 'English', which in this connotation means the Lowland Scots dialect. It will be seen that they have very little in them which relates to Anglo-Saxondom other than the sexual antics and cavortings – which are in any case universal.

Some of these ballads, verses and songs will appear coarse and rude to the modern reader, but they accurately reflect the actual life, manners and morals, speech and thought of their generations. It is noteworthy that nearly all of them deal with straightforward sexual desire and straightforward carnal copulation. The very few that deal with buggery or bestiality are deliberate attacks on both perversions and those who practised them. By these criteria even the salacious effusions of the Earl of Rochester or John Wilkes lose much of their pornographic aspect, since they are out-and-out satires in the main.

There are also one or two items dealing with another human habit – farting. In an earlier day this was commonplace in the home and in public, largely due to poor quality foodstuffs badly cooked and difficult to digest. It was not then regarded as disgusting but rather as a matter for humorous comment, especially when it concerned the high and mighty such as those at Court or at the Guildhall, and more particularly when it concerned a queen – Anne – whose chronic ill-health and heavy drinking made her prone to such accidents.

The tunes to which the ballads were sung are largely lost and often differed over the years. The titles are given therefore only for reference purposes; but for those who wish to delve more deeply a pointer is given to one or other work of musical reference.

This collection does not pretend to be an academic or pedantic exercise. It is devised for amusement. To make reading and understanding easier some of the very lengthy ballads have been broken up into stanzas, and in the earliest ones the spelling has been up-dated for the same purpose, without however altering the sense of the work or bowdlerizing it.

The collection does not claim to be comprehensive because there are many broadsheets in private hands in this country and the United States which are unknown to this compiler; but even this small start will help make up in some measure for the bowdlerizing and suppressions since 1720 when Thomas D'Urfey's last unexpurgated edition was published. And for the student of English history these ballads, songs and verses effectively complement all the political and economic histories of the period and put some real flesh into them.

E. J. BURFORD

1
The Seven Sages: The Husbande Shut Out
(*ante* 1400)

[Early English Text Society, *Metrical Poems of the 13–15th Centuries*]

There was a burgess in this town
A riche man of great renown,
That would espouse no neighbour's child,
But went from home as a moppe wild.
He let his neighbours child for a vice
And wente from them as moppe and nice
And bought home a dammazel,
Was full of vices so fell.

He seeth her fair and avenaunt
And with her father made convenaunt
For to have her to wife,
And evermore to righte live.
He sposed her and ledde her home –
Her former leman her after come,
That her had served many a stounde
When on sleepe was her husbande.

Then was the lawe in Rome town,
That, whether Lord or garsoun,
That after curfew if be found rominde,
Fast, men should them take and binde,
And keep him till the sun's uprising
And then before the folk him bringe.

And through the town as he would drive,
The burgess perceived that his wife,
Many nights was gone him from
And in the dawn again she came.

37

He nothing said, well long awhile
But every day concealed his guile.

One night, he him as dronke made
And went to bed all blithe and glad,
And lay still as he slepe he might.
She stole away, about midnight,
And went to her lotebi;
And he perceived it surely.

And went him oute and see and heard
All together how she misfeared,
Then went him in, from out the street
And shut the dore swithe skete,
And spake oute at windowe
And saide, 'Dame, God give thee how!

'I give you up; I have no need,
I have taken thee in this deede,
With thy lecheour; with him thou go!
Of thee ne'er keepe I never mo.'
'Ah! let me in, Sire, paramour!
Men shall soone ring the corfour.'[1]

'Nai, dame, I thee forsake;
In thy folie thou worst I-take.
All thy ken shal knowe and seen
What mester woman thou havest been!'
'Nai, God Almighty thats my shield
I will become wood and wilde
But if thou me in let,[2] I thee telle
I will me drown in the welle!'

1. curfew 2. stop

'Drown thyselfe, or else an-honge[1]
For here thou havest lived too longe!'
She tooke up a great stone
And wente to the welle anon
And saide, after a womanes wrenche,
'Here now, sire, I shall me a-drenche',
She let the stone falle in the welle
And stert under the dore wel snelle.[2]

The silly man bigen to grede
'Alas, what shall me to rede!'.
Anon rightes, he went him oute
And sought his wif in the welle aboute,
And swithe lowde he began to crie:
And she stert in well and highe
And shitte the dore swiche fast:
An he could up his head cast

'What, he saide, who is thare?'.
'I, she said, God give thee care!
Is it now time, by thy snoute
For to have been thus so long there-oute?'
'Ah, dame, he saide, I was asschreint[3]
I thoughte thou haddest been adreint,[4]
Let me in dame, *par amour*,
Men shall soone ringe corfour!'

'The devil hang me then by the tooth!
The watche shall well see the sooth,
That thou art an old lechour
And comest home after corfour.
Thou shalt suffer care, and howe
And drinke that thou hast i-browe!'[5]
With that, the waites come ride
And he heard how they come stride.

1. hang yourself 2. rushed behind the door very quickly 3. afraid
4. drowned 5. brewed

And curfew belle ringe-an;
And taken was that silly man
And never of him no word was heard;
They knewe ful well how it fared.
They bid his wife as she was bending
To let him in ere curfews ending.

She answered them, as all malicious
'He cometh now from the whorehouse!
Thus he is wont me to serve:
An evil death must he deserve!
I have hid his shame ere this
I'll no more now, I wis!'

Curfew belle no longer rong,
The burgess was led forth with wrong.
What helpeth it a longer tale?
That night he sat well sore akale,[1]
And his wif lay warm abed
And solace of her leman had.

Come morning was the burgess forth led
With his hands before him knotted,
And through the town he was paraded,
Harshly driven and degraded
As though a thief! This mischaunce,
Guiltless, he suffered his penaunce.

1. aching

2

A Talk of Ten Wives on Their Husbands' Ware
(*ante* 1460)

[Porkington MS., No. 10, f.56 verso, Ballad Society, 1871]

Leve, lystenes to me
Two wordys or three
And herken to my songe;
And I shall tell you a tale
Howe ten wyffes satt at the nayle
And no men them amonge.

Sen we have no othere songe
For to sing us amonge,
Tales lett us tell
Off oure hosbondes ware,
Wych of them most worthy are
Today to bear the bell.

And I shall nowe begyn att myne:
I knowe the measure well and fyne,
The lengthe of a snayle,
And ever he is warse from day to day.
To great god ever I pray
To gyve him evyll hayle.[1]

The secund wyffe sette her near
And seyd, 'by the roode I have a ware
That is two so meane:[2]
I measured him in the morning tyde
When he was in his most pryde,
The lengthe of three bene.[3]

1. bad luck   2. twice as poor.   3. only three inches

41

'Howe schulde I be served with that?
I wolde gyve, owre gray catt
Were cord thereon!
By saynte peter owte of rome,
I never saw a wars lome
Standynge upon mone.'[1]

The therde wyffe was full of woe
And seyd that 'I have one of thoo
That naughte is at neede;
Owre syre's breeche when itt is torne,
His pentyll peepythe owte beforen
Lyke a warbrede.[2]

'Hit groweth all within the here:
Sychon see I never ere
Stondynge upon scheare,[3]
Yett the schrewe is hodless,
And of all thynge godless!
There Cryste gyve him care!'

The fourth wyffe of the flocke
Seyd 'owre syre's fidecocke
Ffayne wolde I skyfte.[4]
He is longe and he is smalle
And yett he hath the fydefalle;[5]
God gyve hym sorry thryfte!

'The leaste finger on my honde
Is more than he when he doth stonde:
Alass, that I am lorn!

1. a worse one standing so poorly   2. a maggot   3. So I have never seen it standing on his balls   4. My husband's penis I'd like to change   5. yet he can't get it up

Sorry mowntyng come thereon!
He sholde be a womon
Had he bee eere born.'[1]

The fifthe wyffe was full fayne
When shee heard her fellowes playn:[2]
And up shee gan stonde:
'Now ye speke of a tarse![3]
In all the world is not a warse
Than hathy my hosbonde.

'Owre syre's braydes[4] lyke a deer,
He pysses his tarse every yere,
Ryghte as dothe a boke.[5]
When men speke of archery,
He mon stond faste thereby
Or ells hys schotte woll troke!'[6]

The sixthe wyffe hyghte sare;[7]
Sche seyd 'my hosbondes ware
Is of a good assyze.[8]
He is whyte as ony milke
He is softe as ony sylke,
Yett certis, he may not ryse.

'I lyrke[9] hym up with my hond
And pray hym that he woll stond,
And yett he lyeth styll.
When I see that all is naughte
I thynke mony a thro[10] thoughte
Bot cryste wote my wyll.'[11]

---

1. he should have been a woman before he was even born   2. complaint   3. penis   4. moults   5. buck   6. fall-short   7. was called Sarah   8. standard   9. jerk   10. fierce   11. But Christ knows my wishes

The seventh wyffe sat on the bynche
And she cast her legge on wrynch[1]
And bad fyll the wyne.
'By seynt Jame of Galys
In Englond ne in Wales
Is not a warse than myne!'

'When our syre comes in
And lookes after that sorry pynne
That schulde hengge bytweene his legges
He is lyke, by the rood
A sorry laverock[2] satt on brood
Opon two addled egges.'

The eighth wyffe was well I-tayte
And seyd 'seldom am I sayte;[3]
And so well I may:
When the froste freeses
Owre Syre's tarse leses
And all-way gose away.

'When the cuckoo gins to synge
And the schrewe begynnes to sprynge
Lyke a humbulbe:
He cowres up on other two –
I know nott the warse of tho,
I schrew[4] them all three!'

The ninth wyffe sett them nigh
And held a measure up on high
The length of a foot:
'Here is a pyntell[5] of a fayre lengthe
But he bears a sorry strength –
God may do boote:[6]

1. twisted her legs 2. lark 3. sated 4. curse 5. penis 6. give a remedy

'I bow hym, I bend hym,
I stroke hym, I wend[1] hym;
The Devell mot hym sterve!
Be he hotte, be he colde
tho I torn hym two-folde,[2]
Yette he may nott serve.'

The tenth wyffe began her tale,
And sayd 'I have one of the small,
Was wyndowed[3] away.
Of all noughts it is noughte,
Certis, and it schuld be boughte
He is nott worth a Nay!'. Amen.

NOTE: This is a rendering from the original, put into more modern
words to aid the reader.

3.
Ane Catholic Sang
(*c.*1581)

Prefatory Note: Nicol Barne, his testimonie of Theodore Beze, the new
pseudo-prophet and pretended reformer of the world, concerning
his sodomitrie bougerie with the young man Audebertus, and
adulterie with Candida, an other mannes wyf who is his harlet still
for the present. Composed by himself in Latin. 1581.

Beza, why bidest thou, why doest thou stay
Since Candida and Audebert are both away.
Thy love is in Paris, in Orleans thy mirth,
Yet thou would Vezel keep to thy girth,
Far from Candida lust of thy cors,
Far from Audebert thy great pleasors.

1. twist   2. bend it double   3. winnowed

Fare well Vezel, well mot ye fare
Fare well my bretheren who dwelles there.
I may spare Vezel, my father, and you
But neither Audebert nor Candida is mu.
Then which of them prefer should I?
Which should I visit first, or espy.

Candida may only be dearer than thou?
Or Audebert only preferred to you?
What if I cutted my body in tway
And give the one half to Candida gay,
The other to Audebert? yet Candida needy
Would Beza have hail, she is so greedie.

And Audebert would Beza have hail,
So covetous is he for to prevail:
But I would so them both imbrace
To be all hail with both in a place,
She with her cunt, him with his arse,
And I betwix, with a stiff tarse.

Yet the one should I prefer indeed,
But O, how hard a thing is need!
And since the one must be preferred
My forequarters shall be conferred,
To Audebert for bougerie
The chiefest of my volupty:
But Candida, if she complain
I shall her cunt kiss sweet again!

NOTE: This is a rendering from the old Scottish, which would be largely incomprehensible to English-speaking readers.

4

Walkinge in a Meadow Greene
(*ante* 1600)

[Percy MS. III, f.93]

[To the tune of 'And Yett methinkes I love Thee' (Simpson, 490)
'Walkinge in a Meadow Greene', 1618]

Walkinge in a meadow greene,
Fayre flowers for to gather,
Where primrose rankes did stande on bankes
To welcome comers thither,
I heard a voice which made a Noise,
Which caused me to attend it.
I heard a Lasse say to a Ladd
  'Once more, and None can mend it!'

They lay so close together,
They made me muche to wonder;
I knew nott whiche was whether
Until I saw her under.
Then off he came and blusht for shame
So soone that he had end it;
Yett still she lies and to him cryies,
  'Once More, and None can mend it!'

His lookes were dull and verry sadde,
His courage shee had tamed;
Shee hadd him playe the lusty Ladd
Or else he quite was shamed;
'Then stiffly thrust, hee hit mee just!
Fear not, but freely spend it
And play about at in and out:
Once more, and none can mend it!'

47

And then he thought to venture her,
Thinking the fitt was on him;
But when he came to enter her
The point turned back upon him.
Yet she said 'Stay! go not away!'
Although the point be bended,
But to't againe and hitt the vaine
Once more, and none can mend it!'

Then in her armes shee did him folde
And oftentimes shee kist him;
Yett still his courage was but cold,
For all the good shee wisht him;
Yett with her Hand shee made it stand
So stiffe she coulde not bend it,
And then anon shee cryes 'Come on
    'Once more, and None can mend it!'

'Adew, Adew, sweet heart' quoth hee,
'For in faith I must be gone.'
'Nay then, you do me wronge' quoth shee
'To leave me thus alone!'
Away hee went when all was spent,
Whereat shee was offended;
Like a Trojan true she made a Vow,
Shee would have one should mend it.[1]

---

1. She will find someone else

5

A Man's Yard
(*c.*1600)

[Rawlinson MS. (Poet.), 216, f.94ᵛ–95ᵉ]

Reed me a riddle: What is this
You holde in your hande when you pisse?
It is a kinde of pleasinge stinge,
A prickinge and a pleasinge thinge.

It is a stiffe shorte flesshly pole,
That fittes to stopp a Maydens hole;
It is Venus wanton stayinge Wand
That ne'er had feet, and yett can stande.

It is a Penne with a hole in the toppe
To write betwene her two-leav'd booke;
It is a thinge both dumb and blinde,
Yett narrow holes in darke can finde.

It is a dwarfe in heighte and length
And yett a Giant in his strength;
Itt is a bacheloures button, newly cutt:
The finest new tobacco pipe.

It is the Zeus that makes dead use
When he did pull on Vulcans shooes;
It is a grafte Horne on a prettye head,
A staffe to make a Countesse bedd.

There is never a Ladye in this lande
But that will take it in her hande:
The fayreste Mayd that e'er tooke life
For love of this became a weife.

49

And every Wench, by her owne will,
Woulde keepe it in her quiver still.
When sturdie stormes arise
Shall blustering Windes appeare.

I finde oft tymes dust in ashes here,
Live kindled coles of fire.
With good intente, marke well my minde
You shal herein a secrett find.

6

The Merrie Ballad of Nashe His Dildo
(*ante* 1601)

[By Thomas Nashe (1567–1601), Rawlinson MS. (Poet.),
216, ff. 96–106]

It was the merry month of February
When young men in their bravery
Rose in the morning before break of day
To seek their *Valentynes* so fresh and gay.
With whom they may consort in Summer's sheen
And dance the high degree in our Town Green.

And also at *Easter* and at *Penticost*
Perambulate the fields that flourish most
And go into some Village bordering near
To taste the Cakes and Cream and such good Cheer.
To see a Play of strange Morality
Shown by the bachelors of Magnanimity,

Whither our country Franklins flockmeal swarm
And *John* and *Joan* coming marching arm-in-arm.
Even on the hallows of that blessed Saint
That doth true lovers with those joys acquaint,

The Merrie Ballad of Nashe His Dildo

I went, poor pilgrim to my Lady's shrine
To see if she would be my *Valentine*.

But Out, Alas! she was not to be found
For she was shifted to another ground.
Good Justice Dudgeon, with his crabbed Face
With Bills and Staves had scared her from that place
And she, poor Wretch[1] compelled for sanctuary
To fly into a *House of Venery*.

Thither went I and boldly made enquire
If they had *Hackneys* to let out to hire,
And what they craved by order of their Trade
To let me ride a Journey on a *Jade*.
With that stepped forth a foggy-three-chinned Dame
That used to take young Wenches for to tame.

And asked me if sooth was my request
Or only made a question but in Jest?
'In Jest?' quoth I 'that term it as you will;
I come for Game, therefore give me my Jill!'
'If that it be' quoth she 'that you demand
Then give me first a Gods-penny in my Hand,
For in our Oratory, surely
None enters in to do his devours
But he must pay his *Affidavit* first
And then perhaps I'll ease him of his thirst'.

I, seeing her so earnest for the *Box*
I gave her her due and she the Dore unlocks.
Now I am entered, sweet Venus be my speed
But where's the female that must do the deed?

1. Wench?

Through blind meanders and through crooked ways
She leads me onward, as my Author says,
Until I came unto a shady loft
Where Venus' bouncing Vestals skirmish oft.
And there she set me in a leather Chair
And brought me forth, of Wenches, straight a Pair.

And bade me choose which might content my Eye –
But she I sought I could no way espy.
I spake her fair and wished her well to fare
But so it is 'I must have fresher Ware:
Wherefore, Dame Baud, so dainty as you be,
Fetch gentle Mistress *Frances* unto me'.

'By Holy Dame' quoth she 'and God's one Mother
I well perceive you are a wily brother;
For if there be a morsel of better price
You'll find it out, though I be now so nice.
As you desire, so shall you *swive* with her,
But look! your Purse-strings shall abide it dear,
For he who'd feed on *Quayles* must lavish *Crowns*,
And Mistress *Frances* in her velvet Gownes,
Her Ruff and Periwigg so fresh as May
Cannot be kept for half-a-Crown a day!'

'Of price, good Hostess, we will not debate
Altho' you assize me at the highest rate;
Only conduct me to this bonny Belle
And Tenn good Goblets unto thee I'll tell
Of Gold or Silver, which shall like you best –
So much I do her company request.'

Away she went, so sweet a word is *Gold*
It makes invasion in the strongest Hold:
Lo! here she comes that hath my Heart in keeping,
Sing lullaby, my Cares, and fall a-sleeping.
Sweeping she comes, as she would brush the ground
Her rattling Silk, my senses do confound.

Away I am ravished 'Void the Chamber straight,
I must be straight upon her with my weight'.
'My *Tomalyn*'[1] quoth she, and then she smiled.
'Ay Ay' quoth I, 'so more men are beguiled
With sighs and flattering words and tears,
When, in your deeds much Falsehood still appears'.

'As how? My Tomalyn' blushing she replied,
'Because I, in this Dancing,[2] should abide?
If that be it that breeds thy discontent
We will remove the Camp, incontinent:
For shelter only, Sweetheart, came I hither
And to avoid the troublesome stormy weather;
And since the coast is clear, I will be gone,
But for thyself, true Lovers have I none!'

With that she sprung full lightly to my lips
And about my neck she hugs, she culls, she clips:
She wanton feigns and falls upon the bed
And often tosses to and fro, her head:
She shakes her feet and waggles with her Tongue
'Oh! who is able to forbear so long?'

1. Little Tom   2. Dancing school (euphemism for a brothel)

'I come, I come, sweet Lady, by thy leave';
Softly my fingers up these curtains heave,
And send me happy stealing by degrees,
First unto the feet and then unto the knees
And so ascend her manly Thigh –
A *Pox* on lingering, when I come so nigh!

Smock, climb apace, that I may see my Joys,
All earthly pleasures seem to this but Toys
Compared by these delights which I behold,
Which well might keep a man from being old.

A pretty rising *Womb* without a wen,
That shines as bright as any crystal Gem,
And bears out like the rising of a hill
At whose decline there runs a Fountain still,
That hath her mouth beset with rugged Briers
Resembling much a dusky Net of Wires.
A lusty Buttock, barred with azure veins
Whose comely swelling, when my Hand restrains
Or harmless checketh with a wanton gripe,
It makes the fruit thereof too soon be ripe.
A Pleasure plucked too timely from his spring
It is, dies ere it can enjoy the used Thing.
O! Gods, that ever anything so sweet,
So suddenly should fade away, and fleet!

Her Arms and Legs and all were spread
But I was all unarmed –
Like one that Ovid's cursed Hemlock charmed:
So are my Limbs unweildy for the fight
That spent their strength in thought of your delight.
What shall I do to show myself a Man?
It will not be, for aught that beauty can.
I kiss, I clip, I wink, I feel at will,
Yet lies he dead, not feeling good or ill!

'By Holy Dame' (quoth she) 'and Will't not stand?
Now let me roll and rub it in my Hand!
Perhaps the silly *Worm* hath laboured sore
And worked so that it can do no more:
Which, if it be, as I do greatly dread,
I wish ten thousand times that I were dead.
What ere it be, no means shall lack in me
That may avail for his recovery!'

Which said, she took and rolled it on her Thigh,
And looking down on it did groan and sigh:
She handled it and danced it up and down
Not ceasing till she raised it from its swoon.
And then it flew on her as it were Wood
And on her Breech laboured and foamed a-good.
He rubbed and pierced her ever to the Bones
Digging as deep as he could dig his stones,
Now high now low, now striking short and thick
And diving deeper, pierced her to the Quick.

Now with a gird he would his course rebate
Then would be take him to a stately gait;
Play when he list, and thrust he ne'er so hard
Poor, patient, Grisel lyeth at his ward,
And gives and takes as blithe and fresh as May
And ever meets him in the middle of the way.

On her his Eyes continually were fixed
With his eye-brows her melting Eyes were mixed,
Which like the Sun, betwixt two Glasses plays
From the one to the other casting rebounding Rays.
She, like a Star that, to regild his Beams
Sucks the influence of sweet *Phoebus'* streams.
Imbathes the beams of his descending Light
In the deepest Fountains of the purest light.

She, fair as fairest Planet in the sky
Her Purity to no Man doth deny:
The very Chamber that includes her shine,
Seems as the Palace of the gods divine,
Who leads the Day about the Zodiac
And in the even, sets on the Ocean lake:

So fierce and fervent in her Radiance
Such flying breath she darts at every glance,
As might inflame the very Map of Age
And cause pale Death him suddenly to assuage;
And stand and gaze upon those Orient lamps
Where *Cupid* all his Joys incamps,
And sits and plays with every atomie
That in her sunbeams swarme abundantly.

Thus striking, thus gazing, we persevere
But not so sure that will continue ever.
'Fleet not so fast' my ravished senses cries
'Sith my content upon thy life relies!'
Which brought so soon from his delightful seats
Me, unawares, of blissful hope defeats.
Together let us march with one content
And be consumed without languishment.'

As she prescribed, so keep we clock and time
And every Stroke in order, like a Chime.
So she that here preferred me by her pity
Unto our Music framed a groaning ditty.
'Alas! Alas! that Love should be a Sin;
Even now my Joys and Sorrows do begin.
Hold wide thy lap, my lovely *Danae*
And entertain this golden showery sea
That dribbling falls into thy Treasury'.

The Merrie Ballad of Nashe His Dildo

'Now, Oh! now' she trickling moves her Lips
And often to and fro she lightly starts and skips.
She jerkes her legs and frisketh with her Heels;
No Tongue can tell the pleasures that she feels.
'I come, I come, sweet Death; rock me asleep,
Sleep sleep desire intomb me in the deep.'
'Not so, my Dear, and Dearest' she replied
'From us two Sweet, this pleasure must not glide
Until the sinewy chambers of our blood
Withhold themselves from this new-prisoned flood'.

The whilst I speak, my Soul is stealing hence
And Life forsakes his earthly residence.
'Stay but one Hour – an hour is not so much
Nay, half an hour – and if thy haste be such
Nay, but a quarter, I will ask no more
That thy departure, which torments me sore
May now be lengthened by a little Pause
And take away this passion's sudden cause.
He hears me not! Hard-hearted as he is,
He is the scorn of Time and hates my Bliss'.

Time ne'er looks back: the river ne'er returns
A second spring must help, or else I burne.
No, No, the Well is dry that should refresh me,
The Glass is run of all my destiny.
Nature, of Winter leaneth, niggardize
Who, as he overbears the Stream with Ice
That Man nor Beast may of their pleasure taste,
So shuts she up her Conduit all in haste
And will not let her Nectar overflow
Lest mortal man immortal Joys should know.

57

'Adieu, unconstant Love: to thy disport
Adieu, false Mirth, and Melodies too short:
Adieu, faint-hearted Instrument of Lust
That falsely hath betrayed our equal Trust,
Henceforth I will no more implore thine aid
Or thee for ever of Cowardice shall upbraid.

My little *Dildo* shall supply your kind
A Youth that is as light as leaves in wind.
He bendeth not nor foldeth any deal
But stands as stiff as he were made of Steel,
And plays at Peacock twixt my Legs right blithe
And doth my tickling 'ssuage with many a Sigh
And when I will, he doth refresh me well
And *never* makes my tender Belly swell.'

Poor Priapus, thy kingdom needs must fall
Except thou thrust this weakling to the wall:
Behold how he usurps in Bed and Bower
And undermines thy kingdom every hour:
And slyly creeps between thy bark and tree
And sucks the sap while sleep detaineth thee.

He is my Mistress' Page at every sound
And soon will tent a deep intrenched wound.
He waits on courtly Nymphs that are full coy
And bids them scorn the blind alluring Boy.
He gives young Girls their gamesome sustenance
And every gaping Mouth his full sufficience.

He fortifies disdain with foreign Arts
While Wantons chaste delude all loving Hearts.
If any Wight a cruel Mistress serve
And in despair full deeply pine and starve:
Curse *Eunuch Dildo*, senseless Counterfeit
Who sooth may fill – but never can beget

Or Drugs or Electuaries of new devices
That shame my Purse, and tremble at thy Prices.

NOTE. This ballad uncovers another side to Nashe's nature. He is
normally famed for his love poems and also his strictures against
sexual sin. In this however he is recounting his embarrassing
experiences in a brothel with a woman of his own choice, and at
great expense, when his exertions render him impotent and his mate
is compelled to resort to a dildo. This is one of the earliest references
to this masturbatory instrument in English literature.

Towards the end of the ballad, which runs on and on after the
reference to the dildo, Nashe observes:

> 'I pen this story only for myself
> And giving it to such an actual elf
> Am quite discouraged in my Misery.'

7

Thomas, You Cannott
(1603–5)

[Percy MS. III f.521]

[Music, Chappell, II, 17]

Thomas untied his points apace
And kindly hee beseeches
That shee wolde give him time and space
For to untie his breeches.
'Content, Content, Content!' shee cryes.
He downe with his breeches immediately,
And over her bellye he cast his thigh;
But then shee Cryes 'Thomas! you Cannott, you cannott!
  O Thomas, O Thomas, you Cannott!'

Thomas, like a lively Ladd
Lay close downe by her side.

He had the worst Courage that ever had man,
In conscience, the poore ffoole Cryed.
But then he gott some Courage againe
And he crept upon her bellye amaine
And thought to have hitt her in the right vaine;
But then shee Cryes 'Thomas! you Cannott, you cannott!
O Thomas, O Thomas, you Cannott!'

This Mayd was discontented in minde
And angrye was with Thomas:
That hee the tyme so long had space
And coulde nott performe his promise.
He promised her a Thinge, two handfull att leaste,
Whiche made this Mayd glad of suche a Feaste;
But shee coulde not get an Inch for a taste,
Which made her cry 'Thomas! You Cannott, you Cannott!
O Thomas, O Thomas, you Cannott!'

Thomas went to Venus the goddesse of Love
And hartilye he did praye,
That this ffaire Mayde might constant prove
Till he performed what hee did say.
In harte and minde they both were content,
But ere he came att her his Courage was spent,
Which made this Mayde grow discontent
And angry was with Thomas, with Thomas;
And angrye was with Thomas.

[The last stanza is lost, but began:–

Vulcan and Venus with Mars and Apollo
They all four swore they woulde ayde him:]

8
The Courtezan
(1609)

[Sam Rowland's *Doctor Merrie Man*, in
F. J. Furnivall, *Shakespeare's Youth*]

I am a profest *Courtezan*
That live by peoples sinne:
With halfe a dozen *Punckes* I keepe
I have great comming in.

Such store of *Traders* haunt my house
To finde a lusty Wench,
That twentie *Gallants* in a weeke
Doe entertaine the *French*;

Your Courtier, and your Citizen,
Your verie rustique Clowne,
Will spend an *Angell* on the *Poxe*,
Even ready money downe.

I strive to live most Lady-like,
And scorne those foolish *Queanes*
That doe not rattle in their Silkes
And yet have able Meanes.

I have my Coach, as if I were
A *Countesse*, I protest;
I have my daintie Musicke playes
When I would take my rest.

I have my *Serving-men* that waite
Upon mee in blew Coates;
I have my *Oares* that do attend
My pleasure, with their Boates.

I have my *Champions* that will fight,
My *Lovers* that doe fawne:
I have my *Hat*, my *Hoode*, my *Maske*,
My *Fanne*, my cobwebbe *Lawne*.

To give my Glove unto a *Gull*
Is mighty favour found,
When for the wearing of the same
It costs him Twentie Pound.

My *Garter*, as a gracious Thing
Another takes away:
And for the same, a silken *Gowne*
The Prodigall doth pay.

Another lowly-minded Youth
Forsooth, my *Shooe-string* craves,
And that he putteth through his Eare,
Calling the rest, *Base Slaves*.

Thus fit I *Fooles* in humoures still
That come to mee for game;
I punish them for *Venerie*,
Leaving their *Purses* lame.

9
The Westminster Whore
(*c.*1610)

[Rawlinson MS. (Poet.), B 35, f.36 rev.]

As I went to Westminster Abby
I saw a younge Wenche on her backe,
Cramminge in, a Dildo of Tabby
Into her Cunt Till 'twas ready to crack.

'By your leave' said I, 'Pretty Maid,
Methinks your sport is but drye?'
'I can get no better' she said; 'Sir,
And I'll tell you the reason why.'

Madame P. hath a Thing at her breech,
Sucks up all the scad of the Town;
She's a damn'd lascivious Bitch
And fucks for half-a-Crown.'

'Now, the Curse of a Cunt without Hair
And ten thousand Poxes upon her:
We pore Whores may go hang in dispaire;
Wee're undone by the Maydes of Honour.'

Then in Loyalty, as I was bound,
Hearing her speak in this sort.
I fuckt her thrice on the ground,
And bid her speak well of the Court.

10
Why Do You Trifle, Fy Upon It?
(*c*.1610)

[Rawlinson MS., B 35, f.54 verso, rev.]

Why do you trifle? fy upon it, fie upon it,
    fie upon it, fy upon it!
Why do you trifle, fy upon it!
Those are not Men but idle Drones
That stay til Ladyes make their moans
Tis pity, but they lost their Stones;
Fy upon it, fy upon it, fy upon it!
Tis pity, but they lost their labour.

He shall not do so, that I love, that I love, that I love!
He shall not do so that I love.
But as soon as I am sick,
Shall never fail me in the nick
To give me proof of his good Prick
That I love, that I love, that I love
To give me proof of his good Meaning.

Nor can it be too thicke and longe,
    thicke and longe, thick and longe.
If any of you chance to feare
That I am too younge – pray look you here;
Few Maids can show you so much Haire
Thick and long, thick and long, thick and long,
Few maids can show you so much faivour.

Faine would I go both up and downe,
    up and downe, up and downe
No child is fonder of the gig
Than I to dance a merry Jig

Faine woulde I try how I could frig
Up and downe, up and downe, up and downe,
Faine would I try how I could caper.

Come let us do then, you know what,
    you know what, you know what,
Why should not I endure the brunt
As well as other Maids have done't?
I'm sure I have as good a Cunt
You know what, you know what, you know what,
I'm sure I have as good a courage.

Sweet, if you love me, then again,
    then agen, then agen
Had ever Maiden that good luck
For to encounter the first Pluck?
O! 'twould invite a maid to fuck,
Then again, then again, then again,
O! 'twould invite a maid to marry.

11

A-Dallying with a Ladye
(*c.*1610)

[Rawlinson MS. (Poet.), 214, f.73ᵛ rev.]

[Composed by Mr Mark P—. Music in *Pills* (1719), 304]

Nay, Pish! nay fye! nay, out upon it!
For shame! nay, take away your hand!
In faith, you are to blame.
Nay, come! this fooling must nott bee.
Nay, Pish! nay fye, You tickle mee.

Your buttons scrubb me; you crumple my Band;
You hurt my thighs. Pray take away your hand.
The dore standes open that all may see.
Nay, Pish! nay fye, You tickle mee.

When you and I shal meet in place
Both together, face to face,
I'll not cry out: then you, then you shall see.
Nay, Pish! nay fi. You tickle mee.

But nowe I see my wordes are but vaine,
For I have done it; why should I complane?
The way is open and all is free:
Since 'tis no more, pray tickle mee.

12

My Mistriss is a Shittle-cock
(*c*.1620)

[Rawlinson MS. (Poet.), 26, f.68
Merry Drollery Compleat, 1691]

[Music, Chappell, II, 508]

My Mistriss is a Shittle-cock
Composed of Cork and Feather;
Each Battledore sets on her Dock
And bumps her on the Leather:
But cast her off which way you will
She will recoil to another, still.   Fa La La La La.

My Mistriss is a Tennis-ball
Composed of Cotton fine;
She's often struck against the Wall
And banded under-line.

But if you will her Mind fulfill
You must pop her in the Hazard still.   Fa La La etc.

My Mistriss is a Nightingale
So sweetly can shee sing.
She is as fair as Philomel,
The Daughter of a King;
And in the darksome Night so thick
She loves to lean against a Prick.   Fa La La etc.

My Mistriss is a Ship-of-War
With Shot discharged at her:
The Poop hath inferred many a Scar
Even both by Wind and Water;
But as she grapples, at the last
She drowns the man, pulls down her Mast.   Fa La La etc.

My Mistriss is a Virginal,
And little cost will string her;
She's often rear'd against the Wall
For every man to finger;
But to say Truth, if you will her please
You must run Division on her Keys.   Fa La La etc.

My Mistriss is a Cunny fine;
She's of the softest skin:
And if you please to open her,
The best part lies within.
And in her Cunny-burrow may
Two Tumblers and a Ferrett play.   Fa La La etc.

My Mistriss is the Moon so bright;
I wish that I could win her.
She never walks, but in the Night,
And bears a man within her;
Which in his back bears pricks and thorns,
And once a Month she brings him Horns.   Fa La La etc.

My Mistriss is a Tinder-box,
Would I had such a one;
Her Steel endureth many a Knock
Both by the Flint and Stone.
And if you stir the Tinder much
Her Match will fire at every touch.   Fa La La etc.

My Mistriss is a Puritan;
She will not swear an Oath;
But for to lie with any man
She is not very loath;
But Pure to Pure, and there's no Sin
There's nothing lost that enters in.   Fa La La etc.

But why should I my Mistriss Call
A Shittle-cock or Bauble,
A Ship-of-War or Tennis-ball
Which things be variable?
But to commend, I'll say no more,
My Mistriss is an arrant Whore.   Fa La La etc.

13
Do You Meane to Overthrowe Me?
(c.1600)

[Percy MS. III, f.197]

Doe you meane to overthrowe me?
Out; alas, I am betrayed!
What! is this the love you showe mee?
To undo a silly Maide.
Alas! I dye, my heart doth breake.
I dare nott crye, I cannot speake!
What! all alone? Nay then, I finde
Men are too stronge for Women kind.

Out upon the maide that putt mee
In this roome to be alone!
Yett she was no foole to shut mee
Where I shoulde be seene of none.
Hark! Hark! alack! what noyse is that?
O! nowe I see itt is the Catte.
Come, gentle Puss, thou wilt nott tell;
If alle doe so, thou shalt not tell.

Silly foole! why doubt'st thou tellinge
Where thou didst nott doubt to Trust?
If thy belley fall a-swellinge
There's no helpe, but oute it muste.
Alas, the Spite! Alas, the Shame!
For then I quite loose my good Name;
But yett the worst of Maides Disgraced
I am nott the firste nor shall be last.

Once again to try your forces,
Thus I dare thee to the feilde;
Time is lost that time divorces
From the pleasures love doth yeilde.
Ah Ha! Fye, Fye! it comes yett still!
Itt comes, ay! Aye, do what you will!
My breath doth passe, my bloode doth trickle!
Was ever Lasse in such a pickle?

14

A Creature, for Feature, I Never Saw Fairer
(*c.*1600)

[Percy MS. III, f.199]

A creature, for feature, I never saw fairer,
So witty, so Prittye, I never knewe a rarer;
Shee so kinde and I so blinde
That I may say, Another day,
I did complaine and I mett a Swaine
But hee knewe not how to woo me nor do me.
He was so dull conceived.
I gave him a smile him to beguile
I made a show to make him knowe,
I pinched his cheeke to make him seeke
And find some further Pleasure, whose Treasure
Needs not to be expected.

I Stayed him and prayed him and proffered him a favour;
He kist mee and wisht mee to beare with his behaviour;
But Hey tro lolly lolly, the silly willy could not do!
All content with him was spent
When he had clipt and kist mee and missed mee.
And coulde nott . . . kiss . . .
Then thoughte I, and thoughte no lie,
Perhaps his Pipe is nott yett Ripe,
And yett an Hour may have the power
To make itt growe in full Length and full Strength:
But fooles are led in blindness.

But woe is mee and woe is mee! Alas I coulde nott raise!
Itt woulde nott nor coulde nott, do all I coulde to please!
His Inke was runne, his Penne was done.
Jack! Art thou dead? Hold up thy Head!

I will litter thee and water thee
And feed thee with my neet
And better, if thou wilt lie besyde mee.
But all in vaine did I complaine,
His Jacke was tired, he'd not be hired[1]
For all my Prayer and all my Teares.

15
Come All You Wanton Wenches
(1620–30)

[Percy MS. III, f.404]

Come all you wanton Wenches
That longes to be in tradeinge.
Come learne fro me, Love's Mistris
To keepe yourselves from jadeing!
When you expose your Faces
All baytes for to entrapp Men,
Then have a Care to husband your Ware,
That you prove not bankrupt Chapmen.
Be nott at first too Nice nor Coye
When Gamesters you are Courtinge,
Nor forward to be sportinge;
In Speeches free – not Action be
For feare of less resortinge.

Lett nott your outwarde gesture
Betray youre inward Passyon,
But seeme to neglecte, when most you do affect
In a cunninge scornefull Fasshyon.

1. highered

Be sparing of your Favours
When Mens Love growe too Eager;
Yett keepe good Guarde, or else all is marred,
When they your Fort beleaguer.
Grant but a Touche or a Kisse for a taste
And seeme nott to be willinge
Always for to be billinge
With a Touch or a Pinche, or a Nipp or a Wrenche
Disappoint their Hopes fulfillinge.

If once you grow too lavish
And all your Wealthe discover
You cast off hope; for then with too much scope
You do dull your eager Lover.
Then order so your Treasure
And so dispende your Store
That tho' men do taste, their loves may never waste,
But they still may hope for more.
And if by Chance, being wrapt in a Trance
You yeelde them full Fruition
Won by strong opposition,
Yett Nipp and Teare, and with poutinge sweare
'Twas against your disposition.

Thus seeminge muche displeased
With that did most content,
You whett Desire and daylie add Fire
To a Spiritt almoste spent.
Be sure at the next Encounter
To put your live to strive
Yett, be nott rude, if need he will intrude.
So shall your Tradeinge thrive.
So shall you be freshly wooed
Like to a perfect Mayde; and do as I have said
Your Fainings seemes True, and like Venus, ever newe.
And your Tradeinge is not betrayed.

16
Panders, Come Awaye
(1620–30)

[Percy MS. III, f.486]

Panders! come away!
Bring forth your whores by clusters:
Alongst the Lane by Gray
Where Cupid keeps his musters,
    Now, today!

Wenches, do you hear? I tell you not a Fable:
All that do appear and be not warrantable,
    He'll Casheer!

As for Nan Wright, tho' her dealings may compare her,
Yet, for her parts below, there's not a Woman fairer
    To the show!

Little Alice is found seven years to have been a Trader
Yet Tom Todd will be bound, whom (they say) did spade her
    That she's sound!

Garden's ne'er the worse, tho' she hath made her Cunny
As common as the Boursse, yett still she hath theyre money
    In her Pursse!

Boulton is out by, and Luce, among th'infected:
And Frank Todd goeth a-wry, being before detected
    To be dry!

Pitts is to forbear the Trade and so is likewise Pearnit,
For Cupid, in his ear is told that they have had it
    To a hair!

True it is that Babe, for yeares may be a Virgin,
Yet Cupid finds the Drabbe all ready for a Surgeon
    For the Scab!

Winslowe is too young to know the fruits of wooing,
Till Nott have made her strong to know the fruits as doing
    Too, too, long!

Gallants! come not near to brave Venetia Stanley.
Her Lord hath placed her there, that will maintain her mainly
    Without fear!

Haysey's stoope so long to Cupid for acquittance,
Till evidence so strong will speak for your inditement

Alice and James, Cupid will have you armed
For with his hottest flames he hath them roundly warmed
    Mark their names!

Nan James is grown so coy that no man can endure her
Yet I have heard some say, a Barber's boy did cure her
    Of a Toy!

But with the wicked Sire, that yet was ne'er thought on,
By quenching Love's fire, hath ta'en away Bess Broughton's
    One desire!

Its ill that Simix rides, Jane Selby doth oppress her;
With other more besides, unless there were a Dresser
    Of their hides!

Beunkards, how ye speed, 'tis shrewdly to be feared
Ye cannot ask to read, so oft you have been seared
    For the deed!

Foulgam will appeal, from Cupid, as men gather,
Or, in her wand'ring Tail, hath been her holy father:
    He's her Bail!

Dodson is nott ill, yett hath she been a Dealer
The fault was in his skill, who knew not how t'appease her
    With his quill!

Her husband says she's nought, I think, an honest woman,
By lewdness may be brought to be like others, common
    Being sought!

Alice Bradshaw is forgot, the City that Engross'd her
But happy is his lott that never did arrest her;
    For she's hot!

City Wives, they say, do occupy by Charter;
But Cupid grant they may, that ware for ware they barter
    Without pay!

Ladyes name wee none, nor yet no Ladyes women
Your honours may be gone, for Caesar's love will summon
    You alone!

But because that some will not allow the order;
To Moorfields you'll come, your Mayor and Your Recorder
    With a Drum!

Thus farewell ye whores, ye hackneys and ye harlots
Come near my walkes no more, but get ye to your Varlets
    As before!

NOTE: The ballad is a generalized attack on the loose morality of the
Jacobean period, when one of the principal areas of whoredom was
Grays Inn Lane (now Road), off Holborn. Not only was it frequented

by poor *Drabbes* but it was also known by Court Ladies seeking rendezvous with Gallants, or even casual encounters with Citizens. Lady Venetia Stanley, wife to Sir Kenelm Digby, was a noted nymphomaniac, as was Lady Bess Broughton. Both of these beauties died young, Bess actually dying of syphilis. Lady Jane Selby – wife of old Sir John Selby – was another such wanton.

It was thus not necessary for the author to mention the Ladies' names: only to remind the lucky ones that Caesar himself (King James I) was always ready to summon them.

The poor whores, however, whose headquarters were the slums of Clerkenwell and Moorgate, always ran the risk of being taken up by the constables acting on the Lord Mayor's instructions and 'carted' to Bridewell to the sound of the drum. Nonetheless the author has a swing at the 'City Wives', who barter their 'Ware' without pay, in Houses of Assignation, in the absence of their Aldermanic husbands on other business, which 'business' also included regular visits either to *Misses* or to ordinary whorehouses.

17

Off Alle the Seaes
(*c*.1620–50)

[Percy MS. III, f.455]

Of all the seas thats cominge
Of all the woods thats rising
Of all the fishes in the sea
Give me a woman's swiving.

For she hath pretty fancies
To pass away the night
And she hath pretty pleasures
To conjure down a sprite

My father gave me Land
My mother gave me money
And I have spent it every whit
In hunting of a cunny

I hunted up a hill
A Coney did espy
My Ferret seeing that
Into her Hole did hie

My Ferret seeing that
Into her hole did run
But when he came into her Hole
No Coney could be found

I put it in again
It found her out at last
The Cunny then betwixt her legs
Did hold my Ferret fast

Till that it was so weak
Alacke, It could not stand
My ferret then out of her Hole
Did come into my hand

All that you be good fellowes
Give hearing unto me
And if you would a Coney hunt
A Black one let it be;

For black ones are they best,
Their skins will yeeld most Money
I would to God that he were hanged
That does not love a Coney.

18

A Freinde of Mine
(*c.*1620–50)

[Percy MS. III, f.459]

A friend of mine not long ago, desired at my hand
Some pretty Toy to move delight, to those that hearers stand.
The which I mean to gratify by all the means I may,
And move delight in every wight, that with affection stay.

Some thought to prove wherein I should these several
    humours please
The which to do, reason forbids, lest I should some
    displease.
But sith my Muse doth pleasure choose and thereon bends
    her skill
Whereby I may drive Time away and Sorrows quite beguile.

It was my Chance not long ago, by a pleasant wood to walk,
Where I unseen of any one did hear two lovers talk.
And as these lovers forth did pass, hard by a pleasant shade;
Hard by a mighty Pine tree there, their resting place they
    made.

'In sooth' then did this young man say, 'I think this fragrant
    place,
Was only made for lovers true, each other to embrace.'
He took her by the middle small – Good Sooth, I do not
    mock –
Not meaning to do anything but to pull up her smock.

Whereon she sat, poor silly soul, to rest her weary bones.
This maid, she was no whit afraid, but she caught him fast by
    the stones.

Whereat he vex'd and grieved was, so that his flesh did
     wrinkle:
This maid, she was no whit afraid but caught him fast hold
     by the Pintle.

Which he had on his chin likewise – but let the pimple pass –
There is no man here that he may suppose, she were a merry
     lass.
He boldly ventured, being tall, yet in his speech but blunt:
He never ceased, but took up all and catched her by the
     Cunt.

And red-rose lips he kiss'd full sweet. Quoth she 'I crave no
     succour.'
Which made him to have a mighty mind to clip, kiss and to
     fuck her.
Into his arms. 'Nay! soft!' quoth she, 'what needeth all this
     doing?
For if you will be ruled by me, you shall use small time in
     wooing.'

'For I will lay me down' quoth she, 'upon the slippery
     sedges:
And all my clothes I'll truss up round and spread about my
     legs:
Which I have in my Apron here under my girdle tucked:
So shall I be most fine and brave, most ready to be fucked.

Ducked unto some pleasant springing Well, for now its time
     of the year,
To decke and bath and trim ourselves, both head, hands, feet
     and geere.

19
The Sea Crabb
(*c*.1620)

[Percy MS. III, f.462]

It was a man of Africa had a fair wife,
Fairest that ever I saw the days of my life.
    With a ging, Boys, ging, ging, boys, ging.
    Tarradiddle, farradiddle, ging, boys, ging!

This goodwife was big-belly'd and with a lad
And ever she longed for a sea crabb.
    With a ging etc.

The goodman rose in the morning and put on his hose
He went to the seaside and followed his nose.
    With a ging etc.

Says, 'God speed, Fisherman, sailing on the sea;
Hast thou any crabbs in thy bote for to sell to me?'
    With a ging etc.

'I have crabbs in my bote one two three.
I have crabbs in my bote for to sell thee.'
    With a ging etc.

The good man went home and ere he wist
Put the crabb in the Chamberpot where his wife pisst.
    With a ging etc.

The good wife she went to do as she was wont:
Up started the Crabbfish and catcht her by the Cunt.
    With a ging etc.

'Alas!' quoth the goodwife 'that ever I was born;
The Devil is in the pisspot and has me on his horns.
   With a ging etc.

'If thou be a crabb or crabfish by kind,
Thou'll let thy hold go with a blast of cold wind.'
   With a ging etc.

The good man laid to his mouth and began to blow
Thinking thereby that the Crabb would let go.
   With a ging etc.

'Alas!' quoth the goodman 'that ever I came hither;
He has joined my wife's tail and my nose together!'
   With a ging etc.

The good man called his neighbours in with great wonder
To part his wife's tail and his nose asunder.
   With a ging etc.

20
Blame Not a Woman
(*c.*1620–30)

[Percy MS. III, f.446]

Blame not a woman although shee bee Lewd
And that her Faults, they have been knowne.
Although shee do offend, yett in time shee may Amend
Then blame her nott, For using of her Owne.

But rather give them Praise as they deserve
When Vice is banished quite and Virtue in them growne
For thats their only Treasure and For to fly vaine Pleasure
Then blame them nott for using of their owne.

There is many now a dayes that women will dispraise
Out of a drunken humour whenas their Witts are flowne,
Out of an idle Braine, with speeches Lewd and Vaine
They'll blame them still for usinge of her owne.

But if a woman should nott Trade, how sholde the Worlde
increase?
If women were all nice, what seed should then bee sowne?
If women were all Coy they woulde breed mens annoy[1]
Then blame them nott for using of their owne.

If any take offence att this my Songe
I thinke that no good manners he hath knowne.
Wee all from women came: why should we women blame
And for a little usinge of their owne?

21

Narcissus, Come Kiss Us
(*c*.1610–20)

[*Wit and Drollery – Joviall Poems*, 1682, p.285]

As I was a-walking I cannot tell where
Nor whither, in verse or in prose;
Nor know I the meaning altho' they all sate
Even, as it were, under my Nose.
    But ever and ever the Ladies all cried
    'Narcissus, come kiss us and love us beside'.

1. cause annoyance

There came in a Lad from I cannot tell where
With, I cannot tell what, in his hand.
It was a fine Thing tho' it had little sense
But yet it would lustily stand.
   Then ever and ever etc.

Some shaked it, some stroked it, some kissed it, its said;
For it looked so lovely indeed.
All loved it as Honey and none were afraid
Because of their bodily need.
   Then ever and ever etc.

At length he did put his pretty fine Toy
(I cannot tell where twas) below
Into one of these Ladies, I cannot tell why,
Nor wherefore, that he should do so.
   Then ever etc.

But when these fair ladies had sported all Night
And rifled Dame Nature's scant store,
And pleasured themselves with Venus' Delight
Till the Youth could hardly do more.
   Then ever etc.

The Lad being tired began to retreat
And hang down his head like a flower;
The ladies the more did desire a new heat
But alas! it was out of his Power.
   But ever etc.

When full forty weeks were expired
A pitifull story to tell;
These ladies did get what they little desired,
For their bellies began for to swell.
   Still ever and ever Etc.

Lucina in pity then sent them her aid
To cease them all of their sorrow;
But when these fair ladies were once brought to bed
They still had the same mind tomorrow.
And dandling their babies, they rantingly cried
'Narcissus shan't miss us: and be by our side!'

22

When Phebus Addrest
(*c.*1620)

[Percy MS. III, f. 96]

[Tune: Chappell, I, 172 (1634)]

When Phebus addrest himself to the west
And set up his rest below,
Cynthia agreed, in her glittering weed
Her beauty on me to bestow.
And walking alone, attended by none,
By chance I heard one cry
'O! do not, do not, kill me yet,
For I am not prepared to die!'.

With that, I drew near to see and to hear,
And strange did appear such a show.
The Moon it was bright and gave such a Light
As fits not each wight to know.
A Man and a Maid together were laid,
And ever the Maid she did cry
'O! do not, do not, kill me yet
For I am not resolved to die!'

The youth was rough, he took up her stuff,
And to Blind-mans buff they did go.
He kept such a coyle, he gave her the foil,
So great the broil it did grow.
But she was so young and he was so stronge
And he left her not till she did cry
'O! do not, do not, kill me yett
For I am not resolved to die!'

With that he gave o'er and solemnly swore
He would kill her no more that night:
But bade her adieu; full little he knew
She would tempt him to more delight.
But when they should part it went to her heart
And gave her more cause for to cry.
'O! kill me, kill me, once again,
For now I am willing to die!'.

23
As I Was Rideinge by the Way
(1630)

[Percy MS. III, f.104]

[Music: Chappell, II, 558]

[See also Poems 44, 123]

As I was ryding by the way
A Woman proferred me a Bagge
And 40 cattell more, to stay
And give her Belley but a swagge.

A Poxe on the whore, they were but Scrapps
That I supposed was single Money;
The cattell had Lice, or else perhaps
I had light, and tooke her by the Cunny.

I had not further rydd a Myle
But I mett with a market Maide
Who sung, the way for to beguile,
In these same words, and thus shee said:

'I see the Bull doth bull the Cow
And shall I live a Maiden still?
I see the Bore doth brim the Sow
And yet there is never a Jacke for Gill.'

I had some Hope and to her I spoke
'Sweet hart shall I put my Flesh in thine?'
'With all my hart, Sir! your Nose in my Arse'
Quoth shee, 'for to keepe out the Winde.'

Shee rydde upon a tired Mare
And to revenge no time withstoode.
I bluntlye asked for to occupye her:
But first shee wold know wherefore that was good.

'It will make thee lively' I did say
'Put Joye and Spirit instead of Woe.'
'Then occupye my Mare, I pray
Good Sir, for shee can hardly go!'

I milder grew and wolde but feele:
She said she was never felt, but kissed.
I was content, and shee said 'Weele,
You must kiss my Bum and feele my Fiste.'

I was red and pale with Shame and Spight
To be so answered of the Drabbe.
That I swore and spurred and away did ryde
And of my wooing, was no blabbe.

24

Off a Puritane
(1642–50)

[Percy MS. III, f.182]

It was a puritanicall Ladd
That was called Mathyas.
And he wolde go to Amsterdam
To speake with Ananyas.

He had not gone past half a mile
But he met his holy Sister;
He layde his bible under her breeche
And merrilye he kissed her.

'Alas! what wolde the wicked say?'
Quoth shee 'if they hadd seene itt!
My Buttockes, they lie too low: I wished
Appocrypha were in itt!'

'But peace, Sweet hart, or ere wee part –
I speake itt out of pure devotion –
By Yea, and Nay, I'll not away
Till thou feele my spiritts motion.'

They hufft and pufft with many heaves
Til that they both were tired.
'Alas!' quoth shee 'You'll spoyle the leaves;
My peticotes all myred!'

'If wee professors sholde bee knowne
To the English Congregation
Either att Leyden or Amsterdam,
Itt wold disgrace our nation.'

'But since it is, that part wee must
Tho' I am muche unwilling;
Good brother, let's have t'other thrust
And take thee this fine shilling,'

'To beare thy charges as thou goes
And passage o'er the Ocean.'
Then downe shee layde and since 'tis sayd
Shee quenched his spirits motion.

NOTE: This early anti-Puritan broadsheet ballad was very popular
amongst Royalists, as a means of denigration. No music is known,
but it may well have been sung to one of the Puritans' own hymns.

25

A Maid and a Younge Man
(*c.* 1620–50)

[Percy MS. III, f.197]

A Man and a younge Mayd that loved a long time
Were taken in a frenzy in the Midsummer prime;
The Maid she lay drooping, Hye:
The Man he lay whopping, Hey; the Man he lay whopping
    Ho!

Thus talking and walking they came to a place
Invironed about with Trees and with Grass.
The Maid etc.

Hee shifted his hand whereat he had placet
Hee handled her knees instead of her Waist.
The Maid etc.

He shifted his Hand till hee came to her Knees
He tickel'd her, and shee opened her Thyhes.
Yet still shee lay drooping, Hye:
The Man etc.

He hottered and tottered and there was a Line
That drew him on forward: he went on amaine
Yett still shee lay drooping, Hye
The Man etc.

He light in a Hole ere he was aware!
The Lane, it was strait: he had not gone farr,
But shee fell a-kissing, Hye.
And he lay drooping Ho, and he lay drooping Ho.

'My Billy, my Pilly! how now?' quoth shee;
'Gett up again, Billy, if that thou lovest me!'
Yett still he lay drooping, Hye.
The Man he lay whopping Hey: the Man he lay whopping
    Ho.

He thought, 'Mickle shame to lye so longe';
He gott up againe and grew very strong;
The Mayde shee lay drooping, Hye.
The man etc.

The Trees and the Woods did ring about
And every Leaf began to shoute:
And there was such drooping, Hye.
The Man he lay whopping, Hey; the Man he lay whopping
    Ho.

26
In a May Morning
(*c*.1620–30)

[Percy MS. III, f.383]

In a May morning I mett a sweete Nursse
With a babe in her armes, sweetly cold busse.
I would to God itt were mine! I should be glad on't!
For it was a merry mumping Thing, who ere was Dad on't.

I saluted her kindlye and to her I sayde
'Good morrowe, sweet Honey, and you be a Mayde:
Or if you wold show to me, I should be glad on't
Or if you would tell me who is the right Dad on't.'

'The dad of my childe, Sir, I do nott well know
For all that lay with me, refuseth mee now,
From one to the other. Still I wold be ridd on't!'
'But whosoever gott the Childe, I'll be the Dad on't.'

'I'll take itt in mine armes and wisely I'll worke:
I'll lay itt in the high way as men come from Kirke,
And every one that comes by shall have a glegg¹ on't
Untill I have founde out a man the right Dad on't.'

There came a kind Scotsman whose name is not knowne
Says hee to this sweet hart 'This baby is mine owne:

1. glance

90

In a May Morning

Come, bind itt upon my backe, Jone shall be rid on't;
For whosoever gott the childe I'll be the Dad on't.'

'Now! nay! now, nay!' shee says 'So itt may nott be!
Your looke and his countenance do nott agree:
For had hee been sike¹ a swayne, I had ne'ere been great on't
For hee was a blythe young Man that was the right Dad on't.'

'His Lippes like the Rubye, his Cheekes lyke the Rose
He tempted all fair Maydes wherever hee goes;
First hee did salute me, then was I right glad on't:
O! he was a blythe yonge man that was the right dad on't.'

'I'll travell thro' England and Scotland so wyde
And a-foot I will follow him to be his Bryde;
I'll binde itt upon my backe, I'll nott be rid on't
Untill I have found out the man thats the right dad on't.'

'I'll hushe itt, I'll busse itt, I'll lapp itt in say;²
I'll rock itt, I'll lull itt, by Night and by Day;
I'll bind it upon my backe, I'll not be ridd on't
Untill I have found out the man thats the right dad on't.'

'And thus to conclude, tho' it fall to my Lott
To find a dad for my bairne, that I cannot;
If an English man gett a childe and wold be ridd on't,
Let him bring it to a Scotsman and he'll be the Dad on't!'

1. such   2. silk

27
The Three Merry Travellers
(*c.*1630)

Who paid their Shot wherever they came without ever a Stiver of Money

[*Pills* (1719), vi, 177]

[Music in *Pills* (1719) and Chappell, I, 97]

There was three Travellers, travellers three
With a Hey down, Ho down, Lanktre down derry.
And they would travel the North Country
Without ever a stiver of Money.

They travelled East and they travelled West
With a Hey etc.
Wherever they came, still they drank of the best
Without etc.

At length by good fortune they came to an Inn
With a Hey etc.
And they were as merry as ever they'd been
Without etc.

A jolly young Widdow did smiling appear
With a Hey etc.
Who drest them a Banquet of delicate cheer
Without etc.

Both Chicken and Sparrowgrass[1] she did provide
With a Hey etc.
You're Welcome, kind Gentlemen, Welcome, she cryed
Without etc.

1. asparagus

They called for liquor, both Beer, Ale and Wine
With a Hey etc.
And every thing that was Curious and Fine
Without etc.

They drank to their Hostess and merry full Bowl
With a Hey etc.
She pledged them in Love, like a generous Soul
Without etc.

The Hostess, her Maid and her Cousin all three
With a hey etc.
They kist and was merry as merry could be
Without etc.

Full Bottles and Glasses replenished the board
With a hey etc.
No liquors was wanting the House could afford
Without etc.

When they had been merry good part of the Day
With a hey etc.
They called their Hostess to know what's to pay
Without etc.

'There's Thirty good shillings and Sixpence' she cried
With a hey etc.
They told her that she should be soon satisfied
Without etc.

The handsomest Man of the three, up he got
With a hey etc.
He laid her on her back and paid her the Shot
Without etc.

The middlemost Man to her Cousin he went
With a hey etc.
She being handsome, he gave her content
Without etc.

The last man of all, he took up with the Maid
With a hey etc.
And thus the whole Shot it was lovingly paid
Without etc.

The Hostess, the Cousin and Servant, we find
With a hey etc.
Made Courtseys and thanked them for being so kind
Without etc.

And the Hostess said 'Welcome, kind gentlemen all.
With a hey down etc.
If you chance to come this way be pleased to call,
Without etc.

Then taking their Leaves they went merrily out,
With a hey etc.
And they've gone for to Travel the Nation about,
Without etc.

28

News from Colchester

**OR A Proper New Ballad of certain Carnal Passages betwixt a
QUAKER and a COLT at Horsley near Colchester in Essex**
(1642)
[from *Poems and Translations*, with *The Sophy*, a Tragedy, by the
Honourable Sir John Denham (5th edition, 1709). Printed for Jacob
Tonson, Grays Inn Gate next Grays Inn Lane, p. 105 ff. Dedicated To
The King[1]]

[To the Tune of 'Tom a Bedlam']
[See Poems 35, 71]

All in the Land of Essex
Near Colchester the Zealous
On the side of a Bank
Was play'd such a Prank
As would make a *Stone-horse* jealous.

1. i.e. Charles II

Help, *Woodcock Fox and Naylor*
For Brother Green's a Stallion;
Now alas, what hope
Of converting the Pope
When a *Quaker* turns *Italian*.

Even to our whole Profession
A Scandal will be counted,
When 'tis talk'd with Disdain
Amongst the Profane
How Brother *Green* was mounted.

And in the good time of Christmas
Which tho' our Saints have damn'd all
Yet when they hear
That a damn'd *Cavalier*
E'en play'd such a Christmas *Gambal*.

Had thy Flesh, O, *Green*, been pampered
With any Cares, unhallow'd,
Had'st Thou sweeten'd thy Gums
With Pottage of Plums
Or profane minc'd Pie had'st swallowed.

Roll'd up in wanton Swine-flesh
The *Fiend* might have crept into Thee,
Then fulness of Gut
Might have caus'd Thee to Rut
And the *Devil* have so Rid through Thee

But alas, he'd been feasted
With a spiritual Collation
By our frugal Mayor
Who can dance on a Prayer
And sup on an exhortation.

'Twas meer impulse of Spirit
Tho' he used the weapon Carnal
'Filly Foal' quoth he
'My Bride Thou shalt be,
And how this is Lawful, learn all!'

For if no respect of Person
Be due 'mongst Sons of Adam
In a large Extent
Thereby may be meant
That a *Mare's* as good as a *Madam*.

Then without more ceremony
Not Bonnet vail'd nor kiss't her,
But took her by Force
For better or worse
And us'd her like a *Sister*.

Now when in such a Saddle
A Saint will needs be riding
Tho' we dare not say
'Tis a falling away
May there not be some Back-sliding?

'No surely' quoth James Naylor
'Twas but an *Insurrection*
Of the Carnal part: for a Quaker, at Heart
Can never lose Perfection.

For as our Masters[1] teach us
The Intent being well Directed
Tho' the *Devil* Trepan
The Adamical Man
The Saint stands un-infected.

1. the Jesuits

But alas, a Pagan Jury
Ne'er judges what's intended;
Then say what we can
Brother *Green's* outward Man,
I fear will be suspended.[2]

And our adopted *Sister*
Will find no better Quarter,
But when him we enrol
For a Saint-*Filly Foal*
Shall pass herself for a *Martyr*.

Rome, that spiritual *Sodom*
No longer is Thye Debter;
O, Colchester now,
Who's *Sodom*, but Thou
Even according to the Letter?

NOTE: James Nayler (1617–60) was a brave Puritan who served under General Fairfax in the Civil War and was already under attack as early as 1642: he did not meet Fox until about 1655. After a brilliant career he was ruined and imprisoned; poor and ill, he struggled back to his home in Huntingdon, was beset by footpads and grievously battered, thrown into a field and died soon afterwards in the local hospital.

Thomas Woodcock's real name was Timothy Wedlock: and he was actually not a Quaker but a fanatical Puritan. In 1656 he was accused of 'horrible blasphemy' and 'whipt almost to death' on the pillory. Then, over the objections of many other Parliamentarians, he was pilloried and whipped again ten days later, when his tongue was pierced with a red-hot iron and he was branded on his forehead. He was then 'dragged to Bristol' and whipped through the streets of that city 'at the cart-arse', brought back to London and incarcerated in the Bridewell Prison in Fleet Street, which was a real hell-hole. Just after Oliver Cromwell's death he was released from prison 'on a Writ issued by the Speaker of the House of Commons'.

2. hanged for bestiality

29

Upon a House of Office, Over a River
(1650)

Set on Fire by a Coale of TOBACCO

[*Choyce Drollery*, 1656]

NOTE: The houses on Old London Bridge at this time were of wooden construction, and each had a small privy overhanging the river Thames, as may be seen on contemporary illustrations: a 'House of Office' was polite terminology for a privy in those days. Because the excrements were voided into the water, it was said that those who lived on the Bridge were less susceptible to the Plague. Dung Removers – popularly known as *Gong-farmers* – cleared the City streets each night. A *'Sir Reverence'* was a satirical euphemism for a turd. The Great Fire of London occurred ten years later than this ballad.

> Oh! fire, fire, fire, Where?
> The usefull house o'er Water cleare.
> The most convenient in a Shire
>   Which Nobody Can Deny.
>
> The House of Office, that old True Blue
> Sir Reverence, so many knew,
> You now may see turn'd fire new.
>   Which nobody etc.
>
> And to our great astonishment
> Tho' burnt, yet stands to represent
> Both mourner and the monument.
>   Which nobody etc.
>
> *Ben Jonson's* Vulcan would do well
> Or the merry Blades who knacks did tell
> At firing *London Bridge* befell
>   Which nobody etc.

Upon a House of Office, Over a River

They'll say if I of thee should chant
The matter smells, now out upon't!
But they shall have a fit of Fie on't!
   Which nobody etc.

And why not say a word or two
Of she that's just? Witness all who
Have ever been at thy *Haut Gout*
   Which nobody etc.

Earth, Air and Water, she could not
Affront, till cholerick Fire got
Predominant; then thou grew'st hot
   Which nobody etc.

The present cause of all our Woe
But from Tobacco ashes, Oh!
'Twas shitten luck to perish so
   Which nobody can deny.

'Tis fatal to be built on Lakes
As Sodom's fall example makes;
But pity to the innocent Jakes[1]
   Which nobody etc.

Whose genius, if I hit aright
May be conceived Hermaphrodite
To both sex common when they shite
   Which nobody etc.

Of several uses it hath store
As Midwifes some do it implore[2] –
But the issue comes at Postern door[3]
   Which nobody etc.

1. privy   2. abortions thrown down it   3. illegitimate children left in doorways

Retited Mortalls, out of fear
Privily, even to a hair
Did often do their business there
   Which nobody etc.

For Mens and Womens secrets fit
No tale-teller, tho' privy to it
And yet they went to't without fear or wit
   Which nobody etc.

A Privy Chamber or prison'd Room
And all that therein ever come
Uncover must, or bide the Doom
   Which nobody etc.

A Cabinet for richest Gear
The choicest of the Lady's Ware
And precious Stones full many there[1]
   Which nobody etc.

And where in State sits noble duck[2]
Many esteem that use of Nock[3]
The highest Pleasure next to Fuck
   Which nobody etc.

And yet the Hose there down did go
The yielding Smock came Up also
But still no Bawdy-house, I trow
   Which nobody etc.

There, nicest Maid with naked Rump
When straining hard, had made her mump
Did sit at ease and hear it pump
   Which nobody etc.

---

1. Note the two *double entendres* 2. Duke 3. Nockandrew – arse

Upon a House of Office, Over a River

Those female folk that there did haunt
To make their fill'd Bellies gaunt
And with that same the brook did launt[1]
   Which nobody etc.

Like the Dutch Skiper now may skit[2]
When in his sleeve he did do it,
She may skit free, but now *plimp niet*
   Which nobody etc.

Are driven now to do't on grass
And make a sallet for their Arse;
The World is come to a pretty pass
   Which nobody etc.

Now farewell friend, we held so dear
Altho' thou helpst away with our cheer;
An open house-keeper all the year
   Which nobody etc.

The *Phoenix* in her perfumed flame
Was so consumed; and thou the same,
But the Aromaticks were to blame
   Which nobody etc.

That *Phoenix* is but one thing twice,
Thy Patron nobler then may rise
For who can tell what he'll devise?
   Which nobody etc.

Diana's temple was not free,
Nor that world Rome, her Majesty
Smelt of the smoke as well as thee
   Which nobody etc.

1. void their abortions   2. shit

And learned Clerks whom we admire
Do say the world shall so expire;
Then when you shit, remember Fire!
   Which nobody etc.

Beware of fire when you scumber
Tho' to shit fire were a Wonder;
Yet lightning oft succeeds the thunder
   Which nobody etc.

We must submit to what Fate sends;
'Tis wholesome counsel to our friends,
Take heed of smoking at both ends!
   Which nobody etc.

30

Madam, Be Covered, Why Stand You Bare?
(*c.*1650)

[*The Academy of Complements*, 1650, p.228]

Madam! be covered! why stand you bare?
It fits not with your female sex.
We know you carry worthy Ware
Which found may be, without Index.
   These bare signs do but bid us look
   For unknown stuff in your two-leaved Book.

Spartan Ladies some there be
Which to their Suitors naked stood,
And you, your bare Breasts let us see,
Which tells your hidden parts are good.
   Thus wanton *Venus* drew-on *Mars*
   A bare breast shows an open Tarse.[1]

1. penis

Madam, Be Covered, Why Stand You Bare?

They hang forth signs at common Inns
That strangers may know where to lodge;
And you show forth your naked Twins
And use them as a Brothel-badge.
   These wanton Signs direct men *gratis*
   The highway to your *nunquam satis.*

Diana, being naked seen
Did hornify *Actaeon*'s crest.
And the fair stripped *Hebrew* Queen
Her husband's forehead finely dressed;
   Shut up then Madam! fly men's scorns
   For open breasts breed secret horns.

The *Persian* Matrons, when their men
Before the *Medes* did fly and fall;
For to encourage them again
Shewed them their Bellies bare and all.
   You with your fair breasts would belike
   Move even a heartless man to strike.

Our Grandam *Eve* before the Fall
Went naked, and shamed not a whit;
You, not to one but unto all
Show both your Hills and naked Pit:
   Very well read in Rhetorick School,
   You show us but a part for th'whole.

The Mask you wear upon your Face
Upon your Breasts would better shew;
By nature that's a naked place,
Then, Madam, use your Mask below
   Lest that some gazing fellow venture
   And so descend to Love's low centre.

31
The Maid of Tottenham

OR **A Tottingham Frolick**
(*c.* 1650)

[*Choyce Drollery*, 1656]

As I came up from *Tottingham*
Upon a Market-day,
There I met with a bonny Lass
Cloathed all in Gray
Her journey was to *London*
With Buttermilk and Whey
   To fall down, down, derry down
   Down down derry down
   Derry derry Dina.

'God speed Faire Maid' quoth one,
'You are well over-took';
With that she cast her head aside
And gave to him a look.
She was as full of Leachery
As letters, in a Book
   To fall down etc.

And as they walked together
Even side by side,
The young man was aware
That her Garter was unty'd:
For feare that she should lose it
'Aha! Alack!' he cry'd
'Oh, your Garter that hangs down!'
   To fall etc.

Qoth she 'I do intreat you
For to take the pain
To do so much for me
As to tye it up again'.
'That will I do sweetheart' quoth he
'When I come on yonder plain'
 To fall etc.

And when they came upon the plain
Upon a plesant green,
The fair maid spread her legs abroad,
The young man fell between;
Such tying of a Garter
I think, was ne'er seen
 To fall etc.

When they had done their Businesse
And quickly done the Deed,
He gave her kisses plenty
And took her up with speed.
And what they did I know not,
But they were both agreed
 To fall etc.

She made to him low Curtseys
And thankt him for his Paine:
The young man is to *Highgate* gone,
The Maid, to *London* came
To sell off her *Commoditie*,
She thought it for no shame
 To fall etc.

When she had done her Market
And all her Mony told;
To think upon the matter
It made her Heart full cold:

'But that which will away' quoth she
'Is very hard to hold!'
    To fall etc.

This tying of the Garter
Cost her her Maydenhead.
Quoth she 'It is no matter;
It stood me in small stead,
But often-times it troubled me
As I lay in my Bed!'
    To fall etc.

32

On the *Flower-de-Luce* at Oxford
(*c.* 1650)

[*Choyce Drollery* (1656)]

A Stranger coming to the Town
Went to the *Flower-de-Luce*;
A Place that seemed, in outward show
For honest men to use.

And finding all things common there
That tended to delight,
By chance upon the *French Disease*
It was his hap to light.

And lest that other men should fare
As he had done before,
As he went forth, he wrote this down
Upon the utmost door.

'All you that hither chance to come;
Mark well ere you be in.
The Frenchmens Arms are signs without
Of Frenchmen harms within.'

NOTE: The 'French Disease' was syphilis, so called because the
French troops in Italy are alleged to have brought it back to France
after their campaign in 1494. However it was known as the French
Disease at least forty years earlier, according to a report from
Tübingen at that time. The Flower-de-Luce was Oxford's most
famous brothel in Commonwealth and Stuart times.

33
A Story Strange I Will You Tell
(*c.*1650)

[*Choyce Drollery* (1656)]

[A broadsheet street song. Tune: 'With a Fading', Chappell, I, 235]

A story strange I will you tell
But not so strange as True
Of a woman that danced upon the Ropes
And so did her Husband too.
  With a Dildo Dildo Dildo
  With a Dildo Dildo Dee
  Some say 'twas a Man, but it was a woman
  As plain report may see.

She first climbed up the Ladder
For to deceive mens Hopes
And with a long Thing in her Hand
She tickled it on the Ropes.
  With a Dildo Dildo Dildo
  With a Dildo Dildo Dee
  And to her came Knights and Gentlemen
  Of low and high degree.

She jerked them backward and forward
With a long Thing in her Hand,
And all the people that were in the Yard
She made them for to stand.
  With a Dildo etc.

They cast up fleering Eyes
All underneath her Clothes
But they could see no-thing
For she wore Linnen Hose
  With a Dildo etc.

The Cuckold, her husband, capered
When his head in the Sack was in
But grant that we may never fall
When we dance in the Sack in Sin
  With a Dildo etc.

And as they ever danced
In faire or rainy weather,
I wish they may be hanged i' th' Rope of Love
And so be cut down together
  With a Dildo etc.

34

The Merrie Mans Resolution

OR His Last Farewell to His Former Acquaintance
(*ante* 1655)

[*Roxburghe Ballads*, III, 242]

[To the Gallant New Tune, called 'The Highlanders New Rant'. The lyric composed by Laurence Price]

N O W farewel to *Saint Giles*, that standeth in the Fieldes
And farewel to *Turnbul-street*, for that no Comfort yeildes:
Farewel unto *The Greyhound* and farewel to *The Bell*,
And farewel to my Land-lady whom I do love so well.
   With a Come Love, stay Love, Go not from mee
   For all the World Ile forsake for thee.

Farewel to *Long-Acre*, that stands neere to the *Mews*
And farewel to *Drury-Lane* where pretty Wenches use:
And farewel unto S O D O M and all her painted Drabbs
And farewel unto *Bloomsbury* and all their vap'ring Scabbs.
   And come Love etc.

Farewel to *Crosse-lane* where lives some Babes of Graces
Farewel to *Common-Garden* and all her wanton Places.
Farewel unto *West-minster* and farewel to the *Strand*
Where I had choyce of Mopsies, e'en at my own command.
   Sing, Come Love etc.

Farewel to the *Bank-side*, farewel to *Blackmans-street*
Where with my bouncing Lasses I oftentimes did meet.
Farewel to *Kent-street* G A R R I S O N, farewel to *Horsey-down*
And all the smirking Wenches that dwells in *Redriff Town*
   And come Love etc.

N o w farewel unto *Wapping* and farewell to *Blackwall*
Farewel to *Ratcliffe Highway*, *Rosemary-lane* and all
And farewel unto *Shor-ditch* and *More-fieldes* eke also
Where Mobbs, to pick up Cullies, a-night-walking do go.
   Then come Love etc.

In *Whitecross Street* and *Golden-lane* do straping Lasses dwell
And so there do in every street twixt that and *Clarken-well*.
At *Cow-Cross* and *Smithfeild* I have much pleasure found
Where Wenches like to *Fayeries* did often trace the round.
   Yet come Love etc.

Yet something more I'le speak of which seems to many
     strange
There's Store of pretty Wenches lives neere to the *Exchange*
And many more there are sure that dwelleth in *Cheapside*
And other streets in *London*, whiche are both broad and wide
   Yet come Love etc.

To all the Country Mopsies wherever they do dwell
In this, my last Conclusion, I likewise bid farewel,
Tho' they were used in former times to come when I did call
I take thee for the boldest and best among them all.
   Then come Love etc.

At *Bristol* and at *Glocester* I had of Loves, great Store
But now I find enough of thee I will desire no more.
And what I have said to thee thou shalt find true and right,
I'le do thee trusty Service, at Morning and at Night
   Then come Love etc.

Farewel unto Black-Patches and farewel Powder'd Locks
And farewel *Luthners* Ladies, for they have got the Poxe.
Farewel the *Cherry-Garden*, for evermore Adue
And farewel to *Spur-alley* and all that wanton Crew
   And come Love etc.

NOTE: This merry ballad is a round-up of every red-light district in London and valuable evidence as to locations and the quality of the wenches available. All of these areas kept their reputations until the end of the eighteenth century. *Redriff-town* is Rotherhithe; *Bankside*, the most ancient whorehouse district in England; *Rosemary Lane* was in the shadow of the Tower of London; the Royal *Exchange* was the rendezvous of doxies for the merchants and brokers; *Lewknor*'s Lane, in Holborn was most notorious between 1670 and 1700 – although nobody seems to have been able to spell it – it was called indifferently Lutenors, Luthners and similar synonyms; it was a pleasant conceit to describe the ladies who haunted *Smithfield* and Bartholomews as *Fairies* – they were amongst the roughest and toughest of all London's whores; *The Cherry Garden* in St Martin-in-the-Fields was famous in its time, the Madam being known as Mother Cunny, well known to Lord Rochester and his *confrères*: but from 1650 through to the end of the century, when whoredom shifted its centres to Westminster and Covent Garden, the main red-light district was Clerkenwell and Moorfields, whose most famous Madams were Mother Cresswell and Priss Fotheringham.

35

The Four Legg'd Elder

OR A Horrible Relation of a Dog and an Elder's Maid
(1647)

[*Wit and Mirth* (1684), p. 10, attributed to Sir John Birkenhead]

All Christians, and Lay Elders too,
For shame, amend your lives;
I'll tell you of a Dog-trick now
Which much concerns your Wives.
An Elder's Maid, near Temple Barr
(Ah! what a *Quean* was she!)
Did take an ugly Mastiff cur
Where Christians use to be.
   Help! House of Commons, House of Peers,
   Oh! Now, or never help!

Th'Assembly having sat Four Years
Has now brought forth a Whelp.

One evening late she stept aside
Pretending to fetch Eggs;
And there she made herself a Bride
To one that had four Leggs.
Her Master heard a Rumblement
And wonder she did tarry,
Not dreaming (without his Consent)
His Dog would ever marry.
   Help etc.

Her Master peep'd, but was afraid;
And hastily did run
To fetch a Staff to help his Maid,
Not knowing what was done.
He took his Ruling Elder's cane
And cry'd out Help Help here:
For *Swash* our Mastiff and poor Jane
Are now fight-Dog fight-Bear.
   Help etc.

But when he came he was full sorry
For he perceiv'd their Strife;
That according to th'Directory
They two were Dog & Wife.
Ah! then (said he) thou cruel *Quean*
Why hast thou me beguil'd?
I wondered *Swash* was grown so lean,
Poor Dog, he's almost spoyl'd.
   Help etc.

I thought thou had'st no carnal Sense,
But what's akin our Lasses;
And could have quenched thy 'Cupiscence
According to the Classes.

But all the Parish sees it Plain
Since thou art in this Pickle,
Thou art an *Independent* Quean
And lov'st a Conventicle.
   Help etc.

Alas! now each *Malignant* Rogue
Will all the World perswade
That she that's Spouse unto a Dog
May be an Elder's Maid.
They'll jeer us if abroad we stir,
Good Master Elder, stay.
Sir! what of Classes is your Cur?
And then, what can we say?
   Help etc.

They'll many graceless Ballads sing
Of a *Presbyterian*,
That a Lay Elder is a thing
Made up half-Dog, half-Man.
Out! Out! said he (and smote her down)
Was Mankind grown so scant?
There's scarce another Dog i'th'Town
Had took the *Covenant*.
   Help etc.

Then *Swash* began to look full grim:
And Jane did thus reply:
Sir! you thought nought too good for Him,
You fed your Dog too High!
'Tis true he took me in the lurch
And leap'd into my Arm:
But (As I hope to go to Church)
I did your Dog no harm.
   Help etc.

Then was she brought to Newgate Jail
And there was nak'd stript;
They whipp'd her till the Cords did fail
As *Dogs* used to be whipp'd.
Poor City Maids shed many a tear
When she was lash'd and bang'd:
And had she been a *Cavalier*
Surely she had been hang'd!
   Help etc.

Hers was but *Fornication* found
For which she felt the Lash.
But his was Bugg'ry presumed;
Therefore they hanged *Swash*.
What will become of *Bishops* then
Or *Independency*?
For now we find both Dogs and Men
Stand for *Presbytry*!
   Help etc.

She might have took a *Sow-gelder*
With *Synod-men* great store;
But she would have a Lay-Elder
With two Legs, and two more.
Go tell th'Assembly of Divines,
Tell Adoniram Blue:
Tell Burgess, Marshall, Case and Vines,
Tell *Now-and-Anon* too!
   Help etc.

Some say she was a *Scottish* Girl
Or else (at least) a Witch.
But she was born in Colchester;
Was ever such a *Bitch*?
Take heed all Christian Virgins now,
The *Dog-Star* now prevails:

Ladies! beware your *Monkeys* too
For Monkeys have long Tails.
   Help etc.

Bless King and Queen and send us Peace
As we had Seven Years since:
For we remember no Dog-days
While we enjoy'd our Prince.
Bless sweet Prince Charles, Two Dukes, Three Girls;
Lord Save His Majesty.
Grant that his Commons, Bishops, Earls,
May lead such lives as he!
   Help etc., etc.

NOTE: Sir John Birkenhead (1616–79) was a fine satirical poet and the editor of the pro-Royalist magazine in Oxford entitled *Mercurius Aulicus*. He wrote this marvellous anti-Puritan ballad in 1647. It was usually sung to the ancient tune of 'Gather Ye Rosebuds While Ye May'. He was exiled in 1648 but at the Restoration he was knighted and became an M.P.

The men lampooned were all Parliamentarians and anti-monarchists, including such diverse elements as Independents, Presbyterians and other Dissenters; 'Now-and-Anon' is Oliver Cromwell himself.

Essex and Colchester were non-conformist strongholds, particularly of Quakers, and the canards linking them with buggery and bestiality are to be found as early as 1642 in *The Sophy* (see Poem No. 28). Indeed in the 1684 edition of *Wit and Mirth* this satire has a sub-title, 'The Colchester Quaker who attempted to bugger a Mare neare Colchester', based on a similar effusion in the 1682 edition, entitled *The Four-Legg'd Quaker*, which can be dated to 1659. (See Poem No. 71.)

The Puritans had made fornication a misdemeanour instead of a felony, thus avoiding the death penalty, and punishable by a spell in the pillory and 'correccion' in a Bridewell or *House of Correccion*, deemed to be less stringent than a prison. But they had not abolished the death penalty for buggery which had been instituted in Henry VIII's *Act Against Buggerie* – indeed that penalty for the offence was not abolished until late Victorian times.

Cornelius Burgess (1589–May 1665) was a Calvinist held in great esteem, and one of the 'Seventeen Divines' set up by the House of Lords in 1641 to try to reach a solution of 'ecclesiastical differences'. He opposed the Church of England's ecclesiastical system; he also opposed the King's execution. The most famous and influential was Stephen Marshall (1594–1655), a Presbyterian Divine, son of a 'poor Glover' of Godmanchester in Huntingdonshire, a Puritan demanding 'the utter abolishing of the existing episcopacy'. He was buried in Westminster Abbey, but at the Restoration his remains were 'cast into a pit at the back Dore of the Prebendary's lodgings in St Margaret's Church Yard' at the Royal command.

Richard Vines (1600–1656), a Puritan, supported 'a modified episcopacy', thus earning the enmity of Burgess and Marshall: he eventually became chaplain to St Lawrence Jewry next to the Guildhall.

Thomas Case (1598–1682), a Presbyterian, was known as 'The Confessor of the Long Parliament' but did not play an important religious or political role. Pepys's *Diary* for 26 November 1667 refers to the 'two daughters of the great Presbyterian Marshall . . . at the King's Theatre'. Neither enjoyed good repute. Beck Marshall had a row with Nell Gwyn, wherein Nelly riposted that she was only one man's mistress whereas Becky was mistress to three or four 'altho' a Presbyterian's praying Daughter!' The fate of her father's bones clearly did not bar Becky's advancement at Court.

36
The Dub'd Knight of the Forked Order
(*c.*1620)

[By Abraham Miles, *Roxburghe Ballads*, II, 114]

[Tune: 'I am Fallen Away', Simpson, 66]

Twas a Lady born, of high degree
In her aged days was youthful – yet she
So youthful was at three-score years old
A young man she esteemed more precious than Gold
　So old, so old, so wondrous old, till threescore years and
　　ten
　Old women are willing to play with Young Men.

This Lady one day in her Parlour did walk
Unto her head serving-man she began to talk;
She told him his feature was comely and rare
Few men that she looked on might with him compare
   So old, etc.

A Lily-white hand, fair face and a nose
Hair crisping and curled, his breath like a Rose,
Straight leg and a foot, and his body tall
But that in the middle is rarest of all
   So old, etc.

'Madam' he said, 'as I am alive
Unto an ancient Lady 'tis a present revive;
It will make them merry either at night or by day
And clear every vein like the dew of May'.
   So old, etc.

'Then note what I say and obey my command,
For I'll make use of thee now straight out of hand,'
The bargain was made unto their own Will
The serving-man had, and the Lady her fill
   So old, etc.

When the Jig was ended the Lady threw down
Unto her good Serving-man, seven score pound;
She gave this Gold freely his courage to maintain
That he will but Ride in the Saddle again.
   So old, etc.

Then the wanton Lady to her Knight she did hie
And like to a meretrix[1] she did reply
That she was much altered and she had caught harm.
'Why then' quoth the Knight 'Lady, keep thyself warm!'
   So old, etc.

1. whore

117

'I'll send for a Doctor, thy grief for to find,
For to ease thy Body and troubled Mind'.
'I will have no Doctor, my grief for to ease
But only one man: Sweetheart, if you please!'
  So old, etc.

'Let me see this Artist' the Knight did reply.
'O!' quoth the Lady, 'Lo, here he stands by,
That can give me cure with a Syrup, that he
Brought from the *Venetian*, and from Italy.'[1]
  So old, etc.

'How came you acquainted with your Man's rarity?'
'Sir, in a sad Passion being ready to die,
I dreamed; that his judgement was right, I do find
And his Physick was healthful, to old women kind.'
  So Old, etc.

'And if by the virtue thou Pleasure do find
I doubt then, by Venus that I am made blind:
I dreamed I was hunting and pleasure did see,
But a vision mine eyes in, much troubleth me.'
  So old, etc.

'The Deer did run swiftly and Hounds after ranged,
And I, like *Actaeon*, most strangely was changed.
I thought that my lower part seemed like a Man
My head like a Buck and horns like a Ram.'
  So old, etc.

'And riding on swiftly, sweet pleasure to find
An Oak burst my horns, and his blood made me blind.
The Huntsman did hollo and great shouts did make
And forth of my dream I straight did awake.'
  So old, etc.

1. an aphrodisiac from an Italian quack

'I told my fair Lady of my dream so strange;
Quoth she, 'Tis the better when thy Life doth change;
For the Forked Order the evil doth expel
And being a dub'd Knight, thou needs't not fear Hell.'
  So old, etc.

From the Poor to the Rich, even to the Ladies gay
Young women are wanton, old women will play;
And mumble their husbands and jeer them to scorn,
And point them a Beaker, and give them a Horn.
  So old, etc.

37
The Lowse's Peregrination
(*ante* 1630)

[From *Musarum Delicae* by Sir John Mennes and Dr James Smith;
1655]

[Tune: 'The Lincolnshire Poacher']

My Father and Mother when first they joyn'd Paunches
Begot me between an old Pedlers haunches.
Where, grown to a Creeper I know how a Pox I
Got to suck by chance of the Bloud of a Doxie,
Where finding the sweetnesse of this my new Pasture
I felt the bones of my pockified Master
  And there I struck in for a Fortune.

A Lord of this Land that lov'd a Bum well
Did lie with this Mort one night in the Strummel.
I cling'd me fast to him and left my Companions:
I scorn'd to converse more with Tatterdemalians:
But sued to Sir Giles to promise in a Patent
That my Heires might enjoy clean Linnen and Sattin
  But the Parliament cross'd my Intention.

This Lord that I follow'd delighted in Tennis
He sweat out my fat with going to Venice.
Where with a brave Donna in single Duello
He left me behinde him within the Bordello,
Where leacherous Passages I did discover
Betwixt *Bonna Roba* and Diego her Lover
    You'ld wonder to heare the discourse of't.

The use of the Dildo they had without Measure
Behind and Before, they have it with Pleasure.
All Aretine's ways they practice with labour
An Eunuch they hate like Dethlem Gabor.
Counting the English man but as a Stallion
Leaving the Goat unto the Italian
    And this is the Truth that I tell you.

Thus living with Wonder, escaping the Talent
Of Citizen Clown Whore Lawyer and Gallant,
At last came a Soldier; I nimbly did ferk him
Up the greazy Skirts of's rabufluous buff Jerkin,
Where finding Companions, without any harm I
Was brought before Breda, to Spinola's army
    And there I remaine of a Certain.

NOTE: In 1625 the Dutch city of Breda surrendered after a year's siege to the General Ambrogio de Spinola, an Italian general in the Spanish army service.

38
My Mistris Is a Lady
(*ante* 1658)

[By Thomas Prestwick.
Rawlinson MS. (Poet.), 214, f.75, verso, rev.]

My Mistres is a Lady
And she's as fine as maybe.
She is as fine as the Muses Nine
Or any Bartholomew Baby.

Her buttock is a round one
And her Cunt is perfum'd too.
And she hath more haire upon her Ware
Than will stuff a Trooper's saddle.

God Bless my Lord Protector
And also his Protectoress;
Let all men live in fear of him
And every man love his mistress.

My Mistress is a Woman,
And her Cunt is grown so common;
Have a care of your Tarse,
Lest she fir't with her Arse,
For she is free for all men.

Her eyes are as bright
As the Stars of the night;
Oh! how they do twinkle!
If she had a thousand Pound,
She would through it, on the ground,
For the love of a standing Pintle.

NOTE: This is an attack on Oliver Cromwell and his mistress, the promiscuous Bess Dysart, afterwards Duchess of Lauderdale.

39
There Is a Thing
(*c.*1660)

[*Pills* (1719), vi, 106]

There is a Thing, which in the light
Is seldom used; but in the Night
It serves the maiden Female crew,
The Ladies and the good Wives too:
They used to take it in their Hand
And then it will uprightly stand;
And to a Hole they it apply,
Where by its good will it could die.
It wastes, goes out, and still within
It leaves its Moisture thick and thin.

40
John and Jone
(*ante* 1651)

[*Merry Drollerie* (1656), II, 46]
[Tune: *Pills* (1719), iv, 191]

If you will give Ear
And hearken awhile what I shall tell
I think I must come near
Or else you cannot hear me well.

It was a Mayd as I heard say
That in her Master's Chamber lay
For Maydens must it not refuse
In Yeomans Houses, they it use
In a Truckle-bed to lye
Or in a Bed that stands thereby;

Her Master and her Dame
Would have the Mayd do the same.

This Mayd she could not sleep
Whenas she heard the Bedstead crack
When Captain Standish stout
Made his Dame crye out 'You hurt my Back,
Fie!' she said 'you do me wrong,
You lye so sure my Breaste upon;
But you are such another Man
You'd have me do more than I can!'
'Fie! Master!' then quoth honest *Jone*
'I pray you let my Dame alone:
'Fie!' quoth she 'what a Coyl you keep,
I cannot take nor rest nor sleep!'

This was enough to make
A Mayden sick and full of Pain
For she did fling and kick
And swore she'd tear her Smock in twain.
But now to let you understand
They kept a Man whose name was *John*,
To whom this Mayden went anon
And unto him she made her moan
'Tell me, *John*, tell me the same
What doth my Master to my Dame?
Tell me *John*, and do not lye,
What ails my Dame to Squeak and Crye?'

Quoth *John* 'Your Master he
Doth give your Dame a *Steel* at Night,
And tho' she find such Fault
It is her only Heart's Delight:
And you, *Jone*, for your part,
You would have one with all your Heart?'

'Yes, indeed' quoth honest *Jone*
'Therefore to thee I make my moan;
But *John*, if I may be so bold
Where is there any to be sold?'
'At *London* then' quoth honest *John*
'Next Market-day I'll bring thee one.'

'What is the Price?' quoth *Jone*
'If I should chance to stand in need?'
'Why, twenty Shillings' then quoth *John*
'For twenty Shillings you may speed!'
The Mayd then went unto her Chest
And fetch'd him Twenty Shillings just.
'There *John*' quoth she, 'here is the Coyne
And prithee have me in thy Mind
And, honest *John*, out of my Store
I'll give thee two odd Shillings more'.

To Market then went *John*
When he had the Mony in his Purse:
He domineer'd and swore
And was as stout as any Horse.
Some he spent in Wine and Beer
And some in Cakes and other good Cheer,
And some he carried Home again
To serve his turn another Time.
'O! *John*' quoth she 'thou'rt welcome Home'
'God-a-Mercy!' quoth he 'gentle *Jone*.
'But prethee *John*, now let me feel,
Hast thou brought me home a Steel?'

'Yes, that I have' quoth *John*
And then he took her by the Hand
And led her straight into a Room
Where she could see nor Sun nor Moon.

124

The Dore to him he straight did clap
And put the Steel into her Lap,
And then the Mayd began to feel
'Cods foot!' quoth she 'tis a goddey Steel,
But tell me *John*, and do not lye,
What makes these two things hang herebye?'
'O! *Jone*, to let thee understand,
They're the two odd Shillings thou put'st in my Hand'.
'If I had known so much before,
I would have given thee two Shillings more!'

NOTE: The same ballad, slightly up-dated, appears in Thomas
D'Urfey's *Pills* (1719) wherein it is described as a Broadside Ballad;
and a few bars of music are given, but whether they are the original
or not cannot be ascertained.

The story discloses a social habit, that maidservants were expected
to lie on a bed or pallet in their masters' bedrooms.

41
She Lay All Naked in Her Bed
(*ante* 1654)

A Dream
[*Wit and Drollery* (1656), p.56]

[Tune: Simpson, 156]

She lay all naked in her Bed
And I myself lay by;
No Vail, but Curtains about her spread,
No covering but I.
Her Head upon her Shoulders seeks
To hang in careless-wise;
All full of Blushes was her Cheeks
And of Wishes, were her Eyes.

Her Blood still fresh into her Face
As on a Message came
To say, that in another Place
It meant another Game;
Her cherry Lip, moyst Plump and faire
Millions of Kisses crown,
Which ripe and uncropt dangled there
And weigh the Branches down.

Her Breasts, that swell'd so plump and high
Bred plesant Pain in me;
For all the World I do defie
The like Felicity.
Her Thighs and Belly, soft and faire
To me were only shewn:
To have seen such Meat and not to have eat
Would have ang'red any Stone.

Her Knees lay upward, gently bent
And all lay hollow under,
As if on easie terms they ment
To fall, unforc'd asunder.
Just so the *Cyprian* Queen did lye
Expecting in her Bower:
When too, long stay had kept the Boy
Beyond his promis'd Hour.

Dull Clown, quoth she, why dost delay
Such proffered Bless to take?
Can'st thou find out no other Way
Similitudes to make?
Mad with Delight I thundering
Threw my Arms about her;
But Pox upon 't, 'twas but a Dream
And so I lay without her.

42

The Willing Lover
(*ante* 1650)

An Answer, being a-dreamed

[*Merry Drollery Compleat* (1691)
Wit and Drollery (1656), p.58]

[Tune: Simpson, 657]

She lay up to the navel bare
And was a willing lover;
Expecting between hope and fear
When I would come and cover.
Her hand beneath my waistband slips
To grope in, busy wise,
Which caused a trembling in her lips
And shivering in her eyes.

The blood out of her face did go
As it on service went
To second what was gone before
When all its strength was spent.
Her cheeks and lips as Coral red
Like Roses, were full blown:
Which fading straight, the leaves were spread
And so the Thorn comes down.

Her Breasts then both panting were
Such comfort wrought between us,
That all the world, I dare to swear
Would envy to have seen us.
Her Belly and its provender
For me was kept in store;
Such news to hear, and not to have share
Would have made a Man a Whore.

Her legs were girt about my waist
My hands under her Crupper;
As who should say 'now break your Fast
And come again to Supper,'
Even as the God of War did knock,
As any other Man will,
For haste of work at twelve o'clock
Kept Vulcan at his anvil.

'Mad wag' quoth she, 'Why dost thou make
Such haste thyself to rear?
Cans't thou not know, that for thy sake
The Fair lasts all the year?'
Quiet and calm as are Love's streams
I threw myself about her.
But a Pox upon true Jests and Dreams –
I had better have lain without her!

43

A Puritan
(*c.*1650)

[*Merry Drollery* (1656)]

A Puritan of late
And eke a holy Sister,
A-catechizing sate
And fain would he have kissed her
   For this Mate.

But she, a Babe of Grace,
A child of Reformation,
Thought kissing a Disgrace –
A Limb of Profanation,
   In that place.

He swore by Yea and Nay
He would have no denial;
The Spirit would it so,
She should endure a trial
   Ere she go.

'Why swear you so,?' quoth she
'Indeed, my holy Brother,
You might have forsworn be
Had it been to another,
   Not to me.'

He laid her on the ground
His spirits fell a-ferking;
Her zeal was in a sound,
He edified her Merkin
   Upside down.

And when their leave they took,
And parted were asunder,
My Muse did then awake
And I turned Ballad-monger
   For their sake.

44

Riding to Dunstable
(*ante* 1630)

[*Merry Drollery* (1656) p.200
J.S.F., 135]
   [See also Poems 23, 123]

Riding to *London* on *Dunstable* way
I met with a Mayd on *Midsummer* Day.
Her Eyes they did sparkle like Stars in the Sky

129

Her Face it was fair and her Forehead was high:
The more I came to her the more I did view her,
The better I lik'd her pretty sweet Face.
I could not forbear her, but still I drew near her
And then I began to tell her my Case.

'Whither walk'st thou, my pretty sweet Soul?'
She modestly answer'd, to *Hockley-i-th'-Hole*.
I asked her her Business; she had a red Cheek,
She told me she went a poor Service to seek.
I said it was pitty she should leave the City
And settle herself in a Countrey Town.
She said it was certain it was her hard Fortune
To go up a Mayden, and so to come down.

With that I alighted and to her I stept
I took her by th' Hand, and this pretty Mayde wept:
'Sweet, weep not' quoth I: I kist her soft Lip;
I wrung her by th' Hand and my Finger she nipt.
So long there I woo'd her, such Reasons I shew'd her
That she my Speeches could not controul,
But curtsied finely and got up behind me
And back she rode with me to *Hockley-i-th'-Hole*.

When I came to *Hockley* at the Sign of *The Cock*,
By alighting I chanced to see her white Smock;
It lay so alluring upon her round Knee
I call'd for a Chamber immediately:
I hugg'd her, I tugg'd her, I kist her, I smugg'd her
And gently I laid her down on a Bed;
With nodding and pinking, with sighing and winking
She told me a Tale of her Maydenhead.

While she to me this Story did tell
I could not forbear, but on her I fell;
I tasted the Pleasure of sweetest Delight,

We took up our Lodging and lay there all Night:
With soft Arms she roul'd me and ofttimes told me,
She lov'd me deerly, even as her own Soul.
But on the next Morrow we parted with sorrow,
And so I lay with her at *Hockley-i-th'-Hole*.

NOTE: Hockley in the Hole was an alley off Farringdon Street (today known as Ray Street) running into the infamous Turnmill Street, in which every house was a brothel. Hockley was renowned for its cockpits and bear-pits and as a place where every form of vice was practised. So that the young lady was not on her way for any respectable Service, and it is doubtful whether she had a maidenhead to sell there.

45

The Old Fumbler
(*c.*1695)

[*Pills* (1719), ii, 312]

[A broadsheet song. Music composed by Henry Purcell]

Smug, rich and fantastic Old Fumbler was known
That wedded a juicy brisk Girl of the Town;
Her face like an Angel, fair, plump, and a Maid,
Her Lute well in tune too – could he have but play'd.

But lost was his Skill, let him do what he can,
She finds him in Bed, a weak silly old man.
He coughs in her ear ''tis in vain to come on,
Forgive me my Dear, I'm a silly old man.'

She laid his dry Hand on her snowy white Breast;
And from those white Hills gave a glimpse of the Best.
But Ah! what is age when our youth's but a span;
She found him an infant instead of a Man.

131

'Ah! pardon' he'd cry 'that I'm weary so soon:
You have let down my Base, I'm no longer in tune.
Lay by, the dear Instrument; Prithee lie still.
I can play but one Lesson, and that I play ill'.

46

An Historical Ballad
(*c.*1670)

[*Ane Plesant Garland* (1835)]

Much has been said of Strumpets of yore,
Of Laïs, whole volumes; of Messaline, more,
But I sing of a lewder than e'er lived before
    Which nobody can deny.

From her Mother at first she drew the infection,
And as soon as she spoke, she made use of injection;
And now she's grown up to a girl of perfection
    Which nobody etc.

If you told her of Hell, she would say 'twas a Jest
And swear, of all gods, that Priapus was best,
For her Soul was a Whore when she suck'd at the breast
    Which nobody etc.[1]

She once was called Virgin but 'twas but a sham
Her Maidenhead never was gotten by man;
She frigg'd it away in the womb of her Dam
    Which the Midwife couldn't deny.

1. alternatively – 'Which her Nurses can't deny.'

An Historical Ballad

At length Mr Fopping made her his bride
But found (to bring down his ambition and pride)
Her Fortune but narrow and her Cunt very wide
   Which he himself can't deny.

In vain, he long strove to satiate her lust
Which still grew more vigorous at every thrust,
No wonder the puny Chit came by the worst
   Which nobody can deny.

For, when he grew sapless she gave him her blessing
And left him to painting, to patching and dressing;
But first dubbed him Cuckold – a strange way of jesting
   Which nobody etc.

And now she is free to swive where she pleases
And where e're she swives she scatters diseases;
And a Shanker's a damn'd loving thing where it seizes
   Which nobody etc.

There's Haughton and Elland, and Arran,[2] the sot
(She deserves to be pox'd that would fuck with a Scot)
All charged the lewd harlot, and all went to pot
   Which they themselves can't deny.

For that she has buboed and ruined as many
As Hinton or Willis, Moll Howard[3] or any
And, like to those Punks, will fuck for a penny
   Is what nobody will deny.

2. Lord Haughton, Lord Elland and the Earl of Arran were notorious lechers at
the Court of Charles II.   3. Mary Hinton, Sue Willis and Mary Howard were
three of the many prostitutes haunting the court. Sue Willis was highly praised
by Lord Rochester.

To scour the Town is her darling delight
In breaking of windows, to scratch and to fight,
And to lie with her own brawny Footman at night
   Which she herself can't deny.

Who, though they eternally pizzle her breech
Can't allay the wild rage of her lecherous Itch,
Which proves our good Lady a monstrous Bitch
   Which they themselves can't deny.

But now, if there's any – or Christian or Jew,
That say I've belied her, I advise 'em to go
And ask the fair creature herself if 'tis true
   Which I'm certain she won't deny.

NOTE: Supposed to refer to Lady Anne Carnegie, later Lady
Southesk, mistress to the Duke of York, later James the Second.

47

Contentment
(*ante* 1655)

[*Merry Drollery* (1661), p.161]

[Tune: Simpson, 474]

What tho' the Times produce effects
Are worth our Observation;
He's mad that at it once dejects
Or does remove his Station.
Give me the Wench that's like a Tench
In holding up her Belley
For to receive, and to conceive
The most heroick *Jelly*.

Altho' she be a Saint that's free
From any such intention;
She may be bold; Hang her that's cold,
With a timorous apprehension.
Let Danger come, have at her Bum
Give me the Girle that stands to't.
And when its lank, does advance her Flank
And lay a helping Hand to't.

To make it rise between her Thighs
And fuck her is a Pleasure;
Tho' he be stout, he ne'er comes out
But he wants of his Measure.
If he have a *Yard*, it will be hard
If he half a one produces:
When he's so short, you may thank her for't:
Oh! these are gross Abuses.

My *Mistris* she is very free
And fancies well my Temper:
Sweet Rogue, she loves the merry Shoves
And is clear from all Distemper.
When I stand to't she needs must do it
For she is compos'd of Pleasure,
And does invite me to delight:
I exhaust my chiefest Treasure.

My *Mistris* she is very free
And sings and frolicks neatly:
Besides all this she does nobly Kiss
And does her work compleatly;
For which I love her, and none above her
And she loves me for the same too:
But that I fear you'd soon be there
I would disclose her Name too!

48
Love's Tenement
(*ante* 1655)

[*Merry Drollery* (1661), II, p.64]

[See also Poem 105]

If any one do want a House
Prince, Duke, Earl, Lord or Squire,
Or Peasant, hardly worth a Louse,
I can fit his Desire.

I have a Tenement, the which
I know can fit them all,
'Tis seated near a stinking Ditch –
Men call it *Cony-Hall*.

It stands below *Bum Alley*
At foot of *Belly-Hill*
This Tenement is to be taken
By whosoever will.

For term of Years, for Months, or Daies,
I'll let this pleasant Bower:
Nay! rather than a Tenant want
I'll let it for an Houre.

About it grows a pleasant *Wood*
To shade you from the Sun
Well watere'd 'tis, for through the House
A pleasant *Stream* doth run.

If hot, you there may cool you
If cold, you there find Heat;
For little, it not greatest is,
For least, 'tis not too great.

My *House*, indeed, I must say is dark
Be it by Night or Day:
But if that you be gotten in
You cannot miss the Way.

None ever yet within my *House*
Did ever weep or wail
You need not fear the Tenure o't
For it is held *In Tayle*

But I must covenant with him
That takes this *House* of mine
Whether for Years or else for Months
Or for some shorter Time,

That once a Day he wash it
And sweep it round about
And that if he do fail of this
I'll seek a new Tenant out.

Thus if you like my *Tenement*
Your house-room shall be good
Of such a Temper as you shall
Need burn neither Cole nor Wood;

For be it Cold or be it Hot
To speak I dare be bold
As long as you keep your Nose within Dores
You never shall be a-cold.

49

Mine Own Sweet Honey-bird-chuck
(*ante* 1655)

[*Merry Drollery* (1661), II, p.155]

[Tune: Simpson, 74]

Mine own sweet Honey-bird-chuck
Come sit thee down by me
And thou and I will truck
For thy Commoditie.

The weather is cold and chilly
And heating will do thee no harm,
I'll put a hot Thing in thy Belly
To keep thy Body warm.

Our Landlady hath brought us
All that the House affords;
'Tis time to lay about us,
Then prithee, make no words.

I know thou art young and tender
Although thy Cunt be rough;
Thy Fort, if thou'lt to me surrender,
I'll man it well enough.

50
The Souldier
(*c*.1660)

[*Merry Drollery* (1661), p.168]

[Tune: Simpson, No. 108]

Hey Ho! have at all!
Fair Lady, by your leave,
He that chanceth low to fall
The higher must he heave.
Nay! Faith, good Sir, you are to blame
'Tis Fashion for a Clown:
For he that mounts too high at first
Is soonest taken down.

I am a Souldier, bonny Lass
And oft have fought in Field
In Battles oft, as fierce as *Mars*,
Yet ne'er was forced to yield.
A *Standard-bearer* still am I
And have broke many a Lance,
I have travell'd Countreys far and nigh
Yet ne'er was bound for *France*.

My *Weapon*, it will stiffly stand
And make a cunning Thrust
If I lye open to your Hand
So that you hit me just:
You are no cunning Marks-man sure
You lye so long at Lure:
Oh! thrust, thrust, thrust, far, far, far, far
Be sure I will endure.

Fie! Fie! your *Lance* doth bend.
Full little I account you
Courageously, if you'll not Spend.
Sit fast, or I'll dismount you;
Such Cowards fight I do disdain
That can endure no longer
But see that when you come again
Your *Lance*, it may be stronger.

So! so! now I see you have Tricks by Arts:
Low! low! not so high.
You make my Thighs to smart.
[*a line missing here*]
Your mounting high 'twill not be,
'Twill bring you soon to Wrack.
I do not doubt the Victory
Tho' I lye on my Back.

51
A Young Man Lately in Our Town
(*ante* 1665)

[*The New Academy of Complements* (1671), No.191]

[Tune: *Pills* (1719), vi, 180]

A young man lately in our Town
He went to bed one Night,
He had no sooner lay'd him down
But was troubled with a Sprite.
So vigorously the Spirit stood –
Let him do what he can –
Sure then, he said, it must be lay'd
By woman, not by man.

A handsome Maid did undertake
And into bed she leaped,
And to allay the Spirit's power
Full close to him she crept;
She having such a guardian care
Her office to discharge,
She opened wide her Conjuring Book
And lay'd the leaves at large.

Her office she did well perform
Within a little space;
Then up she rose, and down he lay
And durst not show his Face.
She took her leave and away she went
When she had done the Deed;
Saying, if it chance to come again,
Then send for me with speed.

52
Come Let Us Be Friends
(*ante* 1666)

[*The New Academy of Complements* (1671), No.149]

[Tune: 'Come Hither to Me', Simpson, 143]

Come let us be Friends and most friendly agree
For the Pimp, the Punk and the Doctor are Three
Which cannot but thrive when united they be.
The Pimp brings in Custom, the Punk gets the Treasure
Of which the Physitian is sure of his Measure
For work that she makes him in Sale of her Pleasure
For which when she fails by Diseases or Pain
The Doctor new vamps, and Up sets her again.

53
A Pox on the Goaler
(1671)

[*The New Academy of Complements* (1671), No.59]

[Tune: 'Let Caesar Live', Simpson, 435]

A Pox on the Goaler and on his fat Jowl
There's Liberty lies in the bottom of the Bowl.
A Fig for what ever the Rascall can do
Our Dung'on is deep, but our Cups are so too.
Then drink we a Round in despight of our Foes
And make our cold Iron cry chink in the Close.

NOTE: 'Goaler': The word is frequently spelt as above in
contemporary literature.

54
There Was a Fair Maiden Came Out of Kent
(1671 [originally *c*.1568])

[*The New Academy of Complements* (1671), No.101]

[Music originally composed *c*.1568; later version Chappell, I,348 and Simpson, 385, 'Jig-a-Jogoo']

There was a fair Maiden came out of Kent
To be fuck'd by a Joyner was her Intent.
To be fuck'd by a Joyner was her Intent:
I have a jobbe of Work for you to doe
To make me a Bed to go jig-a-jogoo.

And when would you have this jobb of Work done?
By the faith o' my Body, soone as you can.
By the faith of my Body, soone as you can
To make me a Bed for to go jig-a-jogoo.

When this jobb of Work it was thoroughly done,
Then he laid this fair Maiden there upon.
Then he laid this fair Maiden there upon
To make her a Bed for to go jig-a-jogoo.

He knockt in a Pinn where a Pinn should be,
Which made the Bed go jig-a-jogee.
But in her old Mother came full of Wo
With 'Oh! fie! Daughter, who would you do so?

Since it must be done, Mother, why not he,
That would with my Bed go jig-a-jogee?

55

The Wooing Rogue
(*ante* 1612)

[*Westminster Drollery*, I, p.16[1]
J.S.F., V, 50]

[A broadside song. Tune: Chappell, I, 215, 'My Freedom is All My
Joy'; Chappell, I, 123, 'Come Live with Me and be My Love']

Come live with me and be my Whore
And we will beg from door to door,
Then under a hedge we'll sit and louse us[2]
Until the Beadle come to rouse us.
And if they'll give us no relief
   Thou shalt turn Whore and I'll turn Thief
   Thou shalt turn Whore and I'll turn Thief.

If thou can'st rob then I can steal
And we'll eat Roast-meat every meal:
Nay! we'll eat White-bread every day
And throw our mouldy Crusts away,
And twice a day we will be drunk
   And then at Night I'll kiss my Punk
   And then at Night I'll kiss my Punk

And when we both shall have the Pox,
We then shall want[3] both Shirts and Smocks
To shift each other's mangy hide
That is with Itch so pockified:
We'll take some clean ones from a hedge
   And leave our old ones for a Pledge
   And leave our old ones for a Pledge.

1. The original was 'Come Live with Me and be My Love'.
2. delouse   3. shall be needing or lacking

56
Have Y'Any Crackt Maidenheads?
(*c*.1672)

[*Windsor Drollery*, p.102]

[A broadside ballad]

Have y'any crackt Maidenheads to new leach or mend?
Have y'any old Maidenheads to sell or to change?
Bring 'em to me; with a little pretty gin[1]
I'll clout 'em, I'll mend 'em, I'll knock 'em in a pin
Shall make 'em as good Maids agen,
As ever they have been.

NOTE: From even before the time of James I there had been Quacks who specialized in renewing maidenheads. Midwives were particularly esteemed for this service. The main chemical used was alum: or other astringents designed to tauten up the vaginal walls to give the impression of virginity. In many cases, however, serious damage was caused and the enraged pimps frequently assaulted the Quacks, who usually fled to the Netherlands or France whence they had come. Dutch Quacks were attacked in the famous petition of the Whores to the Prentices in 1668 after the Shrove Tuesday riots which so upset Charles II and 'vex'd my Lady Castlemaine'.

1. engine, device

57
A Song
(1661)

[*Wit and Drollery* (1661), p.38]

When Young folks first begin to love
and undergo that tedious Taske
It cuts and scowres throughout the powers
much like a Running-glass.

It is so full of sodain joyes
Proceeding from the Heart
So many Tricks, so many Toyes
and all not worth a Fart.

For *Venus* Loves *Vulcan*
yet the world would lye with *Mars*:
If these be honest Tricks, my love
Sweet love – come kiss my Arse.

If this which I have writ
be unworthy in Speech
Yet when occasion serves to shit,
will serve to wipe your breech.

Thus kindly and in Courtesie
these few lines I have written,
And now, O Love, come kiss my Arse
for I am all beshitten.

NOTE: The author of this effusion is most probably Sir William
Davenport, described as 'one of the most refined Wits of the Age'.

58
An Account of Cuffley
(*c.*1670)

[By John Wilmot, Earl of Rochester.
Gyllenstolpe MSS., Stockholm]

This may suffice to let you know
That I to Cunt am not a Foe
Though you are pleas'd to think me so
'Tis strange his zeal shou'd b'm suspition
Who dies a Martyr for's Religion.

But now to give you an Account
Of CUFFLEY that Whore paramount
CUFFLEY whose Beauties warms her Age
And fills our youth with Love and Rage

Who like feirce Wolves pursue the game
While secretly the leacherous Dame
With some choice Gallant takes her flight
And in a Corner fucks all night

Then the next morning we all hunt
To find whose fingers smell of Cunt
With Jealousy and envy mov'd
Against the Man that was belov'd

While you within some neighbouring Grove
Indite the Story of your Love
And with your Penknife keen and bright
On stately Trees your Passion write

So that each Nymph that passes through
Must envy and pitty you

Wee at the Fleece or at the Bear
With good Case-knife well whett on Stair
A gentle weapon made to feed
Mankind, and not to make him bleed

A Thousand amorous fancies scrape
There's not a Pewterdish can 'scape
Without her Name or Arms which are
The same that Love himselfe does beare

Heere one to show Love's no glutton
I'th' midst of's supper leaves his mutton
And on a Greazy plate with care
Carves the bright Image of the fair

Another though a Drunken sott
Neglects his wine and on the Pott
A Band of Naked CUPIDS draws
With Pricks no bigger than wheat-straws

Then on a nasty Candlestick
One figures Love's Hierogliphick
A Couchant Cunt and Rampant Prick

And that the sight may more enflame
The lookers on subscribe her Name
CUFFLEY, her sexes Pride and Shame

There's not a Man but does discover
By some such Action hee's her Lover
But now 'tis time to give her over.

NOTE: In 1663 Lord Rochester indicates that it was the Court pro-
curess Mrs Temple 'who made me friends with Mrs Cuffley, whom
we indeed had us'd most roughly'. In that winter Rochester and
some of his cronies enticed this young and lovely girl with a com-

panion over the Thames to Lambeth and in the drunken frolicking the girls took refuge by climbing a tree, whereby Cuffley (whose Christian name is never mentioned) sustained an injury serious enough to alarm Rochester. He took her under his wing and helped her build up an enthusiastic clientele, part of their pleasure being that young Cuffley 'would fuck for Ten Pound', and that 'Her pow'rful Cunt whose very name, kindles in me an am'rous Flame'. By 1688 she was well established and well liked.

59

A Merry Discourse between a Country Lass and a Young Taylor
(c. 1672)

How the Taylor lost his Plight & Plesure
His Yard not being, by the Standard, Mesure.

[*Roxburghe Ballads*, II, 80
J.S.F., II, 70]

[Tune: 'The Kester Crab']

In harvest-time I walked
Hard by a corn-close side:
I, hearing people talk
I looked about and spy'd.

A young Man and a Maid
Together they did lye;
When you hear it told,
You'll laugh full heartily.

She was as buxsome a Lass
As any in our Town;
She will not let you pass
But she'll call you to sit down.

A Taylor passing by
She hit him on the heel:
You are very welcome Sir,
To sit you down, and feel!

What money's in my Purse
At your command shall be,
If you will go along
To *Marston Wake* with me!

He, hearing her say so
And seeing her to smile
Was charmed with her, so
He sate him down awhile.

And having groped her Purse
And taken all her Money;
He groped again and missed
And caught her by the Cunny.

Where am I now (quoth he)
Another I have found:
Its not the same (quoth he)
For this is tufted round!

If it be tufted round (quoth she)
There is good reason for't;
Therein such Treasure lyes
Will make a taylor sport.

He, hearing her say so,
Being a frollicksome Ladd
Was willing for to know
More of the fringed Bag.

With that he eagerly
to feel, put forth his Hand;
Nay! hold, good Sir (said she)
Go not before you Stand.

Except you take your Yard[1]
The depth of it to measure,
You'll find the Purse so deep
You'll hardly come to th' Treasure.

He hearing her say so,
It put him to a Stand:
She, seeing him dismay'd,
She took his Yard in Hand.

Is *this* your Yard (quoth she)
Is *this* your Taylors' measure?
It is too short for me –
It is not Standard-measure.

The Taylor, being abashed
She told him that it was
More fitter for a Man
Than such a penny Ass.

She bids him now begone
Since he could make no sport
(and said) thou art too dull
To enter such a Fort.

She, looking fiercely at him
(she said) thou sneaking Fool:
Go straightaway to *Vulcan*
And let him mend thy Tool.

1. penis

And tell him that Dame *Venus*
At him is almost mad
For sending to her School
Such an unfit Ladd.

You Taylors that attempt
Fringed Baggs to measure:
Be sure your Yards be sealed
And of full Standard Measure.

60

Dildoides
(1672)

[By Samuel Butler (in *Hudibras*)
Harley MS., 7319, B.M.]

Such a sad Tale prepare to hear
As claims from either Sex a Tear
Twelve Dildoes (meant for the support
of aged Lechers of the Court)
Were lately burn'd by th'impious Hand
Of Trading rascals of the Land,
Who envying their curious Frame
Exposed these PRIAPUS's to the Flame.

O! barbarous Times when *Deities*
Are made themselves a Sacrifice.
Some were composed of shining Horns
More precious than ten *Unicorns*.
Some were of Wax, where every Vein
And every Fiber were made plain.
Some were for tender Virgins fitt
Some for the wide salacious *Slit*
Of a Rank Lady[1] – tho' so torn
She hardly feels when child is born.

1. Castlemaine

Dildo has a Nose and cannot smell
No Stink can his great Courage quell
At sight of *Plaister* he'd not fail
Nor faintly ask, What do you ail?
Women must have both Youth and Beauty
Ere the damn'd Rogue will do his Duty
And that perhaps he will not stand to
Do what *Gallant* and *Mistress* can do.

But I too long have left my Heroes
Who fell in worse hands than NERO'S.
Twelve of them shut up in a Box
Who ne'er gave Maid nor Wife the Pox.
Deep under lawful Traffic hidden
Were seized upon as Goods forbidden.
When Counsell grave of deepest Beard
Was call'd from out the City's herd.

But see the Fate of cruell Treachery –
Those Goats in head but not in Lechery,
Forgetting each his Wife and Daughter
Condemn's these *Dildoes*, to the slaughter;
Cuckolds, with rage were blinded so
They did not their Prisoners know.
One less fanatickall than the rest
Stood up, and thus himself address'd.

These *Dildoes* may do harm, I know,
But Pray! what is it may not so?
Plenty has often made men proud
And above Law, advanced the Crowd;
Religion's self has ruined Nations
And caused vast *Depopulations*.
Yet nowhere people have refused 'em
Because that *Fools* sometimes abuse 'em.

Unless you fear some merry Grigs
Will wear false *Pricks* and Perriwiggs,
And being but too small was born
Will great ones have of *Wax* and *Horn*;
Since even that promotes our Gain
Methinks, unjustly, we complain
If Ladies rather choose to handle
In *Wax* in *Dildo* than in Candle.

Much good may't do them, so they pay for't
And that the Merchants never stay for it;
For *Neighbours*, is't not all one whether
In *Pricks* or Shoes, they wear our Leather?
Whether of Horn they make a Comb
Or *Instrument* to chafe the *Womb*?
Like you I *Monsieur Dildo* hate,
But the Invention let's translate.

You treat them may, like *Turks* or *Jews*
But I'll have two for my own use.
PRIAPUS was a Roman deity,
And such has been the World's variety
I am resolved, I'll none provoke
From the humble Garlick to the Oak.
He paus'd. Another strait stept in
With limber *Prick* and grisly Chinn
And then began

For Souldiers maim'd in chance of War
We artificial Limbs prepare;
Why then should we bear such a Spight
To Lechers hurt in am'rous Fight,
And what the French send for relief
We thus condemn as Witch, or Thief.

Dildoides

Dildo that Monsieur sure intends
For his *French Pox* to make amends
For such without the least disgrace
Might fill the lusty Foreman's place
And make our elder Girls ne'er care for't
Tho' 'twere their Fortune to Dance barefoot.

Lechers whom *Drink* or *Clapp* disable
Might here have *Dildo* to their *Navil*
And with false Heat (and Member too)
Such Widdows, for convenience, woo;
Did not a Lady of Great Honour
Marry a Footman waiting on her?
Were one on these, timely apply'd
It had eased her Lust and saved her Pride.

Safely her Ladyship might have spent
While *Gallants* such, in Pocket went.
Honour itself might use the Trade
While *Pego*[1] goes in Masquerade.
Which of you able to prevent is
His Girl from lying with his Prentice?

Unless we other means provide
For Nature to be satisfied?
And what more proper than this *Engine*
Which would outdo 'em, should thee men joyn.
I therefore hold it very foolish
Things so convenient to abolish;
Which if you burn, we safely may
To your own Act the Ruin lay
Of all that cast themselves away.

1. penis

At this all Parnets' hearts began
To melt apace: and not a man
In all th'Assembly but found
His Reasons solid were, and Sound.
Poor Widdows strait, with Voices shrill
With shouts of Joy the Hall did fill,
For wicked *Pintles* have no mind to her
Who hath no Money nor no *Jointure*.

When one in haste brake through the Throng
And cry'd aloud, Are we among
Heathens or Infidels, to let 'scape us
This Image of the lewd PRIAPUS?
Green-sickness Girls will soon adore him
And wickedly fall down before him,
For him each superstitious Hussy
Will Temples build to *Tussey-Mussey*.

Idolatry will fill the land
And all true *Pricks* forget to stand.
Curst be the Wench who found those Arts
Of losing us the Women's Hearts.
For Pray! henceforth who'd not refuse one
When she has all that she has use on?
Or how shall I e'er make her pity me
Who enjoys man in this *Epitome*?

Besides, what greater Derogation
From sacred Rites of *Propagation*
Than turning th'action of the Tool
(whence we all came!) in Redicule?
The man that would have Thunder made
With brazen Head for Coursers laid
In my mind did not so ill do
As he that found the wicked *Dildo*.

Let's then with common indignation
Expel the *Priapuses* out of the Nation.
These cursed Instruments of Lewdness,
And Ladies, take it not for Rudeness;
For never was so base a Treachery
Designed by Man 'gainst female Lechery.

Men would kind Husbands' seem, and able
With feigned Lust and borrow'd *Bauble*;
Lovers themselves would rest their Passion
In this fantastick new French fashion.
But the wise City will take care
That men shall vend no such false Ware.

See here th'unstable Vulgar's mind
Shook like a Leaf with every Wind.
No sooner had he spoke but all
With a deep Rage, for Faggots call.
The Reasons that before seemed good
Now are no longer understood.
This last Speech had the cruell Power
To bring these *Dildoes* latest Hour;
PRIAPUS thus, in Box opprest
Burnt like a PHOENIX in its nest,
But with this fatal difference dyes –
We find no *Dildo* from his Ashes rise.

NOTE: This satire refers to the incident in February 1671 when the lordly clique known as 'Buff-Ballers' tried to import these dildoes without paying customs duty. Sir Charles Sedley and Lord Henry Saville went down to the City to try and prevent the dildoes from being destroyed by the Customs officers (the Trading rascals of the Land) but were told that 'these filthy things had been burnt without Mercy'. Seemingly, at this time they were made of both leather and wax in France, although Lord Rochester in his play *Sodom* implies that they were made by specialists in London. The earliest mention of dildoes in use is to be found in Thomas Nashe's 'The Merrie

Ballad of Nashe His Dildo' (see poem No. 6), wherein Nashe, being worn out by sexual excess, is chagrined to find his partner, a courtesan, still untaxed, and she threatens to use a dildo instead.

61
A Ramble in St James's Park
(1672)

[By John Wilmot, Earl of Rochester
Rochester 1732]

Much wine had passed, with grave Discourse
Of who fucks who, and who does worse.
(Such as you usually do hear
From those who diet at *The Bear*[1]),

When I, who still take care to see
Drunkenness relieved by lechery,
Went out into St James's Park
To cool my head and fire my heart.

But tho' St James's has th'honor on't,
'Tis consecrate to Prick and Cunt.
There, by a most incestuous Birth,
Strange woods spring from the teeming Earth.

For they relate how heretofore
When ancient Pict began to whore
Deluded of his assignation
(Jilting, it seems, was then in fashion),

1. a chop-house in Drury Lane

A Ramble in St James's Park

Poor pensive lover, in this place
Would frig upon his mother's face:
Whence rows of Mandrakes tall did rise
Whose lewd Tops fucked the very skies.

Each imitative branch does twine
In some loved fold of Aretine;[1]
And nightly now beneath their shade
Are buggeries, rapes and incests made.

Unto this all-sin-sheltering grove,
Whores of the Bulk,[2] and the Alcove,
Great Ladies, chambermaids and drudges,
The Rag-picker and heiress trudges.

Carmen, Divines, Great Lords, and tailors;
Prentices, poets, pimps and jailers,
Footmen, fine Fopps do here arrive,
And here, promiscuously they swive.

Along these hallowed walks it was
That I beheld Corinna pass.
Whoever had been by to see
The proud disdain she cast on me,

Through charming eyes, he would have swore
She dropped from Heaven that very hour,
Forsaking the divine abode
In scorn of some despairing God.

But mark, what creatures women are:
How infinitely vile, when fair!
Three Knights o'the Elbow and the Slur[3]
With wriggling tails, made up to her.

1. Pietro Aretino (1492–1556)   2. a bench in front of shops   3. gamblers, cardsharps, dice-rogues

The first was of your White-hall blades,
Near kin to th' Mother of the Maids;[1]
Graced by whose favour, he was able
To bring a friend to th'Waiters' Table.

Where he had heard Sir Edward Sutton[2]
Say how the King loved Banstead mutton.[3]
Since when he'd ne'er be brought to eat
By 's good will, any other meat.

In this, as well as all the rest
He ventures to do like the best,
But wanting common sense, th'ingredient
In choosing well, not least expedient,

Converts abortive Imitation
To universal affectation.
Thus he not only eats and talks
But feels and smells, sits down and walks,

Nay looks, and lives, and loves by rote
In an old tawdry birthday Coat.
The second was a Grays Inn wit,[4]
A great inhabiter of the Pit[5]

Where critic-like he sits and squints,
Steals pocket-handkerchiefs, and hints
From 's neighbour, and the comedy,
To court and pay his Landlady.

1. matron in charge of the Maids of Honour at Court 2. Gentleman Usher
and Daily Waiter to the King 3. cheap whores from the countryside 4. a
lawyer 5. rear seats in the theatre

A Ramble in St James's Park

The third, a Lady's eldest son
Within few years of twenty-one,
Who hopes from his propitious fate
Against he comes to his estate.

By these two worthies to be made
A most accomplished tearing Blade.
One, in a strain twixt tune and nonsense
Cries 'Madam, I have loved you long since.

'Permit me your fair hand to kiss!';
When, at her mouth, her Cunt cries, 'Yes.'
In short, without much more ado
Joyful and pleased, away she flew;
And with these three confounded asses
From park, to Hackney Coach, she passes.

So, a proud Bitch does lead about
Of humble curs, the amorous rout;
Who most obsequiously do hunt
The savoury scent of salt-swol'n Cunt.

Some Power, more patient, now relate
The sense of this surprising fate.
Gods! that a thing admired by me
Should fall to so much infamy.

Had she picked out, to rub her Arse on
Some stiff-pricked Clown or well-hung Parson[1]
Each job of whose spermatic sluice
Had filled her Cunt with wholesome Juice,

1. one with very large genital equipment

I, the preceding should have praised
In hope she'd quenched a fire I raised.
Such natural freedoms are but just:
There's something generous in mere lust.

But to turn, damned abandoned Jade
When neither head nor tail persuade:
To be a Whore in understanding
A passive Pot for Fools to spend in!

The Devil played booty,[1] sure, with thee
To bring a blot on infamy.
But why am I, of all mankind
To so severe a fate designed?

Ungrateful! Why this treachery
To humble, fond, believing me,
Who give you privilege above
The nice allowances of Love?

Did ever I refuse to bear
The meanest part your lust could spare!
When your lewd Cunt came spewing home
Drenched with the seed of half the Town.

My dram of sperm, was supped up after
For the digestive surfeit water.[2]
Full gorged at another time
With a vast meal of nasty slime

Which your devouring Cunt had drawn
From Porters' backs and Footmens' brawn,
I was content to serve you up
My Ballock-full for your grace cup.

1. conspired to cheat   2. antiflatulence drinks

Nor ever thought it an abuse
While you have Pleasure, for excuse –
You that could make my Heart away
For noise and colour, and betray
The secrets of my tender hours
To such knight-errant Paramours.

When, leaning on your faithless breast
Wrapped in security and rest,
Soft kindness all my powres did move,
And Reason lay dissolved in Love!

May stinking Vapours choke your womb
Such as the men you dote upon
May your depraved appetite
That could, in whiffling Fools delight

Beget such frenzies in your mind
You may go mad for the North Wind;
And fixing all your hopes upon't
To have him bluster in your Cunt,

Turn up your longing Arse to th'air
And perish in a wild despair!
But cowards shall forget to rant,
Schoolboys to frig, old Whores to paint;

The Jesuits' Fraternity
Shall leave the use of buggery;
Crab-louse, inspired with grace divine
From earthly codd, to Heaven shall climb.

Physicians shall believe in Jesus,
And disobedience cease to please us,
Ere I desist with all my power
To plague this woman, and undo her.

But my revenge will best be timed
When she is married that is limed.
In that most lamentable state
I'll make her feel my scorn and hate;

Pelt her with Scandals, truth or lies,
And her poor cur with jealousies,
Till I have torn him from her breech,
While she whines like a dog-drawn Bitch;
Loathed and despised, kicked out o' th' Town
Into some dirty hole, alone.

62

A Panegyrick upon Nelly
(1672)

[By John Wilmot, Earl of Rochester
Rochester, 1732]

Of a great Heroin, I mean to tell
And by what just degrees her Titles swell
To Mrs Nelly, grown from *Cinder Nell*.

Much did she suffer, first on Bulk and Stage
From the blackguard and Bullies of the Age;
Much more her growing Virtue did sustain
While dear *Charles Hart*, and *Buckhurst* sued in vain.

In vain they sued; cursed be the envious Tongue
That her undoubted Chastity would wrong;
For should we Fame believe, we then might say
That thousands lay with her, as well as they.

A Panegyrick upon Nelly

But, Fame, thou liest; for her Prophetick mind
Foresaw her Greatness, Fate had well designed
And her Ambition chose to be, before
A Virtuous Countess, an Imperial Whore.

Ev'n in her Native dirt her Soul was high
And did at Crowns and shining Monarchs fly;
Ev'n while the cinders raked, her swelling Breast
With thoughts of Glorious *Whoredom* was possessed.

Still did she dream (nor could her Birth withstand)
Of dangling Sceptres in her dirty Hand.
But first the Basket her fair arm did suit
Laden with Pippins and Hesperian Fruit;

This first step raised, to th' wondering Pit she sold
The lovely fruit, smiling with streaks of Gold.
Fate now for her, did its whole Force engage,
And from the Pit she's mounted to the Stage.

There in full Lustre did her glories shine,
And, long eclipsed, spread forth their Light divine;
There, *Hart* and *Rowley's* Soul she did insnare
And made a King a rival to a Player.

The King o'ercomes, and to the Royal Bed
The Dunghill Offspring is in Triumph led;
Nor let the envious her first Rags object
To her, that's now in tawdry Gayness decked.

Her Merit does from this much greater show,
Mounting so high, that took her rise so low.[1]
Less Famed that *Nelly* was, whose Cuckold's rage
In ten years Wars did half the World ingage.

1. Helen of Troy

She's now the darling Strumpet of the Crowd;
Forgets her State, and talks to them aloud;
Lays by her Greatness and descends to prate
With those, 'bove whom she's raised by wondrous Fate.

True to th' Protestant Interest and Cause,
True to th'Established Government and Laws:
The choice Delight of the whole *Mobile*,
Scarce *Monmouth's* self is more beloved than she.

Was this the Cause that did their Quarrel move,
That both are rivals in the People's Love?
No! 'twas her matchless Loyalty alone
That bid Prince *Perkin*[1] pack up and begone.

'Ill-bred thou art' says Prince. Nell does reply
'Was *Mrs Barlow*[2] better bred than I?'
Thus sneak'd away the Nephew, overcome
By his Aunt-in-law's severer Wit struck dumb.

Her Virtue, Loyalty, Wit and Noble Mind,
In the foregoing Doggerel you may find.
Now for her Piety, one touch, and then
To Rymer I'll resign my Muse and Pen.

'Twas this that raised her Charity so high
To visit those that did in Durance lie;
From *Oxford Prison* many did she free:
There died her father, and there gloried she
In giving others Life and Liberty.

So pious a Remembrance still she bore,
Ev'n to the fetters that her Father wore.

1. the Duke of Monmouth   2. Monmouth's mother

Nor was her Mother's funeral less her care,
No Cost, no Velvet did the Daughter spare.

Fine gilded Scutcheons did the hearse inrich
To celebrate this Martyr of the ditch;
Burnt Brandy did in flaming Brimmers flow
Drunk at her funeral; while her well pleased Shade
Rejoiced ev'n in the sober Fields below
At all the drunkenness her death had made.

Was ever Child with such a Mother blest?
Or ever Mother such a Child possesst?
Nor must her Cousin be forgot – preferred
From many years Command in the black-guard
To be an Ensign – whose tattered Colours well do represent
His first estate i' th' ragged regiment.

Thus we in short have all the Virtues seen
Of the incomparable Madam Gwyn:
No wonder others are not with her shown,
She who no equal has must be alone.

NOTE: Charles Hart was one of the players in the Drury Lane
theatre, and Nell Gwyn's first lover. Then Lord Buckhurst fell in love
with her and would have married her, but the King (*Old Rowley*
when he wandered incognito about the town) was the successful
suitor. Rochester's savage satire contains some historical nuggets:
The Duke of Monmouth's mother was the low-class whore Lucy
Barlow, so that she and Monmouth – the King's favourite nephew –
were equally ill-bred. Monmouth left the Court after this snub. To
this later generation Nelly's actions in freeing poor prisoners and
showing great respect to her father and mother would be deemed
highly commendable, but Rochester's aristocratic senses were out-
raged. Later, however, Rochester and Nelly became friends. Nelly
was affectionately known to the populace (the *mobile*, now mob) as
the Protestant Whore – all the King's other mistresses being Catho-
lics. Monmouth too was popular because he was a Protestant prince
in line for the throne, but after his rebellion he was executed – an act
forced upon the King, James II, who was very much attached to his
nephew.

63
A Satyr on Charles II
(*ante* January 1674)

[By John Wilmot, Earl of Rochester
Rochester, 1732]

I' th' isle of Britain, long since famous grown
For breeding the best cunts in Christendom,
There reigns, and oh! long may he reign and thrive
The easiest King and best-bred man alive.

Him no ambition moves to get renown
Like the French fool, that wanders up and down
Starving his people, hazarding his crown.
Peace is his aim, his gentleness is such,
And love he loves, for he loves fucking much.

Nor are his high desires above his strength:
His sceptre and his prick are of a length;
And she may sway the one who plays with th'other,
And make him little wiser than his brother.

Poor prince! thy prick, like thy buffoons at Court,
Will govern thee because it makes thee sport.
'Tis sure the sauciest prick that e'er did swive,
The proudest, peremptoriest prick alive.

Though safety, law, religion, life lay on't,
'Twould break through all to make its way to cunt.
Restless he rolls about from whore to whore,
A Merry Monarch, scandalous and poor.

To Carwell, the most dear of all his dears,
The best relief of his declining years,
Oft he bewails his fortune, and her fate:
To love so well, and be beloved so late.

For though in her he settles well his tarse,
Yet his dull, graceless ballocks hang an arse.
This you'd believe, had I but time to tell ye
The pains it cost to poor laborious Nelly,
Whilst she employs hands fingers mouth and thighs,
Ere she can raise the member she enjoys.

All monarchs I hate, and the thrones they sit on,
From the Hector of France to the cully of Britain.

NOTE: Carwell: Madame Louise de Querouaille, Duchess of Portsmouth. Charles at this time was only forty-three. Nelly was Nell Gwyn. For this poem, which Rochester had handed to the King by mistake, he had to flee the Court and it took the King a long time to forgive him.

64

The Maim'd Debauchee
(*c.*1676)

[By John Wilmot, Earl of Rochester
Rochester, 1732]

I'll tell of Whores attaqu'd, their Lords at home,
Bawds' quarters beaten up, and Fortress won,
Windows demolish'd, Watches overcome
And handsome ills by my contrivance done.

Nor shall our love-fits, *Cloris*, be forgot
When each the well-look'd *Linkboy* strove t'enjoy
And the best Kiss was the deciding Lot,
Whether the boy us'd You, or I the boy.

NOTE: This satire concerns the spate of scandals during the reign of
Charles II, when the *Sparks* and *Mohocks* ran amok, and burnt down
and ransacked whorehouses and beat up the whores. It also reflects
the growth amongst the nobility of buggery, which was to remain
and increase during the whole of the next century.

65

Advice to a Cunt-monger
(*c.*1675)

[Yale MS., b.105, ff.394–5
Osborne Library, Yale, U.S.A.]

Fucksters, you that would be happy
Have a care of Cunt it clap ye.
Escape disease of evil Tarse-hole
Gout, and Fistula of Arse-hole,
Swollen Codds, Colon descending,
Prick still weeping, never spending.
Pocky Nodes, Carnosities,
Cunt-botch, Stone and Stranguries.
But take the Councell I have sent yee,
Then fuck on and ne'er repent ye.

Citty Cunts are dangerous sport,
Who, since Prentices ply at Court,
Trudge to Moseley's where ye fatt things
Fuck with Shaftesbury and Judge Atkins.

Advice to a Cunt-monger

Whitehall Cunts are grown so common
Foule and wide, as fitt for no man;
Torn and Tear's from Prince to Carmen,
Grubb'd by Porters, rammed by Chairmen,
Frigg'd at Chappell, fuck'd i'th'Entryes
By the Singing-boys and Sentries;
Pepper'd as they come from Prayers
The next Oares at ye Water-stairs.
Taile turn'd up to all they know
From Doctor Crew to Coachman Crow.

Countrey Cunts have nasty whites;
The Parsons' Daughters and ye Knightes,
Daintily refusing others,
Fuck with their Fathers and their Brothers.
But follow me and you shall prove
Safe varieties of Love.
Every Tarse-indulging Sparke
Shall enjoy, in Whetstone Parke,
A Drunken, Sounde, Obedient Whore:
What can Mortall wish for more?

NOTE: Mother Moseley was a prominent brothel-keeper in that period, whose principal residence was in Whetstone Park, next to Lincoln's Inn Fields, off Holborn. The references are to certain of her clients, such as Lord Shaftesbury, Lord Justice Atkins and Lord Bishop Crewe. The diseases mentioned in verse 1 were often treated in Madame Fourcade's Mercury baths in nearby Leather Lane.

66

The Ladies of London
(*c*.1680)

[A broadside street ballad]

Come listen awhile and you shall hear
How the poor Whores fare in the Winter
They've hardly a rag to hide their *Ware*
Indeed, 'tis a desperate thing, Sir.
With their draggl'd Tails nine inches deep
And hardly a Shoe or a Stocking,
Yet if a Cull[1] they by chance should meet
At him they will be bobbing.

Says *Molly*, 'I think my case very hard
For I can get no Mony'.
Says Nancy, 'I think mine's as bad
Last night I earn'd but a penny'.
All night we freeze with our Cull in the cold
'Til the Constable, he comes early
And packs us away for being so bold,
So we pay for our whoring severely.

Says *Sally*, 'I think I've the worst Luck of all;
Since I have been a-whoring,
I've never before been without a Smock,
Altho' it was ne'er such a poor one.
Tho' I trudge the streets all Night in the cold
At my rags, men are pulling and haling:[2]
Old Nick I am sure, would not be a Whore,
It's grown such a Hell of a calling'.

1. 'cully' – dupe, customer   2. hauling

Then straightway young *Nell* replied
'What signifies complaining?
You know you're all pox'd, and so am I
And that indeed's our failing.
We swarm like Bees at each street-end
Catching at ev'ry Fellow,
Be he ever so pox'd, or clean
We're always ready to follow.'

There's some that wear Silk and Satin gay
'Tis they who gets the Mony;
With their next neighbour, they slyly play
And call him their Joy and their Honey.
While he with Mony can supply
They're always ready to serve him,
While his poor Wife & Children are left at home,
For Bread they are almost starving.

Likewise all you Men with handsome Wives
Take care they don't forsake you:
For if they lack Mony, as sure as your Life
They will a *Cuckold* make you.
They'll graft such a pair of Horns on your head
That you can hardly bear them:
They're such cunning *Jades*, if you don't take care
They'll force you for to wear them.

Before the *privy* Whores were known
In Town to be so plenty,
We common girls had better Luck;
Men then were not so Dainty:
They brought to us brave English *quills*[1]
And we would bit and pinch them:
If we set them afire[2] both ends at once
The *Devil*, he may quench them.

1. penises   2. give them the 'pox'

NOTE: One of a number of broadside ballads supposed to be sung by street prostitutes: the 'privy whores' are the courtesans maintained and patronized by noblemen and rich City merchants subsequent to the Restoration in 1660, and who reached their peak of wealth and influence about 1680–90.

67

Last Night's Ramble
(1687)

[Bodleian MS., Firth, c.15, pp.268–74]

Warm'd with the pleasures, which debauches yeild
Brain, stufft with fumes excess of Wine had fill'd,
I took last night a Ramble, being drunk,
To visit old acquaintance Bawd and Punk.

'Twas Madam *Southcott* near Old Dunkirk Square,[1]
That House of Ease for many a rampant Peer,
For only the lewd Quality fuck there.

The first Divertissement I found was this;
I heard the treble note of yeilding Misse,
Whisp'ring, 'Lord, Sir, what pleasant Tales you tell!
You'll find th'enjoyment worth your mony well.'

Then in Base viol Voice I heard him swear
'Dam me, a Guiney, Madam's very fair,
The utmost fee I ever gave to Swive!'

She answer'd, 'How d'ye think that we can live?
I'll swear Sir William Rich, Sir, gave me five!'
While thus I listened I observed at last,
Tho she asked more, she held the Guinea fast.

1. Lady Jane Southcott's exclusive whorehouse was in Old Dunkirk Square, off Piccadilly – where now Albemarle Street stands.

When Grand Procuress to each standing Prick
Came in, half flustered, from her stallion *Dick*,
With varnish'd face of Paint three inches thick
Daub'd on by Art and wise industry laid
To hide the Wrinkles envious Time had made.

This necessary Freind I would have stayed
When came in Implement she call'd her Maid,
Bred in the Art and skillfull in the Trade,
And whispered her away. I guess'd the matter
And at a little distance, sauntered after.

Anon, I heard one knocking at the Door
Who entering, cry'd 'Give me a ready Whore;
Let her be clean and sound, and bring her strait,
You know me Bawd – I am not used to wait.'

'At *Grayden's*,[1] such a damned defeat I've had
With *Lady Mary Ratcliffe*[2] – I am mad,
And must the flame that's kindled by her eyes
Quench 'twixt some common vulgar Beauties' thighs.'

'And to advance my gust of Lèchery,
Just in the act, dear *Ratcliffe*, I will cry
Fancying at least I swive with Quality!'

By that same cock'd up Nose, Thought I, and mein,
That haughty Spark should be Lord Chamberlain.
To be convinced, I follow'd, but mistook
The room, and did into another look.

Where who the devil do you think I found?
But one, Oh! frailty! of the reverend Gown.

1. Grayden's was another brothel nearby, where gaming was also ventured   2. Mary, Countess of Radcliffe

Stinking-mouth'd *Chester*,[1] to my best discerning,
Who gravely was a fine young Whore confirming.

'Nay! if it be so' cry'd I, 'We need not doubt,
Since our good Clergy-Men are so devout,
But we shall keep all fears of Popery out!'

Then down I went, and thro' a wainscot flaw,
Wallowing upon a tired out Whore I saw
Fumbling in vain, old Griping *Ranelagh*;[2]
With Whores and Pox, these forty years worn out,
He sweats and stinks for one poor single Bout,
'Til wench, half-stifled, cry'd 'My Lord! I'll frig
Your Prick's too short, your Belly is too big!'

I left them at it – when I heard a noise
Of gentle rage in an affected Voice.
'What have we here' thought I, 'for a Sir Nice?'

'Twas *Cavendish*,[3] who th'faithless Bawd was schooling
For giving him a Heat, instead of cooling.
'God damn me, Madam, were you not a Bitch
Last Sunday, with a Clap to cure mine itch,
Just when I should have had an assignation
With the most courted Beauty of the Nation!'

'How clapt! Gad! this my reputation touches!'.
'Twas my best ware, my Lord. Zounds! 'twas my Dutchess,
Who never yet was by foul gamester leap't,
And so uncommon, by the Lord she's kept!'

'And is she sound, may I depend upon her?'
'Your fears are vain, for she's a Whore of Honor;

---

1. The Bishop of Chester – a notorious rake, but a staunch anti-popist 2.
Richard Johne, 1st Earl of Ranelagh (1638–1712) 3. Lord Cavendish

Last Night's Ramble

Altho' Your Lordship bilk'd her, as they say
You do the hacks, and boxes, at the Play.
Which tho' so often used, you never pay.'
So out he went, quite eased of his despair
By knowing he might venture with *Kildare*.[1]

Then in comes *Newburgh, Grey and Manchester*.[2]
'Oh!' cry'd the Matron, 'Have I got you, Sir?
And would you think it? Damme! my Lord Grey,
This *Manchester* stole my best Whore away!
I-gad, hence forth I'll watch Your Lordships waters
And bring you City Wives – but no more Daughters.

But you, my little *Ruthven*,[3] kind and true
I have most delicate fine things for you;
My Lady Litchfield's woman,[4] Brisk and New!'

Quoth *Newburgh* 'Have you no fine things for me?
For I am tired with fucking Quality?'.
'Yes, i' the next room I've such a Rarity.'

'The Lady within's tis, whose husband's old.
She comes to swive for Pleasure, not for Gold:
While quondam Judge is taking fees at home,
She, for that same, sometimes abroad does roam,'

"Such a Belle tall, such a Bon Mein and Air
So witty, so well-shap'd and such a Hair!
A snowy skin, such sparkling eyes, and then
Rough as you'd wish, strait as a girl of ten!'

This dear description did my nerves assail
And over all my faculties prevail:

---

1. the Countess of Kildare 2. Lord Newburgh, Earl Grey, and Charles Montagu, Earl of Manchester 3. Lord Ruthven 4. Lady Lichfield's maid of honour

And while they bartered, I stole in before
Where longing Beauty was, and barred the door.

There, on a couch, all carelessly extended
I saw what Bawd before, so much commended,
Just as she said, fair as the morning skies:
Lust heav'd her Breasts and Lechery drest her Eyes.

I saw to court her was but time ill spent,
She, by my looks, guessed at my kind intent;
Yet that fair play might on both sides be shown
(As soldiers parley ere beseige a Town)
I her unguarded Virtue so assailed
That showing *Pego*,[1] she her Cunt unveil'd.

I could not longer hold, but rushing on
The short, but pleasing, sally we begun.
So eager and so vigorously free
We gave not o'er 'til we repeated three.
Our raptures hardly finished were, before
The Peer and Bawd were knocking at the door!'

'Open! fair *Venus* to a fair *Adonis*!'
'The youth must wait' said I, 'she not alone is.'
Mars now possesses all with pleasure fervent.'
'Is't so? Then Damn me, Sir, Your humble Servant!'[2]
Then cursing wondering Bawd, he went away,
While I alone, was master of the day.

I need not tell you when with toying tired
We sought, with Clarret to be new inspir'd;
Or how we kiss'd and laughed, and towsed again,
And try'd so often that we try'd in vain.

---

1. current slang for penis, particularly when erect   2. Lord Newburgh took his
leave with the formal salutation 'Your Humble Servant'.

This only, therefore, I'll recount you more,
My Body weak, My Prick severely sore,
My Linnen foul, my Hair with feathers stuck
And half Ten Guineas spent in Wine and Fuck;
I like a ruffled Bully Rock came trudging
And just, at five this morning, found my Lodging.

68

A Westminster Wedding

OR Like unto Like, Quoth the *Devil* to the *Collier*
(*ante* 1685)

[*Westminster Drollery* (1685), Item 167]

There lived of late in *Luteners Lane*
A painted *Whore* and a *Rogue* in Grain
    Tom come tickle me
    Tom come tickle me
    Tom come tickle me once again.

They often meeting at *Venus*' play
Agreed to be married without delay
    Tom etc.

This girl was the finest of all the Flock
With her Taffety Gown and her Holland Smock
    Tom etc.

Her Hair it was powdered, her Locks was curled
In Rings, like a Lady, for all the World.
    Tom etc.

And she of a Bargain was very well sped
To take a rude *Royster* unto her Bed
    Tom etc.

One that was thrice of *Newgate* made free
And hardly escap'd the Three-legg'd Tree
    Tom etc.

A hopefull couple in mischief deep
A thousand times better to hang than to keep
    Tom etc.

But hap at a venture it must be so
To bind up the Bargain, they needs must go
    Tom etc.

The Wedding appointed and Day being set
Mark what a Company there was met
    Tom etc.

First came Dorothy with her Mate
Bonny Bridget and bonny Kate
    Tom etc.

Jumping Joan that can play in the dark,
Sue and Sarah from Whetstone Park
    Tom etc.

Matt so merry came with good will
Pegg and Prudence, from Saffron-Hill
    Tom etc.

Smiling Cissily worthy regard
Frank and Mary from *Dog & Bitch Yard*
    Tom etc.

Beck and Maudlin, as it was meet
Hasted thither from Turnbull Street
    Tom etc.

A Westminster Wedding

Quoth Gillian, Ile go tho' it cost me a Fall
And call all my Sisters from *Hatton-Wall*
    Tom etc.

As far as from Ratcliff thither they came
From *Well-Close* and from Rosemary Lane
    Tom etc.

But she, of all others that bore the Bell
Came, as they told, from Clerkenwell
    Tom etc.

Thus Tag Rag and Sorrell came flocking amain;
I think, at a Wedding, was ne'er such a Train
    Tom etc.

For *Luteners Lane*, it was never so grac't
With so many Girls of the Game, at a Feast
    Tom etc.

Nor never at Westminster went such a Pair
A Couple so exactly match't to a Hair!
    Tom etc.

They had not been married above one Hour
But there was 'Thou Rogue, and Thou'rt a Whore'.
    Tom etc.

I wish th' Apprentices had been there
That time, to frighten them from their cheer
    Tom etc.

But now I must leave them to shake up their Bedding
And there is an end to a Westminster Wedding,
    Tom etc.

NOTE: *Luteners Lane* – properly Lewknor's Lane, not far from the present Drury Lane, was one of the most notorious streets of whore-houses in London. The ballad describes actually a slice of the lowest London life in those days, from the almost mandatory Holland smock worn by prostitutes, to the overhanging threat of the three-legged tree – the gallows at Tyburn – for other malefactors. Of equal social importance is the linking with the other centres of whoredom: Whetstone Park (off Lincoln's Inn Fields); Saffron Hill and Turnbull Street in Clerkenwell (Turnbull Street was the most notorious of them all, known from as early as the time of Henry III); Dog and Bitch Yard in Covent Garden – frequented by Pepys and friends – described as a nest of strumpets; Hatton Wall – now Hatton Garden; Wells Close and Rosemary Lane close by the Tower of London and the infamous Ratcliff Highway. The reference to the apprentices is their annual Shrove Tuesday rampage, during which brothels were pulled or burnt down and the whores assaulted. 'She of all others that bore the Bell', that is to say, the champion of them all, may be a reference to the famous Mother Cresswell, the greatest Bawd known, whose famous brothels were situated in Clerkenwell and Moorfields.

69

The Brown Cunts of Old England
(*ante* 1750)

[M.M.C. (1827), 51]

[To the tune of 'The Roast Beef of Old England']

When mighty brown cunts were the Englishman's taste,
With strong curled hair that could tie round the waist.
Our offspring were stout and our wives were all chaste
    Oh! the brown cunts of old England
    And Oh! the old English brown cunt.

But since we have learned from all-vapouring France,
To fuck and to swive as well as to dance,
To a juicy brown cunt we're afraid to advance
    Oh! the brown etc.

Our fathers of old were robust, stout and strong,
And had pricks, report says, full twelve inches long,
Which made their plump dames rejoice in this song,
   Oh! the brown etc.

But now we're dwindled to – I'll tell you what,
A sneaking poor race of small-hunters, most hot,
And a prick of nine inches is hard to be got,
   Oh! the large etc.

King Edward the Third for his prick was renowned,
Had a prick thirteen inches before he was crowned,
He fucked all the ladies and never lost ground.
   Oh! the large etc.

King Henry the Eighth as recorded of old
Had swinging large cods, as you've often been told.
And his royal prick was a sight to behold.
   Oh! the large etc.

In those days our sailors fought most on the main,
They walloped proud Spaniards again and again,
Then fucked all wives, widows and daughters in Spain.
   Oh! the large etc.

King James when he travelled the throne to ascend,
In Yorkshire he found a brown cunt to commend,
And fucked it, then said, there's no prick that would spend
   With the brown etc.

Then, then, we were able to fuck or to fight,
Our swords always drawn and our pricks always right,
But now we're a parcel of shittle-come-shite,
   Oh! the large etc.

70

On One Writing Against His Prick
(*c*.1688)

[Anon.
Harvard MS., Eng., 636 F. Harvard Library, U.S.A.]

Base Mettel hanger by your Masters Thigh
Eternall shame to all Prick's Heraldry;
Hide thy despis'd Head and doe nott dare
To peepe – no nott soe much as take the Aire
But through a Button Hole – but pine and dye
Confin'd within the Codpeice monestry.

The littel childishe Boy that hardly knowes
The way through whiche his Urine flowes,
Touch't by my Mistris her magnetick Hand
His little Needle presently will stand.
Did shee not raise thy drooping Head on high
As it lay noddinge on her wanton Thigh?
Did shee nott clap her Legges about my Backe
Her Port-hole open? Damn'd Prick, what is't you lacke?

Henceforth stand stiffe and gaine your Creditt lost
Or Ile ne'ere draw thee but against a Post!

71

The Four-legg'd Quaker
(1659)

[*Wit and Mirth* (1682), p.81. See also Poem 35]

All that have two, or but one Ear
(I dare not tell ye half)
You, of an *Essex* colt shall hear,
Will shame the very *Calf*.
In *Horsley Fields* near *Colchester*
A Quaker would turn Trooper:
He caught a Foal, and mounted her
(O! Base) below the Crupper.
   Help! Lords and Commons, Once more help!
   O send us Knives and Daggers!
   For if the Quakers be not gelt
   Your Troops will have the Staggers!

Ralph Green (it was this Varlet's name)
Of *Colchester*, you'll swear;
From thence the *Four-legg'd Quaker* came:
Was ever such a Pair?
But tho' 'twas foul 'tween *Swash* and *Jane*
Yet this is ten times worse;
For then a *Dog* did play the Man,
But *Man* now play'd the Horse.
   Help! etc.

The Owner of the Colt was nigh
(Observing their embrace)
And drawing nearer, did espie
The Quaker's sorrell Face:
My Foal is ravish'd (then he cryes
And fiercely at him ran)

Thou Rogue, I'll have thee haltered twice,
As *Horse*, and eke, a *Man*.
   Help! etc.

Ah! Devil, dost thou tremble? Now
'Tis sore against thy Will:
For *Mares*, and preaching *Ladies* know
Thou hast a Colts-tooth still.
But mine's not guilty of this Fact;
She was by Thee compelled:
Poor Thing, whom no *Man* ever backt
Thou wickedly has Bellied.
   Help! etc.

O Friend (said *Green*, with sighs and groans)
Let this thy Wrath appease!
(And gave him then eight new Half-Crowns
To make him hold his Peace).
The Man reply'd, though I for this
Conceal thy *Hugger-Mugger*,
Dost think it Lawfull for a Piece[1]
A silly Foal to bugger?
   Help! etc.

The Master saw his Colt defiled
Which vext his Soul with doubt;
For if his *Filly* prov'd with Child
He knew all would come out.
Then he afresh began to rave
(For all his money-taking)
Neighbours, said he, I took this Knave
I'th very Act of *Quaking*.
   Help! etc.

1. a crown

Then to the *Pinfold* (Gaol, I mean)
They dragg'd him by the Mane:
They call'd him *Beast*; they call'd her *Quean*,
As if she had been *Jane*.
O! stone him, all the Women cry'd,
Nay, geld him (which is worse)
Who scorned us all and took a Bride
That's a Daughter to a Horse!
   Help! etc.

The *Colt* was silent all this while
And therefore 'twas no Rape.
The virgin Foal he did beguile
And so intends to 'scape;
For tho' he got her in a Ditch
Where she could not revolt,
Yet he had no *Scottish Spurr* nor *Switch*
To ride the willing Colt.
   Help! etc.

O! Essex, Essex, England's Pride;
Go burn this long-tail'd *Quean*;
For tho' the *Thames* runs by thy side
It cannot wash thee clean!
'Tis not thy bleating Son's complaints
Hold forth such wanton Courses:
Thy Oysters hint the very Saints
To horn the very Horses.
   Help! etc.

Tho' they salute not in the Street
(Because they are our Masters)
'Tis now reveal'd why *Quakers* meet
In Meadows, Woods and Pastures.
But *Horse-men*, *Mare-men*, all and some
Who Man and Beast perplex,

Not only from *East Horsley come*
But from *West Middle Sex*.
    Help! etc.

This was not Green the *Feltmaker*,
Nor Willow Green the *Baker*
Nor George, the Sea-Green *Mariner*
but *Ralph*, the Grass-Green *Quaker*.
Had GREEN the *Sow-Gelder* but known
And done his Office duly
Tho' Ralph was GREEN when he came on
He had come off most *blewly*.
    Help! etc.

Alass! you by Man's Flesh came
The *Foul-disease* from *Naples*;
And now we fear the very same
Is broke into our Stables.
For Death has stolen so many Steeds
From *Prince* and *Peer* and *Carrier*,
That this new *Murrain* rather needs
A FARRAR than a Farrier.[1]
    Help! etc.

Nay, if this GREEN within the Walls
Of *Colchester* left forces;
Those Cavaliers were *Caniballs*
Eating his humane Horses!
But some make *Man* their *second course*
(In cool Blood will not spare)
Who butcher Men and favour Horse,
Will couple with a *Mare*.
    Help! etc.

1. 'Physician to the Earl of Pembroke who is no Quaker nor Quacker'

This *Centaur*, unquoth *Other* Thing,
Will make a dreadfull Breach:
Yet tho' an Ass may Speak or Sing
O! let not Horses preach![1]
But bridle such wild *Colts* who can
When they'll obey no Summons
For Things begot 'tween *Mare* and *Man*
Are neither Lords nor Commons.
   Help! etc.

O! Elders, Independents too
Tho' all your Powers combin'd,
Quakers will grow too strong for you
Now *Horse* and *Man* are joyn'd;
While *Cavaliers*, poor foolish Rogues
Know only Maids' *Affairs*;
She-Presbyters can deal with *Doggs*
And *Quaking Men* with *Mares*.
   Help! etc.

Now as when Milan Town was rear'd
A monstrous *Sow* untam'd
With black half-Hair, half-Wool appear'd
'Twas *Mediolanum* named:
Colchester must have recourse
To some such four-legg'd Sister,
For sure as *Horsley* comes from Horse,
From *Colt* 'twas call'd Colchester.
   Help! etc.

NOTE: From the close similarity of this ballad to the *Four Legg'd Elder* of 1647 (see Poem 35), it is likely that Sir John Birkenhead was also the author, although the references to Woodcock Fox and Naylor are cribbed from the lampoon of 1642 in *The Sophy* attributed to Sir John Denham. (See Poem 28.) They are only a few of the vicious slanders

1. 'A new Sect of young Men & Women who pray eat and sing *extempore*'

made against the enemies of the Monarchy. In some rural areas
buggery with sheep and horses was reported from very ancient
times, and at least one in the Colchester district had given a handle
to the lampoonists, although Ralph Green – a well known Quaker –
was certainly never involved in any such activity. At this time the
Quakers in particular were singled out for attack, being cruelly
maligned as well as physically attacked.

George Fox (1624–91), after much proselytizing, founded the
Society of Friends in about 1648.

There was no Pinfold Jail either in Colchester or Essex.

72

There Was an Old Man Had an Acre of Land
(*c.*1641)

Merry Drollery Compleat, 1691, p.52]

[A catch. Tune: 'Sellengers Round', *c.*1597,
Chappell, I, p.258]

There was an Old Man had an Acre of Land
He sold it for five pound-a
Then went to the Tavern and drank it all
Excepting Half-a-Crown-a

And as he came home he met with a Wench
And ask'd her whether she was willing
To go to the Tavern and spend eighteenpence
And fuck for the other odd Shilling.

NOTE: The tune 'Sellengers Round' can be traced back to 1597. It was
a dance tune by 1641.

73
Once, Twice, Thrice, I Julia Try'd
(1693)

[A broadside catch. Music composed by Henry Purcell the Younger]

Once, Twice, Thrice I Julia try'd,
The scornfull Puss as oft deny'd,
And since, and since, I can no better, better thrive
I'll cringe to ne'er a Bitch alive.
 So kiss my Arse, so kiss my Arse, so kiss my Arse
 So kiss my Arse, disdainfull Sow!
Good Claret, good Claret is my Mistress now!

74
The Piss-pot's Farewel
(1701)

*Verses on a Silver Chamber-Pot sent to the Tower to be Coyn'd,
occasion'd by the Lady — at St James's unlucky Hand at Bassett
which forc'd her to sell her Plate.*

[Broadsheet. Printed for Robert Barnham at The Goat in Little
Britain, 1701]

Maids need no more their silver Pisspots scoure
They now must jogg like Traytors to the Tower:
A quick Despatch! No sooner are they come
But ev'ry Vessel there receives its Doom,
By Law condemn'd to take their fiery Tryall,
A Sentence that admits of no denial.

Presumptuous Piss-pot! How did'st thou offend?
Compelling females on their Hams to bend?
To Kings and Queenes we humbly bow the knee,
But Queenes themselves are forc'd to stoop to thee.

To thee they cringe and with a straining Face
They cure their Griefe by opening of their Case!

In times of need thy help did they implore
And oft, to ease their Ailments, made thee roar.
Under their beds thou still had'st been conceal'd
And ne'er, but on Necessity, reveal'd!
When overcharg'd, and in Extremitie
Their dearest Secrets they disclos'd to thee.

Long hast thou been a Prisoner close confin'd;
But Liberty is for thee now design'd.
Thou, whom so many Beauties have enjoy'd,
Now in another Use shall be imploy'd,
And with delight be handled ev'ry Day
And oftener occupied a better Way.

But crafty Workmen first must thee refine
To purge thee from thy soder and thy brine,
When thou, transform'd into an other Shape
Shalt make the World rejoyce at thy Escape;
And from the Mint in Triumph shall be sent
New coin'd and mill'd to ev'ry Heart's content.

Welcome to all, then proud of thy new Vamp
Bearing the Pasport of a Royal stamp
And pass as currant, pleasant and as free
As that which hath so often pass'd in thee.

NOTE: Both James II and William III issued ordinances on the
Coinage, demanding that silver plate of all descriptions be handed in
for melting down for coinage. At the Court even the massive silver
chamberpots were called in.

75

Tom Tinker

(*ante* 1698)

[*Pills* (1719), vi, 265]

[Tune: *Pills* (1719), vi, 265]

Tom Tinker's my true love and I am his Dear
And I will go with him his Budget[1] to bear
For of all the young men he has the best luck
All day he will fuddle, all night he will fuck
   This way that way, which way you will
   I'm sure I say nothing that you can take ill.

With hammer on kettle he tabbers all day
At night he will tumble on strumil[2] or hay
He calls me his jewel, his delicate duck
And then he will take up my Smicket and fuck.
   This way etc.

Tom Tinker I say was a jolly stout lad
He tickled young Nancy and made her stark mad
To have a few rubbers with him on the grass
By reason she knew that he had a good Tarse[3]
   This way etc.

There was an old woman, on crutches she came
To lusty Tom Tinker, Tom Tinker by name
And tho' she was aged near threescore and five
She kicked up her heels and resolved to swive[4]
   This way etc.

1. penis 2. straw 3. penis 4. fuck

A beautiful damsel came out of the west
And she was as jolly and brisk as the rest
She'd dance and she'd caper as wild as a Buck
And told Tom the Tinker she would have some fuck
   This way etc.

A Lady called him, her kettle to mend
And she resolved, herself to attend.
Now as he stood stooping and mending the brass
His breeches was torn, and down hung his Tarse
   This way etc.

Something she saw that pleased her well
She called in the Tinker and gave him a spell;
With pig, goose and capon, and good store of suck
That he might be willing to give her some fuck.
   This way etc.

He had such a trade that he turned me away
Yet, as I was going he caused me to stay;
So, as towards him I was going to pass
He gave me a slap in the face with his tarse.
   This way etc.

I thought in my heart he had struck off my nose
I gave him as good as he brought, I suppose
My Words, they were ready and wonderful blunt
Quoth I 'I had rather been stabbed in my Cunt'.
   This way etc.

I met with a butcher, a-killing a calf
I then stepped to him, and cry'd out half.
At his first denial I fell very sick
And he said it was all for a touch of his Prick
   This way etc.

I met with Fencer a-going to school
I told him at fencing, he was but a fool
He had but three rapiers – and they were all blunt
And told him he should no more play at my Cunt.
   This way etc.

I met with a barber, with razor and balls
He fliggered, and told me, for all my brave alls
He would have a stroke – and his words they were blunt
I could not deny him the use of my Cunt
   This way etc.

I met with a fiddler a-fiddling aloud
He told me he'd lost the case of his Croud
I, being good natured, as I was wont
Told him he should make a case of my Cunt
   This way etc.

76
Young John the Gard'ner
(1683)

[A broadside street song. Music composed by Henry Purcell the Younger]

Young John the Gard'ner having lately got
A very rich and fertile garden plot,
Bragging to Joan, quoth he 'So rich a ground
For melons, cannot in the World be found'.

'That's a damn'd lie' quoth Joan, 'For I can tell
A place that does your garden far excell!'
'Where's that?' says John. 'In my Arse' quoth Joan,
'For there is store of Dung and Water all the Year!'

77

The Women's Complaint to Venus
(1699)

[Rawlinson MS. (Poet.), 159, f.32]

How happy were the good old English *Faces*
Till *Mounsieur* from France
Taught PEGO a Dance
To the tune of *Old Sodom's Embraces*.

But now we are quite out of *Fashion*:
Poor Whores may be Nuns
Since Men turn their *Guns*
And vent on each other their passion.

In the Raign of Good Charles the Second
Full many a *Jade*
A Lady was made
And the issue *Right Noble* was reckon'd.

But now we find to our sorrow
We are over-run
By the *Sparks of the Bum*
And peers of the *Land of Gomorrah*.

The *Beaus* too, whom most we rely'd on
At night make a *Punk*
Of him that's first drunk
Tho' unfit for the *Sport* as John Dryden.

The Souldiers whom next we put trust in,
No *Widdows* can tame
Or *Virgins* reclaim
But at the wrong place will be thrusting.

Fair VENUS, thou Goddess of Beauty
Receive our Complaint
Make *Rigby* recant
And the Souldiers henceforth do their Duty.

NOTE: Captain Edward Rigby was convicted in December 1698 of 'an attempt at Sodomy'. He was sentenced to a year's imprisonment, a fine of £1,000, and to stand in the pillory three times. At this time there was a great resurgence in buggery, occasioning many satires of a similar nature. Had Rigby been found guilty of the actual deed he must have been hanged, but juries were reluctant to convict and often used the legal loophole to avoid the capital punishment.

This ballad is attributed by some to Sir Charles Sedley.

78

A Lusty Young Smith
(ante 1700)

[*Pills* (1707), ii, 198]

[A broadside street song. Music set by Richard Leveridge. Music in *Pills* (1719), iv, 194]

A lusty young Smith at his vice stood a-filing
Rub, rub, rub, rub, rub, rub in and out, in and out ho!
When to him a buxsome young Damsel came smiling,
And asked if to work at her Forge he would go;
  With a rub rub rub rub rub, rub in and out
  In and out, ho!

'A match' quoth the Smith, so away they went thither.
Rub rub rub rub rub, rub in and out, in and out ho!
They stripped to go to it, 'twas hot Work and hot Weather,
She kindled a Fire and soon made him blow.
  With a rub, etc.

Her husband, she said, could scarce raise up his Hammer,
His strength and his Tools were worn out long ago.
If she got her Journeymen, could any blame her?
'Look here!' quoth our Workman, 'my Tools are not so.'
   With a rub, etc.

Red-hot grew his Iron, as both did desire
And he was too wise not to strike while twas so.
Quoth she 'What I get, I get out of the Fire,
Then prithee strike Home and redouble the blow!'
   With a rub, etc.

Six times, did his Iron by vigorous heating
Grow soft in the Forge in a minute or so;
As often twas Hardened, still beating and beating,
But the more it was softened, it hardened more slow.
   With a rub, etc.

The Smith would then go. Quoth the Dame, full of sorrow
'O! what would I give, could my Cuckold do so!
Good Lad, with your Hammer, come hither tomorrow;
But pray! can't you use it once more e'er you go?'
   With a rub, etc.

79

As Oyster Nan Stood by Her Tub

(*c*.1705)

[*Pills* (1719), iv, 107]

[A broadside street song. Tune: *Pills* (1719), iv, 107]

> As Oyster Nan stood by her tub
> To show her vicious inclination;
> She gave her noblest Parts a scrub
> And sighed for want of copulation.

As Oyster Nan Stood by Her Tub

A Vintner, of no little fame
Who excellent Red and White can sell ye
Beheld the dirty little Dame
As she stood scratching of her Belley.

'Come in' says he, 'you silly slut
'Tis now a rare convenient minute:
I'll lay the itching of your Scut
Except some greedy Devil be in it.'
With that the flat-capped Fusby smiled
And would have blushed – but that she could not:
'Alas!' says she 'we're soon beguiled
By men, to do those things we should not.'

From door they went behind the Bar
As its by common fame reported;
And there upon a Turkey Chair,
Unseen, the loving couple sported.
But being called by Company
As he was taking pains to please her
'I'm coming, coming, Sir!' says he;
'My dear, and so am I' says she, 'Sir!'

Her Mole-hill belly swelled about
Into a mountain quickly after:
And when the pretty Mouse crept out
The creature caused a mighty Laughter.
And now she has learnt the pleasing Game,
Altho' much pain and shame it cost her,
She daily ventures at the Same
And shuts and opens like an Oyster.

80
My Lady's Coachman, John
(1687)

[A broadside street song. Music by Henry Purcell the Younger]

> My Lady's coachman, John
> Being married to her maid,
> Her Ladyship did hear on't
> And to him, thus she said
> 'I never had a wench, so handsome, in my life!'
> I prithee therefore tell me
> I prithee therefore tell me
> How got you such a Wife?'.
> John stared her in the face
> And answered very blunt
> 'E'en as my Lord got you!'
> 'How's that?' – 'Why, by the Cunt.'

81
The Women-haters' Lamentation
(1707)

A NEW COPY *of* VERSES *on the Fatal End of Mr Grant a Woollen-draper and two others that Cut their Throats or Hang'd themselves in the Counter, with the discovery of near three hundred more that are Accus'd of unnaturally dispising the Fair Sex & Intriguing with one another.*

[Street broadside sheet, printed for J. Robinson in Fetter Lane, 1707]

[To the tune of 'Ye Pretty Sailors All']

> Ye injur'd *Females* see
> Justice without the Laws

The Women-haters' Lamentation

Seeing the Injury
Has thus reveng'd your Cause.

For those that are so Blind
Your Beauties to dispise
And flight your Charms, will find
Such Fate will always rise.

Of all the Crimes that Men
Through wicked Minds to act
There is not one of them
Equals this brutal Fact.

Nature they lay aside
To gratifie their Lust
Women they hate beside
Therefore their Fate was just.

Ye *Women-haters* say
What do's your Breasts inspire
That in a brutal Way
You your own Sex admire.

Woman you disapprove
(The chief of earthly Joys)
You that are deaf to Love
And all the Sex despise.

But see the fatal End
That do's such Crime pursue
Unnatural Deaths attend
Unnatural Lusts in you.

A Crime by men abhor'd
Nor Heaven can abide
Of which, when *Sodom's* shar'd
She justly was destroy'd

But now the Sum to tell
(Though they plead Innocence)
These by their own Hands fell
Accurs'd for this Offence.

A Hundred more we hear
Did to this Club belong
But now they scatter'd are
For this had broke the Gang.

Shop-keepers some there were
And men of good Repute
Each vow'd a Batchelor
Unnatural Lust pursu'd.

Ye *Women-haters* then
Take Warning by their Shame
Your brutal Lust restrain
And own a Nobler Flame.

Woman the Chiefest Bliss
That Heaven e'er bestow'd
Oh! be ashamed of this
You're by base Lust subdu'd.

This piece of Justice then
Has well reveng'd their Cause
And shows unnatural Lust
Is curs'd without the Laws.

82

I Went to the Alehouse
(*c*.1707)

[*Pills*, (1719), iii, 87]

[A song. Tune: 'I went to the Alehouse']

I WENT to the Alehouse as an honest Woman should
And a Knave followed after, as you know Knaves would
Knaves will be Knaves in every degree
I'll tell you by-and-by how this Knave served me.

I called for my Pot as an honest Woman should
And the Knave drank it up as you know Knaves would
Knaves will be etc.

I went into my Bed as an honest Woman should
And the Knave crept into it, as you know Knaves would
Knaves will be etc.

I proved with child as an honest Woman should
And the Knave ran away as you know Knaves would
Knaves will be Knaves in every Degree:
And thus I have told you how this Knave served me.

83

The He-Strumpets

OR A Satyre on the Sodomite Club
(1707)

[From John Dunton, *Athenianism* (1706–10), II, p.93 ff. Printed by
Thos. Darrack in Peterborough Court, Little Britain]

Having given all the Whores a TOUCH
The CRACKS will rave and think it much,

If the new *Sodomitic* Crew
Han't a brisk *Firking* Bout or two
Such MEN, such Brutes I should them call
Whose TAILS are Sodomiticall . . .

Lewd CRACKS repent, for 'tis the News
Your Tails have burnt so many *Beaus*
That now HE-WHORES are come in use.
Yes! Jilts, 'tis prov'd, and must be said
Your Tails are grown so lewd and bad
That now MEN'S TAILS have all the Trade.

Yet CRACKS are Saints compar'd with them
Who leave the Whores to pick up Men;
All CRACKS are found so full of Ails
A new *Society* prevails
Call'd SODOMITES – Men worse than Goats
Who dress themselves in Petticoats
To whom as *Osborne* did to *Oates*.

Modesty can scarce give a Name
To such a *Catamitish* Flame:
This Lust as far as SODOM came
In SODOM *men* were so unclean
That when the Angels, dresst as Men
They'd ask to fornicate with them.

Then *Sodomy* is the abuse
Of either sex, against the use
Of Nature . . .[1]
The men who thus their Lust confuse
Do doat upon HE-CONCUBINE
Do ply (that's whore,) near the Exchange
Here men turn Cracks – 'tis wondrous strange

1. [words lost here]

Yet very true, for these exclude
All women from their Interlude,
Yet ask what's carnal, vile and rude.

The very 'Change can scarce escape
This nasty loathsome Sodom rape.
But what's your Number, brutes? be free
'Tis said your Gang is forty-three
That whore (as 'twere) in Sodomy.

He-Whore, the word's a Paradox
But there's a CLUB hard by the *Stocks*[1]
Where MEN give unto MEN the Pox . . .
These doat on Men and some on Boys
And quite abandon female joys . . .

O Jones! O! sodomitic Wretch
Should you be damn'd, you could not groutch
You make your very Countrey blush
He-Lust, it looks so vile in print
There's none will stand a *Tryall* in't.
They Jones, no sooner did accuse
And two i'th'COMPTER, full as loose
But they strait fly to Hempen noose.

Jermain, a Clerk that liv'd i'th'East
Bearden, a He-whoring Beast
And forty Sodomites at least;
No sooner did their lewdness flame
But cut their very Throats with Shame . . .

[Here follows a number of verses attacking
whores and whoredom for allowing such a

1. The old Stock-market, torn down in 1739 to build the Mansion House.

state of affairs that the sodomites have
succeeded in establishing themselves
so strongly.]

Yea! sodomy they will permit
(a vice *they* never can commit,
Tho' kissing each other's *something* like it)

Then's Buggery, a beastly Sin
Is not a vice too lewd for them?
For 'tis not forty years ago
A CRACK was hang'd for whoring so:
Her Sparks were but a Dog or Two . . .

[The last verses repeat the attack on whores and
whoredom.]

NOTE: Jermain was the 'late Clerk to St Dunstans in the East; who
being charged with buggery cut his throat with a razor'. This must
be the same scandal as mentioned in 'The Woman-haters' Lamen-
tation', 1707, in which the City Woollen-Draper, Mr Grant hanged
himself in the Compter and several others hanged themselves.
Jones and Bearden were two of them.

The last verse refers to the allegations of Quaker women c.1666–8
having sexual intercourse with dogs. Cf. *The Four Legg'd Elder* ballad,
Poem 35.

84

Oh Mother, Roger with His Kisses
(*c*.1707)

[*Pills* (1719), iii, 202]

[A song. Tune: *Pills* (1707), i, 214]

Oh Mother, *Roger* with his Kisses
Almost stops my Breath, I vow;

Why does he gripe my Hand to pieces
And yet he says he loves me too?
   Tell me Mother, pray now do
   Pray now do, pray now do [repeat]
   What ROGER means when he does so,
   For never stir, I long to know!

Nay more, the naughty Man beside it
Something in my Mouth he put:
I called him Beast and try'd to bite it
But for my Life I cannot do't.
   Tell me etc.

He sets me in his Lap whole Hours
Where I feel I know not what
Something I never felt in yours:
Pray tell me Mother, what is that?
   Tell me etc.

85
As I Went O'er Yon Misty Moor
(*c*.1707)

[*Pills* (1707), iii, 307]

[Tune: set by Mr Akeroyde]

As I went o'er yon misty Moor
'Twas on an Evening late Sir,
There I met with a Well-fared Lass
Was spanning of her Gate, Sir.

I took her by the lilly-white Hand
And by the Twat I caught her;
I swear and Vow and tell you True,
She piss'd in my Hand with laughter.

The silly poor Wench, she lay so still,
You'd swear she had been dead, Sir.
The Devil a word, but all she said, but Ay.
And bowed her Head, Sir.

'Kind Sir' quoth she 'you'll kill me here
But I'll forgive the slaughter,
You make such motions with your Arse
You'll split my Sides with laughter.

NOTE: This is described merely as '*A Scotch Song*', and set by Mr
Akeroyde, who was a well-known singer of that time. It is almost the
same as a Scots ballad entitled 'As I Look'd O'er Yon Castle Wa''
(J.S.F. V.222), but the tune is different.

86

The Fryar and the Maid

OR The Fryar and the Nun
(1684)

[*Wit and Mirth*, 3rd edition (1684)]

[A broadside street song. Music in Chappell, I, 275]

As I lay musing all alone
A merry Tale I thought upon:
Now listen a while and I will you tell
Of a Fryar that loved a bonny Lass well.

He came to her when she was going to Bed
Desiring to have her Maidenhead;
But she denied his desire
And said that she did fear Hell-fire.

'Tush, Tush' quoth the Fryar 'Thou need'st doubt
If thou wert in Hell I could sing thee out'.

'Why then' quoth the Maid 'thou shalt have thy request.'
The Fryar was as glad as a Fox in his Nest.

'But one thing more I must request,
More than to sing me out of Hell-fire:
That is, for doing of the Thing
An Angel of money you must me bring.'

87
The Trooper Watering His Nagg
(*c.*1707)

[*Pills* (1707), iii, 13]

[Tune: *Pills* (1719), v, 13]

There was an Old Woman lived under a Hill
   Sing Trolly lolly lolly lolly lo!
She had good Beer and Ale for to sell
   Ho Ho, had she so, had she so, had she so.

She had a Daughter, her name was *Siss*
   Sing Trolly lolly lolly lolly, lo!
She kept her at Home for to welcome her Guest
   Ho Ho, did she so, did she so, did she so.

There came a Trooper riding by
   Sing etc.
He called for Drink most plentifully
   Ho Ho etc.

When one Pot was out he called for another
   Sing etc.
He kissed the Daughter before the Mother
   Ho Ho etc.

It was with the Mother's own consent
   Ho Ho, was it so, was it so, was it so
Quoth she 'What is this so stiff and warm?'
   Sing Trolly etc.
''Tis Ball, my Nagg; he will do you no harm'
   Ho Ho, won't he so, won't he so, won't he so.

'But what is this hangs under his Chin?'
   Sing Trolly etc.
''Tis the Bagg he puts his Provender in'
   Ho Ho, is it so, is it so, is it so.

Quoth he 'What is this?'; Quoth she ''tis a Well
   Sing Trolly etc.
'Where Ball, your Nagg, may drink his fill'
   Ho Ho, may he so, may he so, may he so.

'But what if my Nagg should chance to slip in?'
   Sing Trolly etc.
'Then catch hold of the Grass that grows on the Brim'
   Ho Ho, must I so, must I so, must I so.

'But what if the Grass should chance to fail,'
   Sing Trolly etc.
'Shove him in by the Head, pull him out by the Tail'
   Ho Ho, must I so, must I so, must I so.

88

My Thing Is My Own
(*ante* 1700)

[*Pills* (1707), ii, 234]

[Tune: *Pills* (1719), iv, 216]

I, a tender young Maid have been courted by many
Of all Sorts and Trades as ever was any;

My Thing Is My Own

A spruce *Haberdasher* first spake to me fair
But I would have nothing to do with Small Ware
  My Thing is my own and I'll keep it so still
  Yet other young Lasses may do what they will.

A sweet-scented *Courtier* did give me a Kiss
And promised me Mountains if I would be his,
But I'll not believe him for it is too true
Some *Courtiers* do promise much more than they do.
  My Thing etc.

A fine *Man of Law* did come out of the Strand
To plead his own Cause with his Fee in his hand;
He made a brave Motion but that would not do
For I did dismiss him and Non-Suit him too.
  My Thing etc.

Next came a young fellow a notable Spark
(With Green Bag and Ink-horn – a *Justices Clark*)
He pulled out his Warrant to make all appear
But I sent him away with a flea in his ear.
  My Thing etc.

A *Master of Musick* came with an intent
To give me a Lesson on my Instrument.
I thanked him for nothing but bid him begone
For my little Fiddle should not be played on.
  My Thing etc.

An *Usurer* came with abundance of Cash
But I had no mind to come under his lash;
He profer'd me Jewels and great store of Gold
But I would not Mortgage my little Free-hold.
  My Thing etc.

A blunt *Lieutenant* surprized my Placket
And fiercely began to rifle and sack it;
I mustered my Spirits up and became bold
And forced my Lieutenant to quit his Stronghold.
   My Thing etc.

A crafty young *Bumpkin* that was very rich
And used with his Bargains to go thro' Stitch,
Did tender a Sum but it would not avail
That I should admit him as Tenant-in-tail.
   My Thing etc.

A fine dapper Taylor, with a Yard in his Hand
Did profer his service to be at command.
He talked of a Slit I had above knee
But I'll have no Taylors to stitch it for me.
   My Thing etc.

A *Gentleman* that did talk much of his Grounds
His Horses, his Setting-dogs and his Grey-hounds,
Put in for a Course, and used all his Art
But he missed of the sport for Puss would not start.
   My Thing etc.

A pretty young *Squire* new come to the Town
To empty his Pockets and so to go down
Did profer a Kindness, but I would have none
The same that he used to his mother's maid, Joan.
   My Thing etc.

Now here I could reckon a hundred or more
Besides all the Gamesters recited herefore
That made their Addresses in hopes of a snap
But as young as I was, I understood Trap.
   My Thing is my own etc.

As the Fryar He Went Along

NOTE: This ballad is the earliest – even the only known – of the
expression of a girl's own independence in the matter of to whom
she shall render her maidenhead. All the other ballads deal with
mens' pursuit of the women and their eventual conquest. Some few
ballads show women feigning reluctance before they part their legs;
but none so outspoken as this heroine. Perhaps she was an early
protagonist of Women's Liberation?

89
As the Fryar He Went Along
(*c*.1707)

[*Pills* (1707), iii, 130]

[A broadside street song. Tune: *Pills* (1719), v, 58]

As the Fryar he went along, and a-poring in his Book
At last he spy'd a jolly brown Wench a-washing of her Buck.
      Sing, Stow the Fryar, stow the Fryar
      Some good man and let this fair Maid go.

The Fryar he pulled out and a jolly brown Tarse as much as
    he could handle
'Fair Maid' quoth he, 'if thou carriest Fire in thy Arse, come
    light me this same Candle.'
      Sing, Stow etc.

The Maid she shat and a jolly brown Turd out of her jolly
    brown Hole
'Good Sir', quoth she 'if you will a Candle light, come blow
    me this same Coal.'
      Sing, Stow etc.

Part of the sparks flew into the North and part into the South
And part of this jolly brown Turd flew into the Fryar's
    Mouth.
      Sing, Stow etc.

90

The Lass of Lynn's Sorrowful Lamentation for the Loss of her Maidenhead

(*ante* 1700)

[*Pills* (1707), iii, 131]

[Tune: *Pills* (1719), v, 59]

I am a young Lass of *Lynn*[1]
Who often said thank you too.
My Belly's now almost to my chin
    I cannot tell what to do.

My being so free and so kind
Does make my heart to rue
The sad effects of this I find
    I cannot tell what to do.

My Petticoats which I wore
And likewise my Aprons too
Alass! they are all too short before
    I cannot tell what to do.

Was ever young Maid so crossed
As I, who thanked him too:
For why? my Maiden-head is lost
    I cannot tell what to do.

In sorrowfull sort I cry'd
And may now for ever rue
The pain lies in my Back and Side
    I cannot tell what to do.

1. King's Lynn, Norfolk

Alass! I was kind and mild
But now the same I rue
Having no father for my child
   I cannot tell what to do.

I took but a touch – in Jest
Believe me, this is true
Yet I have proved, I protest
   I cannot tell what to do.

He craved my Virginity
And gave me his own, in lieu
In this I find I was too kind
   I cannot tell what to do.

Each Damsel will me Regarde
And so will the young men too
I'm neither Widdow, Wife nor Maid
   I cannot tell what to do.

A cradle I must provide
A chair and possett too
Nay! likewise twenty things beside
   I cannot tell what to do.

When I was a Maiden fair
Such sorrows I never knew
But now my heart is full of care
   I cannot tell what to do.

Oh! what will become of me
My Belly's as big as two
'Tis with a two-legged Tympany
   I cannot tell what to do.

You Lasses that hear my moan
If you will your joys renew
Be sure, while *married*,[1] lie alone
  Or else you at length may rue.

I came as of good a Race
As most in Lynn's fair Town
And cost a great deal bringing-up
But a little Thing laid me down.

91

Aminta One Night Had Occasion to Pisse: A Parody
(*ante* 1700)

[*Pills* (1707), i, 274]

[Tune: *Pills* (1719), i, 334–; 'When first Amyntas su'd for a Kisse']

Aminta one Night had occasion to Pisse
Joan reach'd her the Pot that stood by her;
I in the next Chamber could hear it to hiss,
The Sluice was small but Stream was strong:
My Soul was melting thinking of bliss
And raving I lay with desire
  But nought could be done
  For alas she Pissed on,
Nor car'd for Pangs I suffer'd long:
  Joan next made hast,
  In the self-same Case;

---

1. The original has *'married'*, but obviously it should have been *'unmarried'*.

To fix the Pot close to her own Arse;
   Then Floods did come,
   One might have swom,
And puff a Whirl-wind flew from her Bum.

Says *Joan*, by these strange Blasts that do rise,
I guess that the Night will grow windy;
For when such Showers do fall from the Skies,
To clear the Air the North-wind blows;
Ye nasty Quean, her Lady replies,
That Tempest broke out from behind ye;
And though it was decently kept from my Eyes
The troubled Air offends my Nose:
   Said *Joan* 'ods-heart
   You have pissed a Quart,
And now you make ado for a Fart;
'Tis still your Mind, to squeeze behind,
But never fell Shower from me without Wind!

92

The Bee-hive
(*ante* 1700)

[*Pills* (1707), ii, 73]

[Tune: *Pills* (1719), iv, 73]

My Mistress is a Hive of Bees in yonder flow'ry Garden
To her they come with loaden Thighs, to ease them of their
    Burden:
As under the Bee Hive lieth the Wax and under the Wax is
    Honey
So, under her Waste her Belly is placed and under that, her
    Cunny.

My Mistress is a Mine of Gold, Would that it were her
    Pleasure
To let me dig within her Mould and roll among her Treasure.
As under the Moss the Mould doth lie, and under the Mould
    is Money
So, under her Waste, her Belly is placed and under that, her
    Cunny.

My Mistress is a Morn of May, which drops of Dew down
    stilleth
Where e'er she goes to sport and play, the Dew down
    sweetly trilleth;
As under the Sun the Mist doth lie, so under the Mist it is
    sunny,
So, under her Waste her Belly is placed and under that, her
    Cunny.

My Mistress is a pleasant Spring that yieldeth store of Water
    Sweet
That doth refresh each withered Thing lies trodden under
    feet,
Her Belly is both White and Soft and downy as any Bunny,
That many Gallants wish full oft to play but with her Cunny.

My Mistress hath the Magick Sprays; of late she takes such
    wondrous Pain
That she can pleasing Spirits raise and also lay them down
    again:
Such Power hath my tripping Doe, my little Pretty Bunny
That many would their Lives forgo to play but with her
    Cunny.

93

Pillycock
(*ante* 1700)

[*Pills* (1707), iii, 50]
[Music by Thomas Wroth, *Pills* (1719), iv, 311]

Pillycock came to my Lady's Toe
And there the Whoreson began to go.
  Had he Feet,
    Ay, Marry had he?
    And did he go,
    Ay, Marry did he?
So bolt upright and ready to fight
And Pillycock he lay there all Night.

Pillycock came to my Lady's Heel
And there the Whoreson began to feel.
  Had he Hands,
    Ay, Marry had he?
    And did he feel
    Ay, Marry did he?
So bolt upright etc.

Pillycock came to my Lady's shin
And there the Whoreson began to grin.
  Had he Teeth,
    Ay, Marry had he?
    And did he grin,
    Ay, Marry did he?
So bolt upright etc.

Pillycock came to my Lady's Knee
And there the Whoreson began to see.
  Had he Eyes
    Ay, Marry had he?

And did he see
Ay, Marry did he?
So bolt upright etc.

Pillycock came to my Lady's Thigh
And there the Whoreson began to fly
Had he Wings
Ay, Marry, had he?
And did he fly
Ay, Marry did he?
So bolt upright etc.

Pillycock came to my Lady's Cunt
And there the Whoreson began to hunt.
Had he Hounds
Ay, Marry had he?
And did he hunt
Ay, Marry, did he?
So Bolt upright etc.

Pillycock came to my Lady's Quilt
And there the Whoreson began to tilt.
Had he a Lance
Ay, Marry had he?
And did he tilt
Ay, Marry did he?
So bolt upright etc.

94
The Suburbs Is a Fine Place – A Satyre
(c.1705)

[*Pills* (1707), iii, 99]

[A broadside ballad. Tune: *Pills* (1719), v, 27]

The Suburbs is a fine Place belonging to the City
It has no Government at all; alack, the more the Pity,
A Wife, a silly Animal, esteemed in that same Place
For there, a civil Woman's now ashamed to show her Face.
The *Misses*[1] there have each Man's Time, his Money, nay! his
    Heart
Then all in all, both great and small, and all in every Part.

Which Part, it is a Thorough-fair so open and so large
One well might sail through every *Tail* even in a western
    Barge:
These *Cracks*[2] that Coach it now, when first they came to
    Town
Did turn *Up-Tail* for a Pot of Ale, in Linsey Wolsey Gown.
The *Bullies* first debauch'd them in baudy Covent-Garden,
That filthy Place where ne'er a Wench was ever worth a
    Farthing.
And when their Maidenheads are sold to sneaking Lords,
Which Lords are *Clapt* at least nine-fold for taking of their
    Words.

And then My Lord, that many tries, she looks so innocent,
Believing he infected her, he makes a *Settlement*.
These are your *Cracks*, who skill'd in all kind of Debauches
Do daily Piss, Spue and whore, in their own Glass-Coaches.

1. Kept women, upon whom often a money 'settlement' is made, either from
affection or through blackmail of pregnancy, real or alleged. 2. Cheap
prostitutes; who may sometimes graduate to *Misses*.

Now *Miss* turns *Night-Walker*, till Lord Mayor's Men she
    meets
O'er Night she's drunk, next day she's finely flogged thro'
    London Streets.
After their Rooms of State are changed to *Bulks* or Cobblers'
    stalls
'Til *Poverty* and *Pox* agree, they dye in Hospitals.

This Suburbs gallant *Fopp*[1] that takes delight in Roaring,
He spends his time in Huffing, Swearing, Drinking and in
    Whoreing.
And if an honest Man and Wife should meet them in the
    Dark
Makes nothing to run the Husband through, to get the name
    of *Spark*.

But when the Constable appears, the Gallant, let me tell ye
His Heart defiles his *Breeches* and sinks into his Belly.
These are the silly Rogues that think it fine and witty
To laugh and joak at Aldermen – the Rulers of the City.

They'd kiss our Wives, but hold for all their plotting Pates
While they would get us Children we are getting their
    Estates:
And still in vain they Court, pretending in their Cares
That their Estates may thus descend unto the lawfull Heirs.

Their Play-houses I hate: are Shops to set off Wenches
Where *Fopp* and *Miss*, like Dog and Bitch do couple under
    Benches.

1. The aristocratic hooligans, sometimes called *Mohocks*, or *Sparks*, who terro-
rized the streets, maiming and killing innocent citizens.

95

The Irish Hullaloo
(*c*.1707)

[*Pills* (1707), ii, 205]

[Tune: *Pills* (1719), iv, 199]

Instead of our Buildings and Castles so brave
Into our Caverns we're forced for to crave.
When we are driven along the Bogs
We root up Potatoes like the wild Hogs.

Instead of their Beavers and Castors so good
In their picked[1] Caps they are forced to the Wood;
And when they are driven along the Passes
They've nothing but Tatters to hang on their Arses.

Instead of their Mantles lined with Plush
They're forced to seek Rags off every Bush.
When they have gotten a very good Cantle
They go to the Butchers and there make a Mantle.

Instead of their Boots with Tops so large
I'm sure they are ridd of that same Charge
Now they have gotten a thin pair of Brogues
And into the Woods among the wild Rogues.

Their Mutton and Beef, they are all wild Runts,
Their Wives are all nasty and so are their Cunts.
But I'll keep my Fiddle-stick out of their Cases:
They stink like Privies: a Pox of their Arses.

1. peaked

96

The Harlot Unmask'd
(*ante* 1655)

[*Musarum Delicae* (1655)
J.S.F., IV, 3]

[A broadside street ballad. Tune: Chappell, II, 53, 'The King and the
Miller']

How happy the State does the Damsel possess
Who would be no greater, nor can be no less?
On her *Quim* and herself depends for support,
And is better than all the Prime Ladies at Court.
What tho' she in Grogram and Lindsey does go,
Nor boasts of fine clothing to make a gay show.
A girl in this dress may be sweeter by far
Than she that is stitched by a *Garter and Star*.
Than she that is stitched by a Garter and Star.

Tho' her hands they are red and her bubbies are coarse,
Her *Quim*, for all that, may be never the worse.
A girl more polite, with less vigour may play
And her passion in accents less charming convey.
What tho' a brisk Fellow she sometimes may lack
When warm with desire and stretched on her back:
In this too, great Ladies example afford,
Who oft put a Footman in room of a Lord.
Who oft put a Footman in room of a Lord.

Or should she endeavour new conquests to make,
In this too, she mimicks the *Punks* of the State,
Whose aim is all one for to get a good Stroke
As all her concern's to supply her *Black Toak*.
Each night when Sport's over and Love's fountain's dry
She, weary with stitching, contented does lie.
Then wakes in the morning so brisk and so keen;

If so happy a *Harlot*, then who'd be a *Queen*?
If so happy a Harlot, then who'd be a Queen?

NOTE: The tune may be traced back to the time of King Edward IV.

97

The Long Vocation

OR **A New Touch of the Times**
(*c*.1707)

[*Pills* (1707), iii, 65
J.S.F., IV, 136]

[Tune: *Pills* (1719), iv, 317]

In the Long Vocation,[1] when Business was scanty
But Cherries – and Whores, extraordinary plenty.

When News came to England, the best e'er was known
All our armies victorious; the French overthrown.

When Quality withdrew to their Grottos of Pleasure
And Ladies to the Wells to spend their Lords' Treasure.[2]

When decrepit old sinners to the Bath did resort
For venereal distempers as well as the Sport.[3]

When the Red Robe was gone to the Country Assizes[4]
And Butchers and Carmen were fighting of Prizes.[5]

1. the long vacation, when the Court went away on holiday in summer 2. nobles went to their country estates and their ladies to Tunbridge Wells to take the waters and gamble 3. Leather Lane mercury baths, to 'cure' syphilis 4. the justices went visiting the provincial assizes 5. butchers and carmen used to fight at the Bull Ring and cockfights on Bankside

When Orthodox also from the Pulpit did roar
'Twas the Sins of the nation made our Taxes so sore.

When young golden Captains did walk the Parade;
But a Draught, once in motion, were always afraid.[1]

When the Cits[2] did retire to their Country-houses
Leaving servants at home, to lie with their spouses.

When wives too, would junket while their Cuckolds did
    sleep
And spend more in a Night than they got in a week.

When high-topping Merchants were daily beset:
And Statutes of Bankrupts filled half our Gazette.[3]

When Lawyers had not money nor Shopkeepers trade
And our Nation preparing, another to invade.

When the Season was too hot for the goggle-eyed Jews
To exercize their faculties in Drury Lane stews.[4]

When Inns of Court Rakes and Quill-driving Prigs
Flocked to St James's to show their long Whiggs.[5]

When Sodomites were so impudent to ply on th' Exchange
And by daylight, the Piazzas of Covent Garden to range.[6]

When the Theatre Jilts would swive for a Crown:
And for want of brisk trading patroll'd round the Town.[7]

1. Spa waters were cathartic   2. the great merchants and citizens of the City   3.
the *London Gazette*   4. the whorehouses   5. lawyers and clerks went to St
James's Park, Westminster   6. homosexuals openly solicited on the prostitutes'
beats at the New Exchange and in Covent Garden   7. the actresses would fuck
for a crown; as well as go on the streets because business was bad

When Debauchees of both sexes from hospitals crept:
Where nine months at least in flannel they slept.[1]

When Drapers smugged Prentices, with Exchange girls most
    jolly;
After Shop was shut up, could sail to 'The Folly'.[2]

When the amorous Thimberkins in Paternoster Row:
With their Sparks, on an evening, could Coach it to Bow.[3]

When Poets and Players were so damnably poor
That a threepenny Ordinary they often would score.[4]

When Defoe and the Devil at leapfrog did play,
And huffing proud Vintners broke every day.

When chambermaids dressed in their Mistresses clothes
Walked in public places to ogle the Beaus.

When Tallymen had no faith with strumpets and whores:
But napped[5] them in the streets by dozens and scores.

When Informers were Rogues and took double-pay
Much worse then the persons they're hired to betray.

When Serjeants were so vigilant 'twas impossible to shame
    'em
But whip see Jethro, immediatly; God eternally Damn 'em.

When Brewers to Victuallers was so cursed severe,
They scarce would give credit for a barrel of beer.

1. the Lock Hospital for venereal diseases 2. masters buggered their apprentices: or went to the showboat on the Thames to pick up whores 3. the whores in Paternoster Row, with their Gallants, might ride to Bow – then a green suburb 4. they would be reduced to eating at the cheapest chophouses 5. fucked

Thus is it not evident, Tap-lashes don't thrive:
Since they swarm in most prisons like bees in a hive.

But you Blue-apron[1] tribe, let this caution prevail:
Be not too saucy lest you rot in a jail.

At this juncture in time I strolled to Moor-fields,
Much used by the Mob to exercise their heels.[2]

Also famed for a Conjurer – the Devils Head Proctor;
Where a little below him dwells the never-born Doctor[3]

Two such impudent Rascals, for lying and prating –
That the series of their lives is not worth my relating.

My pockets being lined well with rhino, good store;
And inclinations much bent after a Thing called a Whore.

To gratify my lust I went to 'The Star';[4]
Where immediately I spy'd a Whore in the Bar.

Whose phiz[5] was most charming and as demure as a saint
But confoundedly bedaubed with Patches and Paint.

'Sweet Lady' cried I, 'I vow and protest
The sight of your charms have so wounded my breast'

'That I'm downright in Love, and my life shall destroy
If you do not admit me your favour to enjoy.'

1. blue-aprons: ambulant City prostitutes   2. a centre of prostitution but also a
popular recreation ground   3. Dr Trotter – a charlatan   4. a notorious Tavern in
the Strand   5. face: probably short for 'physiognomy'

Cringing in her Arse the bawd then replied
'My favour, kind Sir, shall never be denied'

'Will you please to walk up, or be private below?
Here! Boy! with a bed in it, the Gentleman show.'

Then backwards we went to a cavern behind[1]
But such an intricate place the Devil could not find.

Where wine being brought and the fellow withdrawn
I caressed her with Love: she made a return.

No pigs in a sty or goats in bad weather
E'er nussled so close or more amorous together.

We kissed and we billed, we tickled and toyed
And more than once, ourselves we enjoyed.

But the Reckoning grew high – which would make my
     pocket low:
So how for the bilk 'em, I did not well know.

But at last, by a stratagem: pretending to rally,
While she went for more wine I whipped into an alley

And was so dextrous nimble they could not pursue:
So got rid of my Mistress and damned Reckoning too.

Recovering the Fields,[2] I was void of all fear
And the next place to Bedlam my course I did steer.

1. most brothels were in back alleys   2. escaping into nearby Finsbury Fields

Bawdy Verse

Where was such amphibious crowds I ne'er saw before:
Harlots for the Water as well as the shore.[1]

But one above the rest, so wondrous trim:
You would swear she was a Hick,[2] and no common Brim.[3]

Accosted me presently and called me her Love
But I soon did dismss her with a Kick and a Shove;

For the Jade was so homely the Devile wouldn't touch her
Fit only for a Drayman or a Whitechapel butcher.

But had not walked long before a rare one I espied
Bright as a Goddess and adorned like a Bride.

With a rich furbelow Scarf worth at least forty shilling:
And when I asked her a question, was extraordinary willing.

So to the tavern we went – a curse on the place:
For her love was so hot it soon fired my Arse.[4]

The plague of my sins made me damnable sore
That my wife soon concluded I'd been with a Whore

She scolded so loud and continued her clamour
I could not forbear but to Curse and to Damn her.

We made such a noise and confounded a racket
My Landlady knew I'd been searching the Placket

And being good-natured, to make up the matter,
Came down in her smock, with Jenny, her daughter.

1. outside the mad-house there were always great crowds and large numbers of
whores plying 2. country lass 3. short for 'Brimstone' – a sobriquet for
whore 4. she gave him a dose of the clap

'Ah! tenant' quoth she 'Let this fault be remitted:
If he'll beg but your pardon, he shall be acquitted'

For to speak by-the-by, and I'm sure 'tis a fact;
You and I have been guilty of many such act.'

NOTE: As a contemporary document about social and sexual *mores*
this ballad is excellent. The absence of the moneyed people of the
Court and the hangers-on, meant that business in the City was bad,
money was short, and many small traders went bankrupt. The
lawyers earned no fees, and touted for business in St James's Park,
where anybody who was anybody might still be found. The unem-
ployment was reflected in an immense increase in street prostitu-
tion; and from boredom and lack of other entertainment, the citizens
patronized the whorehouses in Moorfields, Clerkenwell and Fins-
bury, bilking the whores as often as they could – sometimes just for
the hell of it, a sort of sport. The poor diseased whores passed on
venereal diseases to their clients, who (if wealthy) patronized the
mercury baths in Leather Lane through which syphilis was sup-
posed to be cured (the poor had to go to the Lock Hospital in
Kingsland, for men, or the Lock Hospital in Southwark, for women).
Either way, venereal disease was regarded as an occupational
hazard – a nothing between friends – and either way there was no
cure. The Old Exchange in the City and the New Exchange in the
Strand, were haunts of prostitutes. This ballad discloses (almost
uniquely) that male prostitutes also frequented these two centres.
The ballad succeeds in communicating to the reader the atmosphere
of frustration and boredom. 'The Folly' was a houseboat on the
Thames, moored off the Bankside; originally meant for music and
concerts or amorous dallying, it deteriorated and became a low-class
place of assignation. Finally it ended up as a Nonconformist house of
worship before it was broken up.

98
Underneath the Castle Wall
(*c.*1700)

[*Pills* (1707), iv, 261
J.S.F., V, 222]

[A broadside street song. Tune: *Pills* (1719), vi, 120]

Underneath the Castle wall the Queen of Love sat mourning
Tearing of her Golden Locks, her Red Rose Cheeks adorning.
With her Lily-white Hand she smote her Breasts
And said she was forsaken.
With that the Mountains, they did skip
And the Hills fell all a-quaking.

Underneath the rotten Hedge, the Tinker's Wife sat shiting,
Tearing of a Cabbage Leaf, her shitten Arse a-wiping;
With her Coal-black Hands she scratched her Arse
And swore she was beshitten.
With that the Pedlars all did skip
And the Fiddlers fell a-spitting.

99
The Maid's Lesson
(*c.*1710)

Being Instructions for a Young She-Beginner

A Spick and Span New Song

[J.S.F., II, 212]

[A broadside ballad]

To play upon a VIOL if a VIRGIN will begin
She first of all must know her CLIFF

And all the STOPS therein.
    Repeat. She first etc.

Her PRICK she must hold long enough
Her BACKFALLS, gently take,
Her TOUCH must gentle be, not rough
She at each STROKE must shake
    Repeat. Her Touch etc.

Her BODY must by no means bend
But stick close to her FIDDLE
Her feet must hold the lower end
Her knees must hold the middle
    Repeat. Her Feet etc.

She boldly to the BOW must fly
As if she'd make it CRACK
Two FINGERS on the Hair must lye
And Two, upon the BACK
    Repeat. Two Fingers etc.

And when she hath, as she would have
She must it gently thrust,
UP, DOWN, SWIFT, SLOW, at any rate
As she herself doth list.
    Repeat. Up, Down etc.

And when she once begins to find
That she grows something cunning,
She'll ne'er be quiet in her Mind
Untill she finds it running.

100
The Lasse with the Velvet Arse
(*ante* 1710)

[J.S.F., II, 214
Pills (1709), vi, 247]

[Tunes: Simpson, 335, a broadside song, with music 'Abroad as I Was Walking'; 'There Was a Buxsome Lass']

There was a buxom Lasse
And she had a Velvet Arse
Which made her to Bounce and to vapour
When E'er she went to Shit
If twas ne'er such a little bit
   O, she always wiped it with brown Paper.
     With brown Paper
     With brown Paper
   She always wiped it with brown Paper.

This Lasse, whose name was *Jane*
O she kept her Arse so clean,
That she won the Heart of one Mr Draper.
He married her outright
So she got a Husband by't,
And all because she wiped her Arse
With brown Paper.
     With brown Paper
     With brown Paper
   And all because she wiped her Arse with brown Paper.

Ye Lasses short and tall
Pray take Example all,
And learn for the Future to use brown Paper.
So here's a Health to every Lasse
That mudifies her Arse,
Not forgetting good Mrs Draper.

Good Mrs Draper
Good Mrs Draper
Not forgetting Good Mrs Draper.

101
The Female Scuffle
(1680–90)

[Wit and Drollery (1682)
Pills (1709), iv, 18]

[A broadsheet ballad. Tune: Chappell, I, 259, 'Packington's Pound',
ante 1596]

Of late in the Park a fair Fancy was seen
Betwixt an old Baud and a lusty young Quean.
Their parting of Money began the uproar;
'I'll have half' says the Baud. 'But you shan't' says the
    Whore.
'Why 'tis my own House
I care not a Louse
I'll have three parts in four, or you get not a Souse!'

'Tis I' says the Whore, 'must take all the Pains,
And you shall be damned e'er you get all the Gains.'
The Baud being vex'd, straight to her did say
'Come off with your duds, and I pray, pack away:
And likewise your Ribbonds, your Gloves and your Hair,
For naked you came, and so out you go bare.'
Then Buttocks so bold
Began for to scold
Hurrydan was not able her Clack for to hold.

Both pell-mell fell to't and made this uproar
With these compliments – 'Th'art a Baud', 'Th'art a Whore!'

The Bauds and the Buttocks that lived there around
Came all to the case, both pocky and sound
To see what the reason was of this same fray
That did so disturb them before it was day.
If I tell you amiss
Let me never more Piss
This Buttocks so bold, she named was Siss.

By quiffing with Cullies, three pounds she had got,
And but one part of four must fall to her Lot.
Yet all the Bauds cry'd 'Let us turn her out bare
Unless she will yield to return her half share.
If she will not we'll help to strip off her Cloaths
And turn her abroad with a slit-o-the-Nose'.
Who, when she did see
There was no remedy
For her from the tyrannous Bauds to get free;
The Whore from the money was forced to yield,
And in the conclusion, the Baud got the Field.

NOTE: The venue was the infamous Whetstone Park, next to
Lincoln's Inn in Holborn, a red-light area for centuries. A *buttock
whore* was an ambulant woman of very low class; the description is
first recorded in 1660. Poor whores who landed in Bridewell prison
often had their noses slit open as punishment.

102
The Fart
(1711)

[*Pills* (1719), i, 28]

[Tune: *Pills* (1719), i, 28]

[Composed by Thomas D'Urfey in 1711, when it was 'Famous for its Satyricall Humour in the Reign of Queen Anne'. It is directed against politicians and the clergy, the Queen's fart being incidental.]

YE *Jacks* of the Town, and *Whiggs* of renown
Leave off your Jarrs and Spleen,
And haste to your Arms, All thronging in Swarms
Be ready to guard the Queen.
   With a hum, hum, hum, hum.

For last Lord's-day, at St James[1] they say
A strange odd Thing did chance,
Which put into the News, all Holland would amuse,
But would make 'em rejoyce, in France.
   With a hum etc.

Each Commoner and Peer, of both Houses was there
And folks of each Rank and Station;
Had thither free recourse, from the Keeper of the Purse
To the Mayor of a Corporation.
   With a hum etc.

When at Noon, as in state, the Queen was at Meat
And the Princely Dane[2] sat by her
A Fart there was heard, that the Company scared
As a Gun, at their Ears had been fired.
   With a hum etc.

---

1. St James's Palace 2. George, Prince of Denmark, her husband

Which irreverent Sound made 'em stare all around
And in each Countenance lower,
Whilst judgement thereupon said, It needs must be done,
As affronting the Soveraigne Power.
 With a hum etc.

The Chaplain in Place had but just said Grace
And then, cringeing behind, withdrawn.
When they called back to examine if the Crack
Came from him, or the Lords in Lawn.[1]
 With a hum etc.

A *Garter and Star*,[2] next censure did bear
Who for all he looked so High
And carry'd it so Great in Intrigues of the State
Yet might condescend to let fly.
 With a hum, etc.

But he, in a Heat, said the Thing in debate
Impose'd on each Sex might be,
And would have made it clear that some Dutchesses there
Were as likely to do it as he.
 With a hum etc.

The colour then rose 'mongst the noble Furbelows
For just by the *Chair*[3] some fat Bishops were there
Whom the *Whigg* boys fain would bespatter
Who with a sober look, declared, *upon the Book*
That the Clergy knew nought of the matter;
 Of the hum etc.

But they would not Swear, for the Parties were there
Of the High Church, and the Low,

---

1. the bishops 2. a Knight of the Garter 3. the throne

The Fart

Who from a mighty Zeal for good of th'Commonweal
Might let some of their Bagpipes blow.
  With a hum etc.

At this, when heard, Late *Comptroller* stroak'd his Beard
And declared, with an Antique bow,
He tho' of some, nothing knew, yet would vouch for two –
Himself and his brother, Jack Howe.
  For the hum etc.

For the Squire was well-bred and his Key might have had
But refused for an old State Trick
And that he that had made Sport with Places of the Court
Now resolved upon Wharton's[1] *White Stick.*
  With a hum etc.

When this was done, and the Crime not yet known,
Came a Law Peer to plead the Case.
How they had no Intent to affront the Government
Nor had he, to regain the Mace.
  With a hum, etc.

But the Giggling Rout that were waiting round about
'Twas likely were heedless *Jades*
So that saving their own Fame, they agreed upon the sham
To have turned it upon the poor Maids.[2]
  With a hum, etc.

Who all drowned in Tears, charged the Ladies there in Years[3]
To tell truth if that hideous Roar
So Thunderlike sent from audacious Fundament
Could consist with *their* Virgin bore.
  With a hum etc.

1. the Duke of Wharton   2. Maids of Honour   3. the older women

Who answering, No! all disputes fell too
For now they believed it was reason
To pass the matter off as a Joke and in a Laugh,
Since they ne'er could make it High Treason.
   With a hum etc.

So that turning the Jest, they agreed it at last
That naught from *The Presence*[1] did come
But the Noise that they heard was some Yeoman of the
   Guard
That brought Dishes into the next Room.
   With a hum etc.

But the Truth of the Sound not at all could be found
Since none but the Doer could tell.
So that hushing up the shame, the Beef-eater bore the blame
And the Queen, God be Praised, dined well.
   With a hum etc.

NOTE: Farting and belching, at home or in public, was a common-place occurrence in those days, when eating and drinking was gross, and the food, in general, was ill-cooked and of poor quality, which led to stomach upsets and indigestion and other complaints. Bad teeth and bad breath afflicted both men and women, and the smell of unwashed bodies at Court was often remarked upon in Courtiers' memoirs. Farting at Lord Mayors' banquets was acceptable, as a mark of appreciation of the good food served. There was, if Ned Ward is to be believed, even a *Farters Club*, which is not so *outré* as may be thought, for those times, when table manners were also gross. Moreover, the Queen was known to be ill of various complaints, was a gourmandizer and a heavy drinker of brandy, and it would not occasion much comment had she been the perpetrator, although it would have been almost *lèse majesté* to have allowed it to be thought at a banquet. Hence the consternation and the need to find a suitable scapegoat from proletarian sources.

The ballad also draws attention to the two political parties, still in their infancy as Whigs and Tories: as well as the two parties in the Church, High and Low; and their attempts to score off one another.

1. the Queen

103
Good Honest Trooper, Take Warning by Donald Cooper
(*c.*1700)

[*Pills* (1719), v, 88]

[A street ballad. Tune: 'Daniel Cooper', *c.*1700]

A bonny Lad came to the Court
His name was *Donald Cooper*,
And he petitioned to the King
That he might be a Trooper.
  He said that he by Land and Sea
Had fought to Admiration;
    And with *Montrose* had many blows
Both for his King and Nation.

The King did this Petition grant
And said he liked him dearly
Which gave to Donald more content
Than Twenty-shillings Yearly.
  This wily Laird rode in the Guard
And loved a strong Beer-barrel
    Yet stout enough to Fight and Cuff
But was not given to quarrel.

Till on a Saturday at Night
He walked in the Park, Sir.
And there he kenn'd a well-fair Lass
When it was almost dark, Sir.
  Poor Donald, he, drew near to see
And kissed her bonny *Mow* Sir,
    He laid her flat upon her back
And banged her side *Weam* too, Sir.

241

He took her by her Lilly-white Hand
And kissed his bonny Mary,
Then did they to the Tavern go
Where they did drink *Canary*.
   When he was drunk, in came a *Punck*
And asked 'gain would he *mow* her
   Then he again with Might and Main
Did bravely lay her o'er, Sir.

Poor *Donald*, he rose up again
As nothing did him ail, Sir
But little kenn'd this bonny Lass
Had *Fire* about her Tail, Sir
   When Night was spent then Home he went
And told it with a 'Hark, Sir',
   How he did kiss a dainty *Miss*
And lifted up her *Sark*, Sir.

But e'er a Month had gone about
Poor *Donald* walked sadly
And everyone enquired of him
What gar'd him leuk so badly.
   A Wench, quoth he, gave *Snuff* to me
Out of her *Placket-box*, Sir
   And I am sure she proved a *Whore*
And given me the *Pox*, Sir.

Poor *Donald* he being almost Dead
Was turned out of the Guard, Sir.
And never could get in again
Altho he was a Laird, Sir.
   When *Mars* doth meet with *Venus* sweet
And struggled to surrender
   Then Triumph's lost – then never trust
A Feminine Commander.

Poor *Donald* he went home again
Because he lost his Place, Sir
For playing at a Game of *Whisk*
And turning up an Ace, Sir.
   Ye Soldiers all, both great and small
A Footman, or a Trooper
   When you behold a Wench that's bold
REMEMBER DONALD COOPER.

104

The Penurious Quaker

OR **The High-priz'd Harlot**
(*c*.1719)

[A broadsheet catch. Tune: *Pills* (1719), vi, 294]

Quaker: My Friend! thy beauty seemeth good;
         We Righteous have our failings;
         I'm flesh and blood; methinks I could,
         Wert thou but free from Ailings.

Harlot: Believe me, Sir! I'm newly broached
         And never have been in yet:[1]
         I vow, and swear, I ne'er was touched
         By Man 'till this day sennight.

Quaker: Then prithee, Friend, now prithee do;
         Nay, let us not defer it.
         And I'll be kind to thee, when thou
         Hast laid the Evil Spirit.

Harlot: I vow I won't, indeed I shan't
         Unless I've Money first, Sir.
         For if I ever trust a Saint
         I wish I may be curst, Sir.

1. in the Lock Hospital for venereal disease in Southwark

Quaker: I cannot, like the Wicked, say
 'I love thee and Adore thee,
 And therefore thou wilt make me pay:
 So here is Sixpence for thee.

Harlot: Confound you for a stingy WHIG
 Do ye think I live by stealing?
 Farewel, you Puritannick Prig,
 I scorn to take your Shilling.

105

A Tenement to Let
(*c*.1680 based upon an original of *ante* 1661)

[*Pills* (1719), vi, 355]

[Tune: *Pills* (1719), vi, 355]

[See Poem 48]

I have a Tenement to let
I hope will please you all
And if you'd know the Name of it
'Tis call'd CUNNY HALL

It's seated in a pleasant Vale
Beneath a rising Hill
This Tenement is to be lett
To whosoe'er I will.

For Years, for Months, for Weeks or Days
I'll let this famous Bower
Nay, rather than a Tenant lack
I'd let it for an Hour

There's round about, a pleasant Grove
To shade it from the Sun
And underneath is Well-water
That pleasantly does run.

Where if you're hot you may be cooled
If cold, you may find heat
It is a well-contriv'd Spring
Not little nor too great.

The Place is very dark by Night
And so it is by Day
But when you once are entered in
You cannot lose your way.

And when you're in, go boldly on
As far as e'er you can
And if you reach to the House top
You'll be where ne'er was Man.

106

The Schoolmaster's Lesson
(*c.*1720)

[J.S.F., II, 227]

[A broadside ballad]

I will fly into your Arms
And smother you with Kisses
I will rifle all your Charms
And teach you amorous Blisses.
For it is my Concern
And a means that you should learn
The pranks of other *Misses*.

Don't be coy when I invade
And kindly yield the Blessing,
For its high time your *Maidenhead*
Were in my possession.
Don't cry out and be a Fool
For if that you come to School
You must peruse your Lesson.

Open then the Books, my Dear
The Leaves shall be separated
All things that comprehensive are
Shall soon be penetrated.
Lessons three, she had that Night
Taking pleasure with delight,
She begged for more next Morning.

Lovely Master, try again
Don't so soon forsake me,
For to learn I am in Pain
Till you a Scholar make me.
Such pretty pretty Things you show
The more you teach, the more I'd know
For now the Fit doth take me.

Never Master pleased me more
To such great Perfection
And of all the schools, I'm sure
Kind is your Correction.
For whenever you give the same,
Never a scholar can you blame
'Tis done with such affection.

Open then my Leaves so fair
And kindly to me show, Sir,
What Knowledge is, how sweet, how rare,

And what I long to know, Sir,
Cupid tells me very plain
That your Learning is not vain
But useful, as his Bow, Sir.

When he was departing then
She said with kind expression
When will you, pray Sir, come again
And teach me t'other Lesson?
He replied with great delight
My Dear! I'll come but every Night
And think it as a Blessing.

Thus each Night he doth repair
To tell her of her Duty
While he's taken in the Snare
Shot to the Heart by Cupid.
When the School-master is LOVE
Then the Scholars kinder prove,
For Love is kin to Beauty!

107
The Turnep Ground
(*c.*1720)

[J.S.F., II, 93]

[A broadsheet song]

I owed my Hostess thirty pound
And how d'ye think I pay'd her?
I met her on my Turnep Ground
And gently down I lay'd her.

She ope'd a Purse as black as Coal
To hold my Coin when counted.
I, satisfied in the Hole,
And just by Tail she found it.

Two stone make pounds full twenty-eight;
And Stones, she had some skill in.
And if good Flesh bare any rate,
A Yard's worth Forty Shilling.

If this Coin pass, no Man that lives
Shall dun for past Debauches;
Zounds! Landlords, send but in your Wives,
We'll scour off all their Notches.[1]

108

The Travelling Tinker, and the Country Ale-wife

OR **The Lucky Mending of the Leaky Copper**
(*ante* 1720)

[*Pills* (1720), vi, 296]

[Tune: 'The Travelling Tinker']

A Comely Dame of Islington,
    Had got a leaky Copper;
The Hole that let the Liquor run,
    Was wanting of a Stopper:
A Jolly Tinker undertook,
    And promised her most fairly;

---

1. Until written book-keeping became usual, payments were recorded by making notches in sticks, called 'tallies'. Smoothing out the notched stick meant that payment had been made.

With a thump thump thump, and knick knack knock,
   To do her Business rarely.

He turn'd the Vessel to the Ground,
   Says he a good old Copper;
But well may't Leak, for I have found
   A Hole in't that's a whopper:
But never doubt a Tinkers stroke,
   Altho' he's black and surly,
With a thump thump thump, and knick knack knock,
   He'll do your Business purely.

The Man of Mettle open'd wide,
   His Budget's mouth to please her,
Says he this Tool we oft employ'd,
   About such Jobbs as these are:
With that the Jolly Tinker took,
   A Stroke or two most kindly;
With a thump thump thump, and knick knack knock,
   He did her Business finely.

As soon as Crock had done the Feat,
   He cry'd 'tis very hot ho;
This thrifty Labour makes me Sweat,
   Here, gi's a cooling Pot ho:
Says she bestow the other Stroke,
   Before you take your Farewel;
With a thump thump thump, and knick knack knock,
   And you may drink a Barrel.

109
The Jolly Pedlar's Pretty Thing
(*ante* 1700)

[*Pills* (1719), vi, 248]

[Tune: 'The Jolly Pedlar's Pretty Thing']

A Pedlar proud as I heard tell,
　He came into a Town:
With certain Wares he had to sell,
　Which he cry'd up and down:
At first of all he did begin,
　With Ribbonds, or Laces, Points, or Pins,
Gartering, Girdling, Tape, or Filetting,
　　Maids any Cunny-skins.

I have of your fine perfumed Gloves,
　And made of the best Doe-skin;
Such as young Men do give their Loves,
　When they their Favour Win:
Besides he had many a prettier Thing
　　Than Ribbonds, etc.

I have of your fine Necklaces,
　As ever you did behold;
And of your Silk Handkerchiefs,
　That are lac'd round with Gold:
Besides he had many a prettier Thing
　　Than Ribbonds, etc.

Good fellow, says one, and smiling sat,
　Your Measure does somewhat Pinch;
Beside you Measure at that rate,
　It wants above an Inch:
And then he shew'd her a prettier Thing,
　　Than Ribbonds, etc.

The Lady was pleas'd with what she had seen,
 And vow'd and did protest;
Unless he'd shew it her once again,
 She never shou'd be at rest:
With that he shew'd her his prettier Thing
  Than Ribbonds, etc.

With that the Pedlar began to huff,
 And said his Measure was good,
If that she pleased to try his stuff,
 And take it whilst it stood:
And then he gave her a prettier Thing,
  Than Ribbonds, etc.

Good fellow said she, when you come again,
 Pray bring good store of your Ware;
And for new Customers do not sing,
 For I'll take all and to spare:
With that she hugg'd his prettier Thing
  Than Ribbonds, etc.

110

One Maid Let a Fart
(*c.*1700)

[*Pills* (1719), vi, 247]

ABROAD as I was walking, I spy'd two Maids a-wrestling
The one threw the other unto the Ground:
One Maid, she let a Fart, struck the other to the Heart:
Was this not a grievous Wound?

This Fart it was heard, into Mr Bowman's Yard
With a great and a mighty Power
For ought that I can tell, it blew down *Bridewell*
And so overcame the Tower.

It blew down *Paul's* steeple, and knocked down many People
Alack! was more the Pity:
It blew down *Leadenhall*, and the Meal-sacks, and all
And the Meal flew about the City.

It blew down the *Exchange*, was not this very strange,
And the Merchants of the City did wounder;
This Maid, she like a Beast, turned her Fugo to the East
And it roared in the air like Thunder!

111

Venus Unmask'd

OR A Merry Song for an Afflicted Sinner
(*c.* 1720)

[J.S.F., II, 183]

[A broadsheet street song]

Of jolly Rakes and pleasing Dames,
Of Claps, Mishaps, and teasing Pains
That do from Venus spring:
Of Love, and every sad effect
Which wanton Jilts, and Fools, neglect;
My Muse intends to sing.

These common Jades that make a Trade
In humouring every lustful Blade,
They're like Pandora's Box:
Whene'er they hug men in their arms
With their deluding 'ticing charms,
Out flies a Clap, or a Pox.

Nay! she that scorns to sin for Bread,
But squeaks and blushes like a Maid

Venus Unmask'd

When men attempt their joys;
Her eager look may yet by Chance
Contract the old disease of France,
Tho' Madam seems so coy.

The Lordly Beau, that keeps his Miss,
More safely to enjoy his bliss
When Love excites his taste:
The wealthy Dame that does depend
Upon her dear and chosen *Friend*
May both be stung at last.

The Statesman, and the Statesman's Tool,
The zealous Wise Man, and the Fool,
Are all to Love inclined:
Great Ladies stray as well as they;
And those who pray three times a day,
A sinful Hour will find.

Since all degrees of human kind
The Rich, the Poor, the Lame, the Blind,
The Queen of Love adore;
But when their Veins are numbed and cold
They all grow angry when they're old,
Because they can sin no more.

Since that all trading Sparks and Dames
Are subject to venereal Flames,
As doctors do agree;
All you that suck the poison in,
When Pins and Needles make ye grin,
I pray, repair to me.

At fucking, both the Rich and Poor
May find a safe and speedy Cure

In every sad degree:
Go East, go South, go West, in vain
Needham, the Man must ease your Pain
Tho' desperate your case be.

Altho' from foot unto the head
Like unto Lazarus, you're spread
    With filthy Ulcers round;
My remedies will burge[1] your Veins,
Heal up your sores, assuage your pains,
    And make you perfect sound.

NOTE: The broadsheet appears to have been reprinted about 1720.
The reference to Dr Needham implies a much earlier date – about
1680 – when the Leather Lane mercury baths for the cure of syphilis
were patronized by the nobility and gentry; they were no longer
operating by 1720.

112
My Little Lodge, Teaze Me No More!
(*c.*1700)

from An Imitation of the First Ode of the Fourth Book of Horace

[Harley MS., 7318, B.M., attributed to Alexander Pope]

My little Lodge, teaze me no more
With promises of the finest *Whore*
    That *Cundum* e'er was stuck in;
Give younger Men the beautious Dame,
Alass! I'm past the am'rous Flame
    And must give over Fucking.

1. purge

My Little Lodge, Teaze Me No More!

I'm not that Hero once you knew
When I the *Tygress* did subdue
   By noble feats of Vigour;
Why then pretend that I can *swive*?
Mother! *You* know, at fifty-five
   A man can only *frigg* her!

Go to Sir Paul, that vig'rous Knight,
Equal in Fucking or in Fight
   Ready for each encounter;
He can a Lady's cause defend
In Senates, when she lacks a Friend,
   Or He, in bed, can mount her.

He says an Hundred tender things
Is generous, gives Ruby Rings,
   In prowess never wanting.
To Operas he'll take the Jades
And Fuck too, at the Masquerades
   Three times, without *discards*.

But Lodge! cold Customers like me,
Intirely lost to Gallantry
   I fear would quickly starve ye:
I value not, tho' e'er I Toast,
Nor care a Rush who pleases most
   Or Lord or Lady Harvey.

And yet, what means my faultering Tongue?
Again I sigh: again am young,
   In Dreams I find her yielding.
Oh! were she so in Daytime too,
Still could I *dangle*, still pursue
   My charming Fanny Fielding!

NOTE: Mother Lodge was a famous procuress of the period 1710–1735, with an extensive clientele amongst the Court and nobility. Lord Harvey is the famous diarist John Hervey, created a baron in 1703, and Earl of Bristol in 1714. The *Tygress* may refer to the lady whom Hervey married, Mary Lepell; Frances Fielding was a well-known beauty of that day, a courtesan, connected in some way with the Fielding family, Earls of Denbigh; she may have been a daughter of the notorious *Beau* Fielding, who bigamously married Barbara Castlemaine, Duchess of Cleveland.

113

John and Susan
(*c.*1700)

[*A Musical Miscellany*, III, 47]

[A broadside ballad to the tune of 'Of Noble Race was Shenkin']

'Twas in the Land of Cyder
At a Place call'd *Brampton-Bryan*
Such a Prank was play'd
Twixt Man and Maid
That all the Saints cry'd Fie on.

For gentle *John* and *Susan*
Were oft at Recreation;
To tell the Truth
This vigorous Youth
Caus'd a dreadfull Conflagration.

Both Morning, Noon and Night, Sir
Brisk *John* was at her Crupper:
He got in her Geers
Five times before Prayers
And six times after Supper.

John and Susan

John being well-provided
So closely did solace her
That *Susan's* Waiste
So slackly lac'd
Shew'd signs of *Babe of Grace*, Sir.

But when the Knight perceived
That *Susan* had been sinning,
And that this Lass
For want of Grace
Lov'd Kissing more than Spinning,

To cleanse the House from Scandal
And filthy Fornication,
Of all such Crimes,
To shew the Times
His utter Detestation,

He took both Bed and Bolster
Nay, Blankets, Sheets and Pillows,
With *Johnny's* Frock
And Susan's Smock
And burnt them in the Kiln-house,

And every vile Utensil
On which they had been wicked,
As Chairs, Joint-stools,
Old Truncks, Close-stools,
And eke the three-legg'd Cricket

But had each Thing defiled
Been burnt at *Brampton-Bryan*
We all must grant
The *Knight* would want
Himself, a Bed to lye on!

114
White Thighs
(*c.*1735)

[J.S.F., II, 242]

[A broadside ballad to the tune of 'The Bob-tailed Lass'. The lyric
attributed to Thomas, Sixth Earl of Haddington]

Let the world run its course of capricious delight
I none of its vanities prize
More substantial the joys I experience each night
From a touch 'twixt my charmer's white thighs.

Poets praise Chloe's shape, her complexion, her air,
Coral lips, pearly teeth, and fine eyes;
A fig for them all, they can never compare
To my charmer's elastic white thighs.

What care I for Phyllis, Maria and Jane
Their beauties may raw ones surprise,
Let others enjoy them – content I remain
Sole Lord of thy lovely white thighs.

If aught can entice me, or aught can allure
My slumbering passions to rise,
Or aught kindle up my desires – be sure
'Tis the sight of these snowy white thighs.

When I revel, dear love, in thy heavenly charms
The joys of the gods I despise;
Nor envy great Mars, though in Venus' arms
Whilst embracing thy beautiful thighs.

Believe me, my dear, there is nothing on earth
Which so fondly – so madly I prize

As that fountain of bliss where delight takes its birth
Which is placed 'twixt thy parting white thighs.

Of Ganymede's beauties we ofttimes have heard
And how Jove buggered him in the skies:
No envy I have, nor care I a turd
Whilst possessing such exquisite thighs.

The Arse of my love is delightful to see
Its plumpness rejoiceth the eyes,
Her lily-white belly is heaven to me,
But, ye Gods! what are these to her thighs.

115
Little Peggy
(1743)

A Prophetic Homily

[By Horace Walpole]

Ye Nymphs of *Drury*, pour a nobler Strain!
I like not rural themes, and scorn the plain:
I sing of Courts and when of Courts I sing,
Notes worthy *Lincoln* flow, or Lincoln's King!

The hour is come, by ancient Dames foretold,
E'er his small *Cock* were yet a fortnight old,
How with majestick Vigour it should rise,
Strong to the Sense and tow'ring to the skies!
Women unfuck'd at sight of it should breed
And other Virgins teem with heav'nly Seed.

But thou, O *Venus*, on the newborn Maid
Thy quintessence of pow'rful Beauty shed,
That impious Loves and barren Vice may cease
And joys of golden fucking only please.
Propitious hear, O goddess of Delight!
Thy fav'rite *Lincoln* reigns, thine own adopted Knight.

While you, my Lord, are stallion of the age
The graceful Virgin shall the men engage;
Her little Veins with warmth paternal glow;
Her monthly Flow'rs, like her chaste mother's, blow!
If any traces still of Sin remain,
Venereal symptoms and the secret pain:
You shall instruct her to remove the fear,
Nor but in *Cundum* armed, embrace her dear.
Oh! what celestial pleasures shall she taste,
Great as Celestial, if they could but last!
The bravest Heroes shall the fair enthrall
And govern with paternal Lust, the Ball.

Presents till then shall strew the Nurs'ry floor
And golden Playthings round the Cradle pour:
To gather coral, Admirals shall sail
And British Navies seek the spicy gale;
Spice for the pap, and silver for the bells
Whose tinkling soothes the throbbing Gum that swells.
The comely Nurse the tumid *Dug* shall press
Nor fear to tempt the mighty Sire's caress.
Dayrolle shall rock thee o'er the Cradle loll,
Present the Rattle or undress the Doll.
The smiling infant in her hand shall bend
The nut-brown *Engine* of her father's friend,
Pleased shall behold the goodly *Member* rise
And innocently touch her titillating Thighs.

Little Peggy

But soon as manifest of Hair, the Maid
Conceives the praises of her beauty paid;
In at both ears her Sire's exploits shall suck
And comprehends, the mighty Joy, to fuck.
The sable down its ringlets shall disclose
And twine crisp tendrils round the pouting *Rose*;
While the stiff *Member* the glad space shall fill
And balmy Honey from each pore distill.

But still some tracks of ancient fraud shall last:
Distended *Cunts* with alum shall be braced;
With foreign Hair the circle shall be bound
And *Dildoes* make an imitative Wound.
Another *Onan* shall new crimes invent
And noble Seed in selfish Joys be spent:
Another *Bateman* shall debauch the boys
And future *Sapphos* practice mimic joys.

But when matured to Love thy breasts shall pant
And conscious Blushes speak the tender want,
Each happy Islander shall own thy sway
Nor foreign Beauties plough the British sea.
All *Pricks* shall stand for thee; no more shall feel
Italia's sons the music-making Steel:
Robust *Hibernians*, muscularly strong
With well-proportioned *Yards* and nobly long,
Yards that ten backs of modern *Beaux* would sprain
Shall *kneel* before thy throne and vindicate thy reign.

Thus spoke the *Fates* as the fair thread they spun
And bade thy years with equal tenor run.
Arise, O Maid, to promised joys arise!
Lincoln's sweet seed and daughter of the Skies!
See joyous Brothels shake their conscious Beds,
See glowing *Pricks* exalt their crimson Heads!

See Sportive *Buttocks* wanton in the Air
And Bawds, *cantharides* and *punch* prepare!
The youth unbuttoned to thy arms advance
And feather-tickled Elders lead the Lech'rous Dance!

Oh! may those *Fates* propitious slowly twine
The thread revolving of my vital line,
That I may live thy wondrous deeds to tell
How oft you may be rogered, and how well!
Pope should not sweeter weave the flowing Tale
Nor Cibber's numbers o'er my verse prevail:
Tho' one has sung of Wortley's loves, and this
How Pope was perch'd on the soft Mount of Bliss.
Nay! should thy Sire himself his acts repeat
Thy Sire should soon acknowledge his defeat.

Begin, sweet Babe, on thy chaste mother smile!
Ten tedious months with thee did *Peggy* toil.
Begin! – on whom no parent smiled, shall fall
A Maid, unkissed by most, unfucked by all!

NOTE: Peggy Lee was a prostitute with whom the young and lecherous Earl of Lincoln was besotted, and by whom he had a baby girl, the subject of Horace Walpole's eclogue. Lincoln's amorous escapades were legion and the cause of much gossip and scandal.

Mr Dayrolle, described as a gentleman of 'very brown complexion' was a captain well liked and trusted by the highest nobility. He eventually became Resident to The Hague. He had been entrusted by Lincoln to be a *duenna* to Peggy.

William Bateman (created Viscount Bateman in 1725) was the brother-in-law of the Duke of Marlborough. An inveterate bugger, he was separated from his wife by the Duke, for his scandalous behaviour.

The Wortley reference is to Lady Mary Wortley Montagu, whose letters and gossip were famous, but whom Walpole described as 'famous for her wit, poems, intrigues and dirt'. Horace Walpole (1717–97) became Earl of Orford in 1791 on the death of his brother. His two concubines, the sisters Alice and Mary Berry, lived with him at his beautiful house at Strawberry Hill.

116
The Fourth Eclogue of Virgil Imitated
(1743)

[By Sir Charles Hanbury-Williams. Yale MSS., V, 70, ff.39–43. Courtesy the Lewis Walpole Library, Yale University]

Ye Druryan Muses loftier Strains begin
King's Coffee House & Bawds & Whores & Gin
Delight not all. Yet if W E there remain
The subject heighten & exalt your Vein
Till Lincoln smiles or Fox approve the Strain.

All the prophetick Muse foretold proves True
See glorious ages opening to our view:
Ev'n Bawds conceive & lustfull Charles' reign
To Bastardy propitious, comes again.

See a new Progeny from Heav'n sent down,
For Man could ne'er perform this Task alone.
Douglas brings forth, suspicious *Cannon* smil'd;
The *Mother*, without Pangs produc'd the Child.

This great event shall *Sandy's* life adorn,
Beneath whose Ministry this Hero's born;
A Hero half Human, half Divine
St James's Square & Covent Garden join,
A *Peer* & *Drab* are authors of his Line.

But if of Prud'ry still then aught remain
That frowns on guiltless Bastards with disdain
(Tho' *Cloës*, *Celias*, *Rufas*, *Mopsas* pains
From *Thraso's* brood have wip'd off all their Stains)
Yet shall he flourish free from all rebukes,
Shall lie with Dutchesses & laugh at Dukes.

Mankind he'll charm with all his Father's grace
And conquer Women with his Father's Face.
East India Captains shall rich presents make
And load the infant for the *Mother's* sake;
Chintzes and *Damasks* from Bengal shall come
And piles of glittering China crowd the room.

Rack *Punch* & *Tea* shall common as small beer
Be drank, and India seem transplanted here.
Noxious *Distempers* shall be known no more,
Nor *Claps*, nor *Poxes* poison ev'ry Whore.
Each man, secure, his *Bunter* shall enjoy
Nor shall the dread of *Pills* his bliss destroy.

But soon as on thy Chin the down appears
(That certain Promise of more vig'rous years)
And first great Youth with *Cundums* in his hands
(A plain but usefull Present Jacobs stands
Of gratitude a small but real Proof
For millions sold beneath thy *Mother's* roof).

Each morning and each night thou shalt receive
The richest *Milk* St James' Park can give
So shall the world thy *Mother's* love be shewn
Who gives thee any milk, except her own.

With various flow'rs thy cradle, ev'ry morn
Thy native Covent Garden shall adorn;
Thy *Mother's* care (and let me call her Mine)
Shall then be shewn, and all her *Arts* shall shine.

She shall procure Thee some untast'd *Lass*
Worthy her mining, and Thy embrace;
Then to Your virgin arms shall lead the Fair
Whose glowing Blushes speak her lust and fear
And having put you both to Bed shall leave you there
Where each shall give what t'other longs for most
And Maidenhead in Maidenhead be lost.

Your *Sire*, who hears what prowess you have shown
Shall own his fondness and confess his son,
And thy fond hopes with a *Commission* crown.
Go then, with well-cock'd Hat and smart Cockade
Bow at the Play and strut on the Parade

Till some rich *Widdow*, longing for thy arms
Shall largely pay her tribute to thy charms;
But sacrifice not to her goatish gust
Thy *Father's* vigour & thy *Mother's* lust,
Unless a *Settlement* at morn requite
The dull distastefull labours of the night.
Such conduct shall encrease thy *Mother's* love
And such thy prudent Father will approve.

But wide, more wide shalt thou extend thy pow'r;
Wives thou shalt violate, and Maids deflow'r.
Impotent Husbands shall thy visits dread
And Cits shall tremble for their nuptial bed.

No bridegroom to his feast shall thee invite
But fear thy Charms e'en on his Wedding Night;
While prudent Mothers, in a cautious fright
Lock up their girls from thy too fatal sight.

But call'd from all the charms of Love & Peace
This Earl's dear son, Fitzwilliam's great Increase,
Shall fly to War – War claims the Hero now
And schemes of Glory in his bosom glow.

What Deeds, for England's cause shall he perform?
Towns he shall take and Citadels shall storm;
And share (or else my Prophecy is vain)
The triumph of some future Dettingen;
Then die, recorded in the Lists of Fame
With *John of Austria's*, and with *Borgia's* name.

Now, all things prosper, at thy birth, behold.
Austria is sav'd, and Gin once more is sold!
France is repuls'd and *Prussia* stands afraid:
The *Dutch* are march'd, and *Hanoverians* paid;
Pelham's preferr'd (long may he there remain)
And *Bath's* disgrac'd, never to hope again.

O! that kind Heav'n would lengthen out my days
Till thy great deeds demand a poet's praise;
To bolder flights I'd stretch my willing wing
Thy *Toils*, Thy *Victorys*, Thy *Amours* to sing.
Nor *Wellstead's* Muse my verses should excel
Nor *Theobald's* – tho' from Shakespear he should steal.
E'en *Orrery* should, we contend, should own
My brighter Genius or my Temple's crown.

Begin, my boy, and as thy Badge of Shame
Blush at the hearing of thy *Mother's* name:
But in thy cradle on thy Father smile
And with thy infant charm his heart beguile.

Prevail at last that he thy claim would own
Else shalt thou live in Poverty, unknown.
For still (Tyrannick Custom makes it so)
To Bastards whom their fathers disavow
No Lady curtsy's & no Lord will bow!

NOTE: Sir Charles's footnotes are here abridged, but for better under-
standing see Horace Walpole's eclogue on Little Peggy (the Earl of
Lincoln's bastard daughter), which Sir Charles was imitating, the
infant on this occasion being the son born to Lord Charles Fitzwilliam,
the alleged mother being the famous procuress, *Mother* Jane Douglas
of Covent Garden. Fitzwilliam dithered over recognizing and admit-
ting paternity, although it was known that he had had sexual relations
with her over several years.

Lincoln was an insatiable lecher, and a frequenter of the Covent
Garden whorehouses, as also the famous 'King's Head' tavern, which

wits and politicians likewise frequented. Lincoln, however, did acknowledge his daughter by Peggy Lee, a prostitute with whom he was admittedly besotted.

Sir Charles observed: 'Charles II – a King of England who fuck'd so well & so much that Lord Lincoln don't care to hear him talk'd of'. The King's bastards were all created Dukes.

He described Mother Douglas as 'a great flabby fat stinking swearing ranting Billingsgate Bawd', but confirmed that she was well known to 'most Men of Quality & Distinction in the Kingdom . . . Bawd to all the world in general & Whore to Lord Fitzwilliam in particular'. Mrs Cannon was a well-known midwife, who had 'delivered Mrs Douglas and also the Princess of Wales'.

Both the Prince of Wales (Poor Fred) and his brother, William, Duke of Cumberland, were patrons of Mother Douglas's establishment – indeed, Duke William had presented her with some massive silver plate, prominently displayed on her sideboard and known as *'Billy's Bread Basket'*. Jane Douglas had started as à prostitute in St James's, where she later owned a luxurious brothel, but by 1735 she was established in Covent Garden Piazza in an equally luxurious establishment, and famous throughout the Kingdom, until she died in 1761.

Cundums, says Sir Charles, were then supplied wholesale to Mrs Douglas and other madams by J. Jacobs from a shop in Oliver's Alley in the Strand, and she sold them to her customers at exorbitant prices.

Before about 1720 Covent Garden was surrounded by green fields which pastured cows, so that milk was freely and cheaply available, but by the 1740s, says Sir Charles, it was a commodity 'formerly very plenty but grown excessively scarce by the infinate number of horses & oxen taken in to graze at so much per head per week'. It was not to be expected that Mrs Douglas could suckle her own babe, and she would not let it be suckled by any of her girls, and 'chose a Cow to Nurse' because it could not have any of the only distemper known to Mrs Douglas.

Samuel Sandys M.P. (1695–1770) was created a baronet in 1743 and helped to displace Robert Walpole from office.

The reference to prudery was Sir Charles's comment about 'natural children' not being regarded in the same light as legitimate ones. He explains that the Chloës and Celias etc. referred to four ladies 'of the Highest Quality & Distinction . . . who introduced the spurious offspring of a bastard into all the best Assemblies . . . and Publick places . . .'

Among the best customers of the Covent Garden brothels were the captains of the East Indiamen who also gave handsome presents to madams and whores. A contemporary, the famous Mother Hayward, is quoted as saying that 'if a dog was to come into her House from India she would give him an handsome Dinner' because of anticipated generosity, in contrast to many Christians who owed her 'long bills'.

A *'bunter'* was a nightwalking, and usually rather elderly or diseased, prostitute who could only get customers after dark in dark places such as St James's Park and Temple Bar; and they were usually so hungry that they would demand a good supper at midnight.

Sir Charles opines that an 'untasted Lass' – a virgin – was the greatest rarity that any brothel could afford its clients, if indeed they could ever afford it. Horace Walpole in this connection refers in his eclogue to 'distended cunts' being braced with alum, and then being passed off as virgins over and over again.

In that period it was the common practice for noble fathers to buy a commission in the army or the navy for their bastard sons. Sir Charles (*passim*) says that Fitzwilliam was not a prodigal man, so that his son could not expect money, although he might be bought off with a commission.

The previous Parliament had banned the sale of gin – then known as *blue ruin* – but after Walpole's fall Sam Sandys was instrumental in getting the decision reversed. Sir Charles described Sandys as being a Principal Courtier 'without the Manners or Fashion of a Gentleman, at the Head of the House of Commons without the Abilities of the wildest Scotch Member, and a Lord of the Treasury without the capacity of the least Clerk in that office!'.

The result of the war was that the French were driven out of the Holy Roman Empire and Queen Maria Theresa was restored to her possessions, mainly owing to the valour of the Dutch and with the help of the Hanoverians, 6,000 of whom had been put on the British payroll. The Earl of Bath was ousted from office and his place was taken by Henry Pelham.

Wellstead, Theobald and Orrery were three minor poets, and Sir Charles – perhaps with tongue in cheek – blows his own trumpet to demonstrate that he was perhaps another Virgil. He shows his liberalism in the last two lines, when trying to persuade his friend Fitzwilliam to acknowledge his son so that he could have a future, otherwise he would be condemned to poverty and ignominy. He would have overlooked the fact that Mother Douglas was a rich woman and could easily have seen her son looked after, much as her equally famous contemporary, Moll King, had sent her son to Eton.

117
An Essay on Woman
(1764)

[Attributed to John Wilkes, M.P.]

AWAKE my Fanny, leave all meaner things,
This morn shall prove what rapture swiving brings!
Let us (since life can little more supply
Than just a few good fucks, and then we die)
Expatiate free o'er that loved scene of man,
A mighty maze, for mighty pricks to scan;
A wild, where *Paphian Thorns* promiscuous shoot,
Where flowers the monthly Rose, but yields no Fruit.
Together let us beat this ample field,
Try what the open, what the covert yield;
The latent tracks, the pleasing depths explore,
And my prick clapp'd where thousands were before.
Observe how Nature works, and if it rise
Too quick and rapid, check it ere it flies;
Spend when we must, but keep it while we can:
Thus, godlike will be deem'd the ways of man.

I

SAY, first of woman's latent charms below,
What can we reason but from what we know?
A face, a neck, a breast, are all appear
From which to reason, or to which refer.
In every part we heavenly beauty own,
But we can trace it only in what's shown.
He who the hoop's immensity can pierce,
Dart thro' the whalebone fold's vast universe,
Observe how circle into circle runs,
What courts the eye, and what all vision shuns,
All the wild modes of dress our females wear,
May guess what makes them thus transform'd appear

But of their Cunts, the bearings and the ties,
The nice connections, strong dependencies,
The latitude and longitude of each
Hast thou gone through, or can thy Pego reach?
Was that great Ocean, that unbounded Sea
Where pricks like whales may sport, fathom'd by Thee?

II

Presumptuous Prick! the reason would'st thou find
Why form'd so weak, so little and so blind?
First, if thou canst, the harder reason guess
Why form'd no weaker, meaner and no less.
Ask of thy mother's cunt why she was made
Of lesser bore than cow or hackney'd jade?
Or ask thy raw-boned Scottish Father's Tarse
Why larger he than Stallion or Jackass?
Of Pego's possible, if 'tis confess'd
That wisdom infinite must form some best,
Where all must rise, or not coherent be,
And all that rise must rise in due degree;
Then, in the scale of various Pricks, 'tis plain
God-like erect, BUTE stands the foremost man,
And all the question (wrangle e'er so long)
Is only this, if Heaven placed him wrong.
Respecting him, whatever wrong we call,
May, must be right, as relative to all.
When frogs would couple, labour'd on with pain
A thousand wriggles scarce their purpose gain:
In Man, a dozen can his end produce
And drench the female with spermatic juice.
Yet not our pleasure seems God's end alone,
Oft when we spend we propagate unknown;
Unwilling we may reach some other goal,
And sylphs and gnomes may fuck in woman's hole.
When the proud Stallion knows whence every vein
Now throbs with lust and now is shrunk again;

The lusty Bull, why now he breaks the clod,
Now wears a garland, fair Europa's God:
Then shall Man's Pride and Pego comprehend
His actions and erections, use and end.
Why at *Celaenae* Martyrdom, and why
At *Lampsacus* adored chief Deity.
Then say not Man's imperfect, Heaven in fault,
Say rather, Man's as perfect as he ought;
His Pego measured to the female Case
Betwixt a woman's thighs his proper place;
And if to fuck in a proportion'd sphere,
What matter how it is, or when or where?
Fly fuck'd by fly may be completely so
As Hussey's Duchess, or yon well-bull'd cow.

III

Heaven from all creatures hides the Book of Fate
All but the page prescribed, the present state,
From boys what girls, from girls what women know,
Or what could suffer being here below?
Thy lust the Virgin dooms to bleed today,
Had she thy reason would she skip and play?
Pleased to the last, she likes the luscious food
And grasps the prick just raised to shed her blood.
Oh! Blindness to the Future, kindly given,
That each may enjoy what fucks are mark'd by Heaven.
Who sees with equal Eye, as God of all
The Man just mounting and the Virgin's fall;
Prick Cunt and Bollocks in convulsions hurl'd,
And now a Hymen burst, and now a world.
Hope, humbly, then, clean girls; nor vainly soar
But fuck the cunt at hand, and God adore.
What future fucks he gives not thee to know
But gives that Cunt to be thy blessing now:

NOTE: John Wilkes, M.P., famous in English history for his staunch defence of democratic principles which earned him the sobriquet of 'Wilkes and Liberty' and the enmity of the Establishment then led by John Stuart, third Earl of Bute, whom he is here pillorying, is credited with this Essay – although it is thought by some to have actually been written by his friend Tom Potter – and he was indicted, on the grounds of obscenity and blasphemy. The alleged obscenity was the minor point: his comparisons of men's sexual organs with those of such excellent animals as the bull and the stallion were deemed blasphemy. He was triumphantly acquitted of all charges.

The Fanny mentioned in the poem is thought to be the then reigning courtesan Fanny Murray, *née* Rudman, who was the toast of the town, although there is no evidence that Wilkes had any connection with her. Wilkes was incidentally a member of the infamous club known as the Friars of Medmenham, in whose 'Abbey' the most fantastically lewd behaviour was allowed. Although most of the famous courtesans of that time were 'invited' there from time to time, there is no record that Frances Murray was ever a participant.

118
Cunno Opt. Min.[1]

OR **The Universal Prayer**
(1762)

[Attributed to John Wilkes, M.P.]

Mother of all! in every Age
In every Clime adored
By Saint, by Savage and by Sage,
If modest, or if whored.

Thou first great Cause, least understood,
Who all my Prick confined,
To feel but this, that thou art good
And that himself is blind.

1. The inscription along the frieze of the great phallic Temple at Lampsacus

Cunno Opt. Min.

Yet gave him, in this dark Estate
To know the Good from Ill;
With God-like Virtue to create
Following his Prickship's Will.

Sound honest Cunts should oft be done;
Unsound, I ne'er would do;
These teach me more than Hell to shun,
Those more than Heaven pursue.

What Seed my God's free Bounty gives
Let me not frig away;
For God is paid when Cunt receives;
To enjoy is to obey.

Yet not one Cunt's contracted span
My vigour e'er shall bound;
I'll think they all were made for Man,
When thousand Cunts are round.

If I am clapt, may this Right-hand
Its happy cunning know;
Let rankling Venom, round this land
Brand Pego as a foe.

If he goes right, thy Grace impart
Still in the right to stay;
Oh! may he ne'er from thee depart
To find the Primate's Way.

Save him alike from foolish Pride
Or impious discontent.
If greater thickness be denied
Or thirteen inches lent.

Teach me to feel a Virgin's Woe;
The maiden Gore I see
In sacred drops from Hymen flow,
Be kiss'd, and wiped by me.

Mean though my Prick, not wholly so,
Since stiffened by thy breath.
Oh! lead him where he ought to go
In this night's Life or Death.

This night be thou, black-haired, my lot;
Or else beneath the Sun.
God knows if best bestowed or not;
But let thy work be done.

To thee, whose fucks throughout all space
This dying World supplies,
One Chorus let all beings raise,
All Pricks in reverence rise.

Fucking's the end and cause of human state,
And Man must fuck, or God will not create.

119
The Sad Disaster
(1766)

[By Thomas D'Urfey the Younger]

[Tune: 'Fair Kitty, Beautiful and Young']

As Lady Jane, devoutly wise,
Upon her arm reclined;
With Yorick's sermons, pored her eyes,
Fit food for such a mind.

A saucy Flea came skipping o'er
Those parts must not be named;
Which, when she rubbed, still itched the more:
Enraged, the Fair exclaimed.

'Shall this vile Reptile boldly dare
My hidden charms to scan,
Which I so long have kept with care
From that base tyrant, Man?
Forbid it, all ye Gods!' – then flew
Like lightning to the bell;
What sad disaster did ensue
I dread, alas! to tell.

'Here, Betty, quickly bring a Light
And help to find him out.
Make haste, or I shall lose him quite;
What is the Wench about?'
Then stooping, with an eager eye
And Breast, brimfull of Ire,
The heedless creature went too nigh
And set her smock on fire.

120
As Roger Last Night to Jenny Lay Close
(1693)

[A broadside street catch. Music by Henry Purcell the Younger]

As Roger last night to Jenny lay close
He pulled out his Budget and gave her a Dose:
The tickling no sooner kind Jenny did find,
But with laughing, she purged both before and behind:

Pox take it, quoth Roger
He must himself be beside,
That gives Pills, Pills against Wind and 'gainst Tide.

121
The Plenipotentiary
(1786)

[By Captain Morris, M.M.C. (1827), p.46]

[Tune: 'Shawbuce' ('Shawnboy')]

The Bey of Algiers, when afraid of his ears,
A messenger sent to our Court, Sir.
As he knew, in our State, the women had weight,
He chose one well-hung for the Sport, Sir.
He searched the Divan till he found out a man
Whose bollocks were heavy and hairy,
And he lately came o'er from the Barbary shore
As the Great Plenipotentiary.

When to England he came, with his Prick in a flame
He showed it his Hostess on landing,
Who spread its renown thro' all parts of the Town
As a Pintle past all understanding.
So much there was said of its Snout and its Head
That they called it the Great Janissary:
Not a lady could sleep till she got a sly peep
At the Great Plenipotentiary.

As he rode in the Coach, how the Whores did approach
And stared, as if stretched on a tenter:
He drew every eye of the Dames that passed by
Like the Sun to its wonderful centre.
As he passed thru' the Town not a window was down,

And the maids hurried out to the area;
The children cried 'Look! there's the man with the Cock,
That's the Great Plenipotentiary.'

When he came to the Court, oh, what giggle and sport
Such squinting and squeezing to view him,
What envy and spleen, in the women were seen,
All happy and pleased to get to him.
They vowed in their hearts, if men of such parts
Were found on the coast of Barbary,
'Tis a shame not to bring a whole Guard, for the King,
Like the Great Plenipotentiary.

The Dames of intrigue, formed their Cunts in a league
To take him in turns like good folks, Sir.
The young Misses' plan was to catch as catch can
And all were resolved on a Stroke, Sir.
The cards to invite, flew by thousands each Night
With bribes to the old Secretary,
And the famous *Eclipse* was not let for more leaps
Than the Great Plenipotentiary.

When his name was announced, how the women all
        bounced
And their blood hurried up to their faces:
He made them all itch, from navel to breech
And their bubbies burst out all their laces.
There was such damned work to be fucked by the Turk
That nothing their passion could vary:
All the Nations fell sick for the Barbary Prick
Of the Great Plenipotentiary.

A Duchess, whose Duke, made her ready to puke
With fumbling and fucking all night, Sir.
Being first for the prize, was so pleased with its size
That she begged for to stroke its big snout, Sir.

'My stars!' cried Her Grace, 'Its head's like a mace,
'Tis as high as the Corsican Fairy.
I'll make up, please the pigs, for dry-bobs and frigs
With the Great Plenipotentiary.

And now to be bored, by this Ottoman Lord
Came a Virgin far gone the wane, Sir.
She resolved for to try, tho' her Cunt was so dry
That she knew it must split like a cane, Sir.
True it was as she spoke; it gave way at each stroke,
But oh! what a woefull quandary.
With one terrible thrust her old piss-bladder burst
On the Great Plenipotentiary.

That next to be tried, was an Alderman's Bride
With a Cunt that would swallow a turtle.
She had horned the dull brows of her Worshipful spouse
Till they sprouted like Venus's Myrtle.
Thro' thick and thro' thin, bowel-deep he dashed in
Till her Cunt frothed like cream in a dairy;
And expressed, by loud farts, she was strained in all parts
By the Great Plenipotentiary.

The next to be kissed on the Plenipo's list
Was a delicate Maiden of Honour.
She screamed at the sight of his Prick, in a fright
Tho' she'd had the whole Palace upon her.
'O, Lord,' she said, 'What a prick for a Maid!
Do, pray, come and look at it, Cary!
But I'll have one drive, if I'm ripped up alive
By this Great Plenipotentiary.'

Two sisters next came, Peg and Molly by name
Two Ladies of very high breeding.
Resolved, one should try, while the other stood by
And watch the amusing proceeding.

Peg swore by the gods that the Mussulman's codds
Were as big as both buttocks of Mary:
Molly cried, with a grunt, 'He has ruined my Cunt
With his Great Plenipotentiary.'

The next for this plan was an old Harridan
Who had swallowed huge Pricks from each Nation.
With overmuch use, she had broken the sluice
Twixt her cunt and its lower relation.
But he stuck her so full that she roared like a bull
Crying out, she was bursting and weary.
So tight was she stuck by this wonderful fuck
Of the Great Plenipotentiary.

The next for a shag came the new Yankee flag:
Tho' lanky and scraggy in figure.
She was fond of the quid, for she had been well rid
From Washington, down to a nigger.
'Oh! my! such a size. I guess its first Prize.
Its a wonder, quite next Nia-gary.
Wa'al, now I'm in luck. Stranger, let's fuck.
Bully for the Great Potentary.'

All heads were bewitched and longed to be stitched;
Even babies would languish and linger.
And the Boarding-school Miss, as she sat down to piss
Drew a Turk on the floor, with her finger.
For a fancied delight, they all clubbed for a shite
To frig in the school necessary,
And the teachers from France, fucked *a la distance*
With the Great Plenipotentiary.

Each sluice-cunted Bawd, who'd been swived abroad
Till her premises gaped like a grave, Sir.
Found luck was so thick, she could feel the Turk's prick
Tho' all others were lost in her cave, Sir.

The Nymphs of the Stage did his ramrod engage;
Made him free of their gay Seminary.
And the Italian Signors opened all their back doors
To the Great Plenipotentiary.

Then of Love's sweet reward, measured out by the Yard
The Turk was most blest of mankind, Sir.
For his powerful Dart went right home to the Heart,
Whether stuck in before, or behind, Sir.
But no pencil can draw, this great-pintled Bashaw;
Then let each cunt-loving contemporary,
As cocks of the game, let's drink to the name
Of the Great Plenipotentiary.

NOTE: The plenipotentiary was Yussuf Adjah Effendi, sent by Sultan Selim III of Turkey (not the Bey of Algiers) in the summer of 1794 to seek support against Russia. His own behaviour and that of his entourage created great excitement, and they were credited with extraordinary sexual powers. The contemporary scandal-sheet *The Rambler* described the immense exertions made by the madams of the King's Place brothels in St James's, to accommodate their requirements. The ballad, *The Plenipo*, is attributed to Captain Charles Morris (1745–1838), a well-known composer of satirical poems and ballads with close connections at Court including friendship with the Prince of Wales. James Gillray caricatured the plenipotentiary's meeting with George III in a savage and lewd cartoon. The ballad was first published in an edition of Robert Burns's *Merry Muses of Caledonia* under the date 1796 in the section entitled 'English Poems'.

122
Una's Lock
(1786)

[M.M.C., 49]

'Twas on a sweet May morning,
When violets were a-springing,

The dew the meads adorning,
   The larks melodious singing;
The rose trees, by each breeze,
   Were gently wafted up and down,
And the primrose that then blows,
   Bespankled nature's verdant gown.
The purling rill, the murmuring stream,
   Stole gently through the lofty grove.
Such wae the time when Darby stole
   Out to meet his barefoot love.
     Tol, lol, etc.

Sweet Una was the tightest,
   Genteelest of the village dames;
Her eyes they were the brightest
   That e'er set youthful heart in flames.
Her lover, to move her,
   By every art in vain essay'd,
In ditty, for pity,
   This lovely maid he often prayed.
But she perverse, his suit denied,
   Sly Darby, being enraged at this,
Resolved, when next they met, to seize
   The lock that scatters Una's piss.
     Tol lol, etc.

Beneath a lofty spreading oak,
   She sat with cow and milking pail,
From lily hands, at each stroke
   In flowing streams the milk did steal
With peeping and creeping,
   Sly Darby now comes on apace.
In raptures the youth sees
   The blooming beauties of her face.
Fired with her charms he now resolved
   No longer to delay his bliss

But instantly to catch the lock
   That scatters pretty Una's piss
     Tol lol, etc.

Upon her back he laid her,
   Turned up her smock so lily white,
With joy the youth surveyed her,
   Then gazed with wonder and delight.
Her thighs they were so snowy fair,
   And just between appeared a crack.
The lips red, and overspread
   With curling hairs of jetty black.
Transported, Darby now beholds
   The sum of all his promised bliss,
And instantly he catched the lock
   That scatters pretty Una's piss.
     Tol lol, etc.

Within his arms he seized her,
   And pressed her to his panting breast,
What more could have appeased her
   But oaths which Darby meant in jest.
He swore he'd adore but her,
   And to her ever constant prove.
He'd wed her, he'd bed her,
   And none on earth but her he'd love.
With vows like these he won her o'er,
   And hoped she take it not amiss,
If he presumed to catch the lock
   That scatters pretty Una's piss.
     Tol lol, etc.

His cock it stood erected,
   His breeches down about his heels,
And what he long expected,
   He now with boundless rapture feels.

Now entered and concentrated,
   The beauteous made lay in a trance,
His bollocks went like elbows
   Of fiddlers in a country dance.
The melting Una, now she cries,
   I'd part with life for joy like this;
With showers of bliss they jointly oiled
   The lock that scattered Una's piss.
     Tol lol, etc.

123
The Ride in London
(*c.*1786)

[M.M.C. (1827), p.67]

[Tune: 'As I was Rideing by the Way']

As I went thro' London City
'Twas at twelve o'clock at night
There I saw a Damsel pretty
Washing her Jock by candlelight.

When she washed it, then she dried it
The hair was black as Coal upon't.
In all my life I never saw
A girl that had so fine a cunt.

'My Dear' said I, 'what shall I give thee
For a go at – you know what?'
'Half-a-crown, if you are willing,
Two shillings, or you shall not!'

'Eighteen pence, my dear, I'll give thee.'
'Twenty pence, or not at all'.

'With all my heart – it is a bargain'
So up she mounts a cobbler's stall.

'My dear' said I, 'How shall I ride you?
The gallop, amble or the trot?'.
'The amble is the easiest pace, Sir.'
With all my heart, so up I got.

The envious cobbler heard our parley,
And through a hole he thrust his Awl,
Which pricked my girl right in the arsehole
And threw the rider from the stall.

124

A Parody on Shepherds, I Have Lost My Love
(1786)

[M.M.C. (1827), p. 58]

[To the tune of 'Shepherds, I have Lost my Love', Thomson, No. 25]

Shepherds I have got the clap
Stroking of my Anna;
My time's filled up, oh sad mishap,
With taking salts and senna.
I, for her, King's Place forsook,
Where girls I had past telling;
But now my pipe's turned to a crook,
My bollocks, how they're hanging.

Never will I stroke her more,
But to the devil pitch her;
Shepherds, mark the dirty whore,
Beware, though, thou fuck her.

With whey and gruel all day fed,
Youth, by me take warning,
Three pills e'er I go to bed.
And four again each morning.

125
The Citadel
(1786)

[M.M.C. (1827), p.59]

I am a sporting amorous maid,
    That ranged this nation up and down,
In every place my fame's displayed,
    In Cupid's wars I've gained renown.
Amongst them all, both great and small,
    With vast applause I've bore the bell,
I've a little fort, 'twas built for sport,
    And by some is called the Citadel.

Through it runs a purling stream,
    Whose force would turn a little mill,
It's in a forest sweetly hid,
    And sheltered by gentle hill.
Such curious art in every part,
    Its architect none can excel;
That workman rare, with wondrous care,
    Had fortified my Citadel.

A captain brave, his skill to try,
    Resolved for to besiege my fort;
I did this son of Mars defy,
    And straight blocked up my sally-port.
For its defence, with cautious care,

Each avenue I guarded well,;
For the attack he did prepare,
  And swore he'd storm my Citadel.

Just in front, upon a plain,
  His battery opened to my view;
Being fully bent the tower to gain,
  Still nearer to the gate he drew.
No art or means I left untried
  This fierce assailant to repel,
A bastion flanked upon each side
  The entrance to my Citadel.

When he the covered way he gained,
  He on the breastwork made a halt,
His vanguard being well sustained,
  He now prepared for the assault.
With furious rage he did assail,
  The town he entered pell-mell;
His metal flew about like hail
  In the centre of my Citadel

By him oppressed and sore distressed,
  My outworks all being beaten down,
One effort I resolved to try,
  In hopes to drive him from the town.
I opened straight my water gate,
  Such a rapid torrent on him fell
As quickly forced him to retreat,
  And quite forsake my Citadel.

The hero being mad with rage,
  Resolved for to attack again.
I was unwilling to engage.
  I found resistance was in vain.

No succour nigh, my fountain dry,
By which I might the foe repel;
  I being afraid, beat the chamade,
And surrendered up my Citadel.

When he entered it I humbly craved
  That he would not the works destroy,
Like a man of honour he behaved,
  And only fired a feu de joie.
He marched away, but now I find
  I've the sad story for to tell,
That to my grief he left behind
  Some wildfire in my Citadel.

If any young man should now dare
  Invade my Citadel again,
To enter it, let him beware,
  For if he does he'll suffer pain.
Should any form this design,
  The truth to him I'll plainly tell,
On him I'll quickly spring a mine,
  'Twill scorch him in my Citadel.

126
Botany Bay
(1786)

[M.M.C. (1827), p.61]

Britannia, fair guardian of this favoured land,
To a scheme gave sanction by the Ministry planned,
For transporting her sons who from honour should stray,
To a sweet spot terrestrial, called Botany Bay.

Now this Bay, by some blockheads, we've sagely been told,
Was unknown to the famed navigators of old,
But this I deny in terms homely and blunt,
For Botany Bay is the spot we call cunt.

Our ancestor Adam, 'tis past any doubt,
Was the famous Columbus that found the spot out;
He braved every billow, rock, quicksand, and shore,
To steer through the passage none e'er steered thro' before.

Kind Nature, ere Adam had put off to sea,
Bid him be of good cheer, for his pilot she'd be;
Then his cables he split, and stood straight for the Bay,
But was stopped in his passage about midway.

Though shook by the stroke, Adam's mast stood upright,
His ballast was steady, his tackling was tight,
Then a breeze springing up, down the Red Straits he run,
And o'erjoyed at his voyage he fired off a great gun.

'Avast,' Adam cried, 'I'm dismasted, I doubt,
If I don't tack the head of my vessel about.'
'Take courage,' cried Nature. 'leave it to me,
It's only the entrance into the Red Sea.'

High from the masthead, by the help of one eye,
The heart of the Bay did old Adam espy,
And alarmed at some noise, to him Nature did say,
'That it was a trade-wind, that blows always one way.'

So transported was Adam with sweet Botany Bay,
He Dame Nature implored to spend their night and day,
And curious he tried the Bay's bottom to sound,
But this line was too short by a yard from the ground.

The time being out Nature's sentence had passed,
Adam humbly a favour of her bounty asked,
And when stocked with provisions, and everything sound,
To Botany Bay he again might be bound.

Nature granted the boon, both to him and his race,
And said, 'Oft I'll transport you to that charming place;
But never,' she cried, 'as you honour my word,
Set sail with a clap, pox, or famine on board.'

Then this Botany Bay, or cunt, much the same,
I have proved is the spot whence all of us came;
May we there be transported with pleasure and speed,
And nourish its soil with sowing our seed.

127

Coming Thro' the Rye – A Parody
(*ante* 1786)

[Attributed to Robert Burns.
M.M.C. (1827)]

O gin a body meet a body
Coming thro' the rye.
Gin a body fuck a body,
Need a body cry?

Gin a body meet a body
Coming thro' the glen.
Gin a body fuck a body
Need the warld ken?

Gin a body meet a body
Coming thro' the grain.
Gin a body fuck a body
Cunt's a body's sin.

Gin a body meet a body
By a body's sel.
Whatna' body fuck a body
Wad a body tell?

Mony a body meets a body
They darena weel avow.
Mony a body fucks a body
Ye wadna think it true!

128

The Pious Parson
(*ante* 1750)

[M.M.C. (1827), p.62]

[To the tune of 'Of Noble Race was Shenkin']

There was a pious Parson
Who lived at Upper Harding,
That loved his lass.
And pretty lass,
And hated dice and carding.

The Parson went a courting,
To ladies was unlucky,
For all he said
To wife and maid
Was, 'Madam, shall I fuck ye?'.

This Parson, when in London
Lodged near to Norton Folgate.
He coached Sal Carr
From Temple Bar,
And fucked her quite to Aldgate.

He once swived Oyster Nelly,
With cunt as black as charcoal;
He fucked so quick
That he fired his prick
With friction in her dark hole.

He finger-fucked the Furies,
He bollocked the bitches,
Jove and all Gods
He beat for Gods,[1]
So large, they burst his breeches.

He stitched the goddess Juno,
That haughty bitch of Thunder.
He rammed his tarse
Into her arse
And split her cunt asunder.

His prick was full twelve inches;
The total he did give her.
He fucked her tight
Twelve times a night,
And the thirteenth, turned her liver.

NOTE: For the same tune see *John and Susan*, No. 113.

1. misprint for 'Cods'

129
The Bumper Toast
(*ante* 1786)

[M.M.C. (1827), p.63]

I can't, for my life, guess the cause of this fuss.
Why drink ye the health of each high-titled Beldame.
What's a Queen or a Princess or a Duchess to us?
We never have spoke to and see them but seldom.

Fill a Bumper, my host, and I'll give you a Toast
We all have conversed with and everyone knows;
Fill it up to the top and drink every drop
Here's Cunt in a bumper wherever she goes.

Your high-sounding titles that Kings can create
Derive all their lustre and weight from the Donor;
But Cunt can deride all the mockery of State
For she's, in herself, the true fountain of honour.

She fixes for life the title of Wife
In her does the Husband his honour repose,
Her titles are bright, all in her own right
Here's Cunt in a bumper wherever she goes.

In Rags or Brocades she is equally great
Her Fountain gives rapture to all that bathe in it;
On a rush-bottom chair or a down Bed of State
To bliss we're transported in less than a minute.

She's banished all Care, is a foe to Despair
She's the loveliest Lethe to soften our woes;
Nothing Nature can boast can rival the toast
Of Cunt, in a bumper wherever she goes.

The Bumper Toast

Your wiseacre critics are puzzling their Brains
How crowns and coronets first came in fashion.
But a peep at her would have saved them the pains
For Cunt wore a coronet since her creation.

A title so old, never bartered for Gold
The whole British peerage would vainly oppose;
Then let Mother Eve due homage receive
Here's Cunt in a bumper wherever she goes.

That Peers, on the Trial of Peers are to sit
Is their highest distinction, beyond all denial.
But Cunt, tho' untitled by Patent or Writ
Can bring *sui jure*, even Kings to a trial.

Condemned to wear Horns, poor G — r scorns
The judgment he passes on impotent Beaux;
So justly severe, may she ever appear
Here's Cunt in a bumper wherever she goes.

That noble are born the advisers of Kings
Is a maxim established in every free Nation.
Then sure a just claim to that title she brings
Whose rhetoric effected the great Reformation.

Teo' Charles lent his ears to his Periwig,
Yet Cunt was the Counsellor under the rose,
She whispered her mind, the Commons grew kind:
Here's Cunt in a Bumper wherever she goes.

That Nobles are sentenced to die by the Axe
For breach of Allegiance, we all must have read it.
Thus Cunt, when the bond of decorum she cracks,
Like a Queen or a Princess, is always beheaded.

The King, without fees, will execute these
While none but the Hangman will meddle with those.
Then since from the Throne, such deference is shown
Here's Cunt in a Bumper wherever she goes.

Your Stars and your Garters and Ribbons profuse
And white Coats of Arms that a beggar might quarter;
How faint are the splendour, how trifling their use
Compared with the Star that shines over the Garter.

The Star in the front is the emblem of Cunt
In a lovely field Argent, Crown, Sable she glows.
And two Rampant Pricks as supporters we fix
Here's Cunt in a bumper wherever she goes.

130
A Burlesque on Stella, Darling of the Muses
(*ante* 1786)

[M.M.C. (1827), p.69]

Kitty, dearer than the Muses
Fairer far than anything,
Though I did, when at Peg Hughes's,
From your Cunt imbibe a sting
While my Prick, enraptured traces,
All your parts for Joy designed,
All the corners, all the mazes
I, in vain, to strive to find.

Love and Joy and admiration,
Cause my Prick at once to rise,
Words can never paint my passion
When your Cunt's before my eyes.
Lavish Nature thee adorning,

O'er your thighs and Smock has spread
Flowers that might shame the morning,
Shining like the Tyrian red.

But, alas! too weak my will is,
Where strong hair in knots combine,
Whoring Jove, or stout Achilles
Might have Pricks for Cunts like thine.
Could my cods, in best condition,
Give your Cunt its utmost due,
Lovely Kitty, their ambition
Would be to beslobber you!

131

The Vigorous Courtezan
(*c.*1786)

[M.M.C. (1827), p.71]

Come hither, my boy, and down by me lie
My smock it is clean, and behold my white thigh,
Survey my soft belly that's both soft and plump,
And besides, I'm all hair from my cunt to my rump.

The lips of my quim red as cherries you see,
And its cockles as juicy as juicy can be;
But stroke it, and pat it, and fuck it apace,
And the spunk that is in it will fly in your face.

Come, lay your leg over, and be not so coy
You son of a whore, you fuck just like a boy;
You have put it in double, I feel it run blunt;
It's a shame such a prick should e'er enter my cunt.

But since it is in, I pray wriggle thine arse,
I'll lather your bollocks and empty your tarse,
I'll spoil you from shagging these ten days or more,
And call you a hook prick son of a whore.

As stung with reproaches, the amorous youth
Lay panting with passion, he told her the truth;
Says he, my dear Molly, in haste I let fly
On the thatch of your cunt, and beslobbered your thigh.

But raised by your hand, put it up to the hilt,
My pintle shall wag and I'll double your milt,
I'll give you such thrusts as you ne'er had before,
Or call me a fumbling son of a whore.

Then pray put that pillow plump under my arse
And with a good home push, push in your stiff tarse:
I'll straight raise your mettle and tickle your codds,
Till in fucking you rival the king of the gods.

Alcemna, nor Leda, nor Io, by Jove,
Were half so well fucked as I then by my love;
Sure Jove was in swiving a fumbler to him,
For he turned up my liver and made my quim swim.

132
David and Bathsheba
(*ante* 1786)

[M.M.C. (1827), p.33]

Twas in the merry month of May
As good King David on a day
Was walking on his terrace;
There he espied fair Bathsheba
A-washing of her bare-arse.

The more he looked the more he liked,
At length his cock stood upright;
A fain he would be doing.
'Ye gods!' said he, 'what's that I see?'
And straight began a-wooing.

'Fair Bathsheba, if you'll be mine
I'll make you Queen of Palestine
And guard you from the Hittite.
Then spread your legs, you nymph divine
For fear that I should split it.'

Fair Bathsheba replied and said
'My dearest Love, be not afraid,
My legs shan't lie together;
You need not fear my Cunt will tear
'Tis made of stretching leather.'

King David then he fucked her once
And fain he would have fucked her twice,
But his cock would stand no longer.
'By Jove!' says she, 'What's this I see
My lord the King's a fumbler?'

'Had ever woman such ill-luck
I could have had a better fuck
From my old man, Uriah.
Oh! sure, says she, this can't be he
That slew the great Goliath?'

Says David 'Thousands of my foes
Have dealt me great and mighty blows
But never could disarm me.
Your cunt, Jove's curse, is ten times worse
Than the whole of the Philistine army!'

133

The Doctors Outwitted
(*ante* 1753)

[*Ane Plesant Garland*
J.S.F., V, 264]

Two able Physicians as e'er prescribed physic
On Burlington's illness, were sent for to Chiswick:
Both took my Lord's pulse and most solemnly felt it
Then call'd for his Urine, view'd, tasted and smelt it.
On sight of the water, cries Meade, 'It is plain
That my Lord has a fever, and must breathe a Vein.'
'You are right, Brother Meade, and besides' added Sloan,
'Who voided this water had doubtless a stone.'
'You are out' quoth the Nurse, 'you both of you miss'd it
For it was not my Lord, but my Lady who piss'd it!'

NOTE: The satire is really aimed at two famous physicians, Dr Richard Meade M.D., F.R.C.S., and a Fellow of the Royal Society; and Dr Hans Sloane M.D. (who is commemorated by Sloane Street and Sloane Square), created a baronet in 1716. Both were known as innovators and hence regarded with suspicion by conservatives. Richard Boyle, third Earl of Burlington and fourth Earl of Cork (commemorated *inter alia* by Burlington Arcade and Cork Street, but especially Burlington House, now the Royal Academy), was a great patron of the arts. Dr Meade, physician to George II, was a pioneer in inoculation, and the constant target of criticism and abuse. ('Breathe a Vein' refers to cupping or bleeding a vein, then the fashionable remedy against high blood pressure but often used in other complaints, frequently unnecessarily and often fatally.)

134
Nine Inch Will Please a Lady
(*ante* 1786)

[Attributed to Robert Burns.
M.M.C. (1827)]

[Tune: 'The Quaker's Wife', Thomson, II, 12]

'Come rede me Dame, come tell me Dame
My Dame, come tell me truly
What length o' gear, when well called home
Will serve a woman duly?'

The old girl scratched her wanton tail
Her wanton tail so ready;
'I learn'd a song in Annandale –
"Nine inch will please a lady!"'

'But for a country cunt like mine
In sooth we're not so gentle;
We'll take two thumb-breadth to the nine
And that's a lively Pintle.'

'O, leeze me on my Charley-lad
'I'll ne'er forget my Charley
Two roaring handfuls and a daud[1]
He squeezed it in full rarely!

'But weary falls the lazy rump
And may it ne'er cease thriving;
Its not the length that makes me jump
But its the double-driving!

1. lump

'Come squeeze me, Tam; come squeeze me Tam
Come squeeze me o'er the navel;
Come loose and pull your battering ram
And thrash him at my gable!'

Index of Titles

Index of First Lines

Come hither, my boy, and down by me lie 295
Come let us be Friends and most friendly agree 142
Come listen awhile and you shall hear 172
Come live with me and be my Whore 144
'Come, rede me Dame, come tell me Dame 299

Doe you meane to overthrowe me? 68

Fucksters, you that would be happy 170

Have y'any crack't Maidenheads 145
Having given all the Whores a TOUCH 203
Hey Ho! Have at all! 139
How happy the State does the Damsel possess 224
How happy were the good old English *Faces* 196

I, a tender young Maid have been courted by many 210
I am a profest *Courtezan* 61
I am a sporting amorous maid 285
I am a young Lass of *Lynn* 214
I can't, for my life, guess the cause of this fuss 292
I have a Tenement to let 244
I'll tell of Whores attaqu'd 169
I owed my Hostess thirty pound 247
I went to the Ale-house as an honest Woman should 203
I will fly into your Arms 245
If anyone do want a House 136
If you will give Ear 122
In a May morning I mett a sweete Nursse 90
In harvest-time I walked 149
In the Long Vocation, when Business was scanty 225
I' th'isle of Britain, long since famous grown 168
Instead of our Buildings and Castles so brave 223
It was a man of Africa had a fair wife 80
It was a puritanicall Ladd 87
It was the merry month of February 50

Kitty, dearer than the Muses 294

Let the world run its course of capricious delight 258
Leve, lystenes to me 41

Madam! be covered! why stand you bare? 102
Maids need no more their silver Pisspots scoure 191

MORE ABOUT PENGUINS
AND PELICANS

For further information about books available from Penguins please write to Dept EP, Penguin Books Ltd, Harmondsworth, Middlesex UB7 0DA.

In the U.S.A.: For a complete list of books available from Penguins in the United States write to Dept CS, Penguin Books, 625 Madison Avenue, New York, New York 10022.

In Canada: For a complete list of books available from Penguins in Canada write to Penguin Books Canada Ltd, 2801 John Street, Markham, Ontario L3R 1B4.

In Australia: For a complete list of books available from Penguins in Australia write to the Marketing Department, Penguin Books Australia Ltd, P.O. Box 257, Ringwood, Victoria 3134.

In New Zealand: For a complete list of books available from Penguins in New Zealand write to the Marketing Department, Penguin Books (N.Z.) Ltd, P.O. Box 4019, Auckland 10.

THE PENGUIN BOOK OF GREEK VERSE

Edited by Constantine A. Trypanis

This selection of Greek verse in the original is the first of its kind to be published in the English-speaking world: it covers approximately three thousand years – from Homer to the twentieth century.

THE PENGUIN BOOK OF ENGLISH VERSE

Edited by John Hayward

A choice of verse reflecting the richness and variety of intellectual and emotional appeal made by the principal poets – some 150 in all – who have written in English throughout the four centuries dividing the first Elizabethan age from the second.

THE PENGUIN BOOK OF IRISH VERSE

Introduced and edited by Brendan Kennelly

Brendan Kennelly explores the origins and development of the Irish poetic tradition, tracing its growth to show its tough capacity for survival despite long silences and methodical oppression and indicating the directions in which he believes it is likely to develop.

THE PENGUIN BOOK OF TURKISH VERSE

Edited by Nermin Menemencioğlu in collaboration with Fahir İz

This anthology is the first published in the English-speaking world to represent the whole span of Turkish Verse from the founding of the Ottoman Empire to the present day.

THE PENGUIN BOOK OF LOVE POETRY

Introduced and edited by Jon Stallworthy

Set by theme rather than chronology, Jon Stallworthy's delightful anthology explores men and women's changeless responses to the changeless changing seasons of their hearts.

THE PENGUIN BOOK OF BALLADS

Edited by Geoffrey Grigson

From both Britain and overseas, this rich and colourful selection of traditional and modern ballads includes stories of court, castle and manor, and themes of social injustice, love and war.

THE PENGUIN BOOK OF
FIRST WORLD WAR POETRY

Edited by Jon Silkin

In this haunting collection of war poetry, poets who were soldiers are joined by others like Kipling and Hardy who were not combatants yet wrote poetry concerned with the War.

THE PENGUIN BOOK OF
UNRESPECTABLE VERSE

Edited by Geoffrey Grigson

The perfect consolation for cynics, black humorists and for anyone who has ever succumbed to a sense of personal disillusionment or social exasperation. This anthology includes insults, outrages, satires, fire-crackers, lampoons and thunderbolts selected from a range of poets, from Burns and Byron, to Beerbohm, E. E. cummings and D. H. Lawrence.

BLAISE CENDRARS

Selected Poems

Translated by Peter Holden

Cendrars' poetry with its startling immediacy and intense visual quality made him a legendary underground figure in his lifetime.

RENGA

A Chain of Poems by Octavio Paz, Jacques Roubaud, Edua do Sanguineti, Charles Tomlinson

Based on the principle of the Japanese *renga* – a sequence of linked poems – this remarkable composition is the work of four poets of international stature.

OCTAVIO PAZ

Selected Poems

A bilingual edition, edited by Charles Tomlinson

A dazzling and mercurial writer equally at home with French Surrealism, American poetry, German Romanticism and Marxist polemic, Paz is clearly established as one of Latin America's greatest poets.

GÜNTER GRASS

Selected Poems

Translated by Michael Hamburger and Christopher Middleton

A bilingual selection of his poetry 'exposing the false identities of modern man, the fragmentation of his world, his puzzlement, his littleness and his curious paradoxical courage in recognizing absurdity and facing it'.

THE PENGUIN BOOK OF LIGHT VERSE

Edited by Gavin Ewart

Never serious or solemn, the anthology contains more than 350 poems by 150 poets. It covers the whole field, from the Anglo-Saxon riddles that had them all in stitches on the mead-benches to the writings of twentieth-century poets, some of them from America, Canada, Australia and New Zealand.

OTHER MEN'S FLOWERS

Selected and annotated by A. P. Wavell

From Shakespeare, Dekker and Marvell to Browning, Yeats and de la Mare, Field Marshal Earl Wavell's collection of his favourite poetry stirs the reader's memory with half-forgotten favourites as well as offering them an excellent selection from less well-known works.

THE PENGUIN BOOK OF WOMEN POETS

Edited by Carol Cosman, Joan Keefe and Kathleen Weaver

This unique anthology represents the work of women poets of many centuries and many cultures. It includes poems not only from North America and Europe, but also from Ancient Egypt, from China and Korea, from Latin America, Africa and the Arab world; and poets from Sappho, Hroswitha and Li Ching-chao to Anna Akhmatova, Stevie Smith and Sylvia Plath.

COLLECTED POEMS 1944–1979

Kingsley Amis

'Amis has no faults. He is clever, witty, ironical' – Gavin Ewart in the *Guardian*. 'Accomplished, literate and entertaining . . . only the fact that he is so marvellously readable can prevent Kingsley Amis from being placed in the front rank of contemporary poets'—Clive James in the *New Statesman*.

'A concrete, tangible, contemporary poet-recorder, writing in the easy-going way people talk' – Peter Lewis in the *Daily Mail*.

THE PENGUIN BOOK OF SPANISH
CIVIL WAR VERSE

Edited by Valentine Cunningham

This collection is the first comprehensive assembly of British poems (some never before published) which have to do with the Spanish Civil War. It includes also supporting prose reports and reviews by the poets, and a selection of poems – notably Spanish romanceros – in translation.

Some of this century's best-known literary figures – Auden, Spender, MacNeice and Orwell among them – are naturally represented, but the anthology also puts firmly on the map the work of several undeservedly neglected poets, such as Charles Donnelly, Clive Branson and Miles Tomalin.

In addition, the detailed and fascinating introduction is the first account of this war's relation to English literatue that has been able to draw on the Archive of the International Brigade Association.

THE PENGUIN BOOK OF HEBREW VERSE

Edited by T. Carrie

Hebrew poetry has been written virtually without interruption from biblical times to the present day, its centres spread through several continents. The result of many years of dedicated research by a poet and translator of international reputation, *The Penguin Book of Hebrew Verse* collects together for the first time the poetic riches from over three thousand years and presents the English translations alongside the Hebrew originals.

THE ANNOTATED SNARK

Lewis Carroll

Edited by Martin Gardner

The inscrutable 'Snark'
leaves us all in the dark . . .
It is psocial or filosofycle?
The dregs from the barrel
of *Alice's* Carroll?
Or a skit on the whole
business cycle?

Martin Gardner's advice
in his notes is concise.
(Once you've
purchased this volume, it's free.)
He reveals the whole core . . .
but we mustn't say more,
for the Snark *was* a Boojum,
you see.

The Annotated Alice, Martin Gardner's edition of the full text of Lewis Carroll's two famous 'Alice' books, is also available in Penguins.

SMALL DREAMS OF A SCORPION

Spike Milligan

They chop down 100ft trees
To make chairs
I bought one
I am six-foot one inch
When I sit in the chair
I'm four foot two
Did they really chop down a 100ft tree
To make me look shorter?

Here's a volume of Millipoems on pollution, population and conversation – serious subjects, overlaid by the inimitable Milligan humour.

PENGUIN ENGLISH POETS

General Editor: Christopher Ricks
Professor of English, University of Cambridge

Robert Browning: The Ring and the Book
Edited by Richard D. Altick

William Blake: The Complete Poems
Edited by Alicia Ostriker

Lord Byron: Don Juan
Edited by T. G. Steffan, W. W. Pratt and E. Steffan

John Donne: The Complete English Poems
Edited by A. J. Smith

Samuel Johnson: The Complete English Poems
Edited by J. D. Fleeman

John Keats: The Complete Poems
Edited by John Barnard

Christopher Marlowe: The Complete Poems and Translations
Edited by Stephen Orgel

Andrew Marvell: The Complete Poems
Edited by Elizabeth Story Donno

Edmund Spenser: The Faerie Queene
Edited by Thomas P. Roche Jnr and
C. Patrick O'Donnell Jnr

Henry Vaughan: The Complete Poems
Edited by Alan Rudrum

Walt Whitman: The Complete Poems
Edited by Francis Murphy

William Wordsworth: The Prelude (A Parallel Text)
Edited by J. C. Maxwell

William Wordsworth: The Poems (in two volumes)
Edited by John O. Hayden

Sir Thomas Wyatt: The Complete Poems
Edited by R. A. Rebholz